Praise for J. Wallis Martin

'In this stylish anatomy of a murder, Martin explores how a single act of violence can wreck not only the life of one person, but of everyone involved with the crime, including those trying to solve it. Intelligent and impeccably plotted, this is one of the best thrillers you'll read this year'
Cosmopolitan

'This is a compelling psychological thriller with echoes of Barbara Vine and Minette Walters. Well written, intelligent and chilling'
Val McDermid,
Manchester Evening News on *A Likeness in Stone*

'Gripping, occasionally ghoulish, psychological thriller in which a body turns up after 20 years and sets in train both new investigations and new crimes. Cracking pace and cleverly plotted'
Mike Ripley,
Daily Telegraph on *A Likeness in Stone*

'Martin cleverly portrays the innocent obstinacy of vulnerable young boys, propelled towards a fate they can neither imagine not believe'
Sunday Telegraph on *The Bird Yard*

'A superb psychological thriller . . . if you like Minette Walters and Ruth Rendell, look out for this talented author'
Choice on *The Bird Yard*

Long
Close Call

J. Wallis Martin

NEW ENGLISH LIBRARY
Hodder & Stoughton

First published in Great Britain in 2000
by Hodder and Stoughton
First published in paperback in 2000
by Hodder and Stoughton
A division of Hodder Headline

A NEL Paperback

10 9 8 7 6 5 4 3 2 1

A CIP catalogue record for this title
is available from the British Library.

ISBN 0 340 72817 5

Printed and bound in Great Britain by
Clays Ltd, St Ives plc, Bungay, Suffolk

Hodder and Stoughton
A division of Hodder Headline
338 Euston Road
London NW1 3BH

Russ – this one is for you.

January 1968

You ran along a railway embankment, long disused and over-grown, a ditch at either side. The track was gone, but you followed the line. It led you to the road. Once on the road, you sat with your feet in the gutter, and you cried.

A woman pulled up in a car. She thought you were hurt and asked if she could help. She gave you a lift into Glasgow, but the night before, a storm had ripped the city apart at the seams, smashing down the chimney stacks and hurling them through the roofs of tenement buildings. The roads had become impassable, and she said she couldn't take you any further; so you ran the rest of the way, weaving past people who stood outside the ruin of their homes.

You reached the railway station and stood on a platform until cold drove you into the buffet. It was dark in there, the windows opaque with filth. The only source of warmth was from a boiler, and a woman who served food let you sit up close, gave you Coke and a sandwich, asked if you'd lost your coat.

You wanted to tell her you'd lost everything, but words to describe what had happened just melted away. She left you alone in the end, and you sat there, picking fat-streaked ham

1

away from crusts too hard to eat. And when the London train came in, you climbed aboard, aware that she was watching; aware that she would remember you when the search for your brother began.

Prologue

Before knocking on the door to that dim, neglected house, Detective Inspector Jarvis took stock of his surroundings. In doing so, he found nothing to suggest that, thirty years from now, this part of north London would become fashionable, that each of these houses would be worth upwards of three hundred thou', or that a future prime minister would live a couple of blocks from here.

Elsa opened the door, her nine-year-old son beside her. It was one of the few times in her life that she had willingly allowed the police to enter her home, and the fact that her husband wasn't simultaneously trying to escape it via the back made a pleasant change.

There was something of the 1940s icon about her face, the suggestion of a starlet who had aged before her time. She had long put Jarvis in mind of the movie star, Jane Russell, and whenever he spoke to her, he tried to ensure that nothing of what he felt for her was betrayed by his tone of voice.

She led him into a room where the furniture was sparse, and her youngster flopped down on the carpet, sorted through Lego that lay on a rug, and started to play with

3

it. Earlier, he had built a small box, the bricks white, the roof green, and when he picked it up, something within it rattled, the boy instantly quelling the sound by holding the box very still.

Jarvis had seen this room on many an occasion over the years, most recently some weeks ago when he and a team of officers had called in search of the boy's father, George McLaughlan. It had been a month before Christmas and Elsa had been pinning paper chains to the Anaglypta walls. Now it was early January but the paper chains remained, their sticky links covered by a film of dust, their colours having faded from their former garish hues.

In seeing those simple, home-made decorations, Jarvis recalled that Elsa had been helping her son to make them, gluing the links, or holding the chains while he stapled them together. That would have been about the size and shape of their Christmas, and his heart went out to them. As a rule, he had no time for the wives of criminals, or at least, no time for those who made excuses for their predicament, but Elsa had made no excuses. *I've made my bed, Mr Jarvis.*

He could relate to her straightforward acceptance of personal responsibility, but couldn't help wondering why she felt it her duty to lie on that bed for the rest of her life. He'd once said, 'You don't have to stick it, Elsa. Nobody would blame you if you cut free of George and made a new life for yourself.' And he had then asked how a girl of her decent, working-class background had managed to get involved with a man like George in the first place, a man who, when she met him, had already served a sentence for armed robbery, a man who was bred in the Gorbals and whose background was so far removed from her own. Jarvis couldn't imagine how they had come to meet.

'Nobody forced me,' said Elsa. 'I wanted him. Thought I could change him, you see.' She had smiled at her own stupidity. 'How many women have you heard say that?'

Plenty, thought Jarvis, who now took his eyes off the paper chains and focused on Elsa's face, finding that this, too, seemed drained of all colour, a washed-out, careworn grey. There had often been times when he had longed to give her husband a piece of his mind. What stopped him was the knowledge that if he did, George would somehow find a way to take it out on Elsa. Besides, he'd be wasting his breath. Men so totally devoid of any sense of responsibility towards their families rarely changed their ways as a result of being told a few home truths. 'You phoned the station,' he said. 'Asked me to drop by,' and Elsa, referring to the older of her two sons, said, 'Tam's gone off somewhere. He hasn't come back.'

'Gone off where?'

'Glasgow.'

'When?'

'A fortnight ago.'

A *fortnight*, thought Jarvis, and Elsa added: 'He went down by train the day before the storm.'

Jarvis knew well enough that Glasgow had just been hit by one of the worst storms in living memory, and his concern deepened. There had been deaths in the poorer parts of the city where roofs that were rotten with age had crashed down on the tenement dwellers below. 'What was he doing there?'

'Trying to find his dad.'

Good luck to him, thought Jarvis, who had been trying to find George for the past six weeks. 'Any particular reason?'

'We needed money,' said Elsa, simply, and she didn't have to elaborate, Jarvis could picture the scene. Christmas had come and gone, and with George on the run from police, it was understandable that either Elsa or Tam would try to get hold of him on the off-chance of getting some money out of him. 'Any luck?' he said.

'I've no idea,' said Elsa. 'He took Robbie with him, but Robbie came back on his own.'

Jarvis now spoke to Robbie. 'Did Tam find your dad, Robbie?'

Robbie kept his head bowed, clicked a small white brick into place, but didn't reply.

Jarvis tried again: 'Why didn't Tam come back with you?'

'You're wasting your time,' said Elsa. 'I can't get a word out of him.'

'Robbie?' said Jarvis, who crouched down low and spoke to the boy very softly.

He straightened as Elsa said: 'What do you think I should do – report him missing?'

Jarvis wasn't sure. Tam was sixteen so, unless they had reason to suspect he had come to harm, the police weren't likely to do anything more than make a few enquiries. There were, after all, more adolescents living on the streets of central London than the authorities knew what to do with.

'It isn't like him,' said Elsa, and Jarvis, who knew Tam well, couldn't deny she was right. When the family had first moved to London, with Tam twelve and Robbie five,

6

Jarvis had been part of a team that was sent to the house in search of stolen money.

Elsa had hovered in the background, an arm around each of her boys, Robbie too young to understand, but Tam clearly traumatised by the way police had come smashing into their home.

There had been a model ship in the room, something Tam had made out of matchsticks salvaged from gutters and ashtrays. It had taken up most of a table that Elsa no longer had, the delicate rigging complex, the varnish applied with care, but an officer had crushed the rigging, had jabbed a fist through the hull. Watching Tam crack as his ship was torn apart had really got to Jarvis. 'This is no place for the lads,' he'd said. 'Let me take them out,' and Elsa had nodded her consent, unable to speak, George in an upstairs room, shouting the odds as another of Jarvis's colleagues read him his rights.

An hour later, he'd returned the boys with ice-cream round their mouths, and the day after he'd turned up on the doorstep with boxes of matches, and glue. Too hamfisted to help, Jarvis had simply watched as Tam put the model back together, and later, when Jarvis was leaving, Tam had mumbled something along the lines of, 'You're all right.'

Jarvis had wanted to tell him that most coppers were 'all right', but that unfortunately they had a job to do, a job that was often unpleasant for all concerned. He had wanted to add that if men like Tam's dad would refrain from committing armed robberies in the first place, it wouldn't be necessary for the police to descend on anybody's house with a view to taking it apart, but he had kept these thoughts to himself.

Now, he reflected on the fact that, despite her circumstances, Elsa had so far managed to bring up the boys as law-abiding, responsible individuals. She didn't deserve to have problems with them, though what people deserved and what they got were often two different things. Even so, he would be disappointed if Tam was about to start causing her concern. He would also be surprised, for he reckoned he knew which of the lads sired by villains would eventually cause problems, and in his view, the McLaughlan boys were cut from a different cloth. 'Supposing something's happened to him?' said Elsa, and because he had no answer for that, Jarvis replied with a question intended to extract some practical information: 'When did Robbie come home?'

'The day after the storm,' said Elsa.

'And how did he get back to London?'

'Same way he got down to Glasgow in the first place – by train.'

Jarvis was staggered that any trains had managed to run from Glasgow the day after the storm and said so, adding: 'What were he and Tam wearing?'

The look that crossed her face made him hasten to reassure her that he only needed to know in case it became necessary for him to put out a description of Tam, and Elsa described the usual clothing of jeans, jumpers and shoes, none of it remarkable, and none of it likely to jog anybody's memory in the event of a description being circulated.

'What about jackets, or coats?' said Jarvis.

'I can't remember.'

Jarvis left it at that for the moment. 'Where were they planning on staying while they were down there?'

'Iris.'

That made sense. George was rumoured to have fled to Glasgow following an armed robbery that had gone badly wrong, and it would be logical for Tam to assume that his grandmother, Iris, might have some idea where he was. After all, Jarvis had recently paid her a visit for precisely that reason.

It had been his first ever visit to Glasgow, and Jarvis recalled a dock stacked with cargo, streetwise gulls stealing food from a wharf, and some kind of iron bridge across the Clyde estuary. It had been a five-minute walk from the red, sandstone tenement where George's mother had raised her lethal offspring, and when Jarvis had poked his nose into the smaller of her two rooms, he had imagined how, in childhood, George and his brother, Jimmy, had slept nose-to-tail on a shake-down bed, the mattress infested by fleas. The mattress was still *in situ*, a writhing, living thing, the material striped in blue and white, like a milk-jug.

Iris was a biggish woman, her features hardened by years of deprivation. Jarvis had questioned her, and had quickly ascertained that she wasn't afraid of the police. At least, she wasn't afraid of Jarvis, who must have seemed soft by comparison with some of the animals Strathclyde had in its ranks. Jarvis had returned to London suspecting she knew where George was, but he had also come back convinced that it would take more of a man than him to get it out of her. He was about to ask Elsa whether, in her view, George was still in Glasgow, when Elsa added: 'I told our Tam he was wasting his time. Iris wouldn't tell him anything, even if she knew.'

'Why not?'

'She'd be worried in case the police got it out of him.'

'Does she know that Tam didn't come back to London?'

'She says it's news to her.'

'Do you think she's telling the truth?'

Elsa had to think about that. 'I can't see why she'd lie,' she said. 'Not to me. And why hasn't he been in touch?'

She had a point, thought Jarvis.

Elsa added: 'She said they stayed with her the night, and then they set off early for the train.'

'How early?'

'Sixish.'

'What time does the express leave for London?'

'About one o'clock.'

Jarvis didn't say anything to that. It would have taken them no longer than thirty minutes to get from the Gorbals to Glasgow's Central Station. Therefore, they'd obviously gone somewhere in the hours between leaving the tenements, and Robbie catching the train. Since Tam had gone to Glasgow to look for their father, it made sense to assume that they'd probably spent the morning trying to find him. Whether they'd found him or not was a different matter.

He turned his attention to Robbie, who was still playing at his feet. He hadn't said a word since Jarvis got there, and he seemed, to Jarvis, unusually withdrawn. It had been the coldest January in Glasgow since records began, and if what Elsa had said about what they were wearing was true, neither boy had been dressed for the weather. Kids could sometimes be very withdrawn when they were sickening for something, thought Jarvis, who wouldn't have been surprised if Robbie was starting with pneumonia. He said, 'Has Robbie shown any sign of illness since coming back?'

Elsa didn't seem too sure what he meant by that, and Jarvis elaborated: 'Has he run a temperature, had any time off school?'

She shook her head.

'I'd get him to a doctor, just to be on the safe side.'

He crouched down by Robbie, and reached for the Lego box. Throughout his conversation with Elsa, he had heard the occasional rattle coming from that box, and he was curious. 'Can I see your box?' he said, and, without looking at Jarvis, Robbie handed it to him.

Jarvis took it and shook it gently. 'Mind if I look inside?'

In the absence of a response, Jarvis tackled the lid. It was jammed down hard on the Lego, and he had to force a fingernail under the hard green plastic in order to get purchase and flick it away. He did it a little more forcefully than he had intended, and the box fell apart in his hands. Pieces of Lego fell from his fingers and, among them, a small golden crucifix.

Reflecting that it was the very last thing he would have expected to fall from the box, Jarvis stooped to the carpet and picked it up. It was old, and very plain. It was also of very high quality, and it had a feel about it, as if it had been—

A word came to mind, a word he couldn't replace with anything more appropriate. It had been *blessed*. Whatever this crucifix was, it was worth a bit, and he suddenly had a vision of it tumbling out of a safety-deposit box in some bank or other. George had a habit of keeping things that took his fancy. On more than one occasion, it had proved an expensive peccadillo, the evidence having been found, if not in the hull of a model ship, then in a hiding place that was equally ingenious, though no less detectable for that.

A chain had also fallen out of the box and Jarvis picked it up, finding it inappropriate for a cross of that size and weight. It was broken, which didn't surprise him. One good yank would have been enough to snap it, thought Jarvis, who was considering what to do for the best with regard to the crucifix: he would have been well within his rights to pass it on to the Antiques Squad to check against their records, but he gave it back to Robbie – he couldn't say why. Maybe he just felt that he could do with something in his life, something that was blessed, as if a little of whatever it was that had blessed it might rub off and improve his lot. In catching Elsa's eye, he saw a glint of gratitude that he hadn't deprived the child of it. 'You keep it safe,' he said. 'Don't go selling it – hear me?'

Robbie took it from him. The *look* that crossed his face. It sent a shudder through Jarvis, and it was then that he realised something had happened to Tam.

'Robbie,' said Jarvis. 'Where's Tam?'

The boy made no response, and in that moment, Jarvis wondered how many other lads of nine had ever had cause to wear the expression that Robbie was wearing now. It was as if he knew that, notwithstanding the charade with the game of Lego, his childhood was over, that he carried a secret of such magnitude it had hauled him out of childhood and into the grown-up world, where secrets aren't merely a game but a matter of life and death.

He curled his fingers around the cross as if attempting

to burn it into his flesh, to hide it for ever within himself
– something to draw strength from in the years and trials
to come.

'Robbie?' said Jarvis.

The boy looked up at him, the cross clutched tight in
his hand, but he didn't say a word.

'Robbie?'

Nothing.

Chapter One

September 1999

The house that Robbie McLaughlan had lived in over thirty years ago had undergone a transformation since he had last seen it. Gone was the drab exterior, and the paintwork gleamed on a brand-new door and windows, recently fitted.

In looking at it now, he found that none of it tied in with his perception of what it had been like to live there, but he didn't doubt that its present occupants had no idea what it had been like in the sixties. Nor would they know that, regardless of the fact that it had been renovated to a high standard, he still saw it pretty much as it had been when he was a boy.

He half expected to see his mother at the door, watching as uniformed men dragged his father out of the house. And then it was Tam he saw – Tam who was still sixteen, his image frozen in time.

Tam had been in the habit of walking round the side to enter via a door that opened straight into the kitchen. The memory was so vivid it brought a tightness to his chest. And then he remembered Jarvis, who had tried to be some kind of father to him after Tam disappeared. *Not all coppers are out to cause grief – remember that.*

McLaughlan had remembered.

He hadn't seen the house in years, and he found it disconcerting to be in such close proximity to it. The memories it invoked weren't pleasant, and he tried not to let them distract him, because it wasn't the house that had brought him back to the area, it was his job.

He was looking through the window of a flat that stood opposite a branch of the Midland Bank. It used to be owned by the grocer who ran the shop below. Now it was owned by someone who had obliged by moving out for the morning, leaving it free for armed police to use for surveillance purposes.

As he took his eyes off the house and trained them back on the bank, an Armed Response Vehicle cruised past and disappeared down a side road.

The sight of that ARV didn't please him, and he knew it wasn't likely to please his guv'nor either. The order to keep a low profile was one that Leonard Orme expected the teams to observe, but for reasons that were lost on McLaughlan, the men in that ARV had driven it past the bank in full view of the public, the police, and maybe even the robbers, thereby jeopardising the entire operation.

'For fuck's sake,' said McLaughlan.

He wasn't alone in that room, and his partner, Doheny, a deceptively weak-looking man who had formerly served in the SAS, spoke into the semi-gloom. 'I don't believe they did that.'

The men inside that ARV carried Smith and Wesson handguns, two carbines, and enough ammunition to quell a revolt in some minor third-world country, and although he wasn't in any way religious, the realisation that those weapons might be fired, and that shots might be returned from hardware equally deadly, made McLaughlan reach for the crucifix rather than for the Glock 17 with which he had been armed since early morning. It was concealed beneath a navy crew-neck sweater, bulky over a bullet-proof vest. Solid. Heavy. Protective.

He had worn it since the day Jarvis handed it back after telling him not to sell it. Initially, he hid it in the box reconstructed from Lego, but when he was slightly older, he plaited it into a leather thong and tied it round his wrist. Later still it dangled from a gold earring that he had given up wearing long ago, and now it hung from a thick gold chain clasped around his neck.

Few of his colleagues had ever commented on it, but those who had were told that he wore it because he had a feeling that it somehow protected him, that if ever he took it off . . .

Most of them could relate to that, if only on the grounds that they each had their own little rituals, their touch-wood devices that they needed to believe would protect them in situations where anything could go down.

The news that an armoured van was about to be hit outside a branch of the Midland had come to McLaughlan courtesy of an informant – Gerald Ash.

It wasn't uncommon for villains to turn grass once, as was the case with Ash, they had grown too old for the game and money was in short supply. At seventy-odd, planning and executing a robbery was rarely seen as an option. Few could face the prospect of another stretch if things should go pear-shaped, and McLaughlan had been benefiting from Ash's desperation for several years, on and off.

They met at a Virgin Megastore in Oxford Street, McLaughlan walking in from pavements that were crowded and a winter's afternoon sky that was already growing dark.

He found Ash thumbing through a rack of golden oldies, and the sight of him came as something of a shock: it had been only a matter of months since McLaughlan had last seen him, but during that time, age had taken hold. His eyes had turned from the steel grey of his prime to the bluish grey of an infant who is not yet able to focus, and his movements, along with his speech, had slowed perceptibly.

It took him a good few moments to realise McLaughlan was there, but when he did, he simply resumed his search for a face from the past. Elvis Presley. Little Richard. Roy Orbison. These were the people who had kept him sane in the type of prison where men such as Ash had only left their cells for an hour a day. *I know every word of every song they ever sang—*

He revealed that an armoured vehicle was due to make a delivery of cash to a branch of the Midland at 11 a.m. that coming Monday, and when McLaughlan complained that it didn't give them much time, Ash had quipped that it gave them two days, and that Flying Squad was always bangin' on about being able to get to the scene of any bank raid in London in under five minutes, so what was he bleatin' about?

It hadn't been getting to the scene, or even ensuring that they had it fully covered, that bothered McLaughlan.

It was getting the robbers under surveillance prior to the job going down.

He asked for names, and more than expected Ash to start screwing him around then, because this was the point at which Ash usually started talking silly money. But on this occasion Ash pocketed fifty quid without even attempting to get more out of McLaughlan. He then said the name *Swift*, and the minute he said it, McLaughlan thought he was either mistaken, or lying.

Calvin Swift, fifty-six years old, was one of London's more notorious villains. He may have started out as a messenger boy for a well-known East End firm, but he'd come a long way since then, and neither he nor his brother Ray needed to dirty their hands by pulling a bank job. Those days were gone for the Swifts, and McLaughlan couldn't imagine either of them returning to the type of activity that had finally earned Calvin a lengthy jail sentence back in the eighties – not unless business was poor, and business, to McLaughlan's knowledge, was currently booming. 'What would Calvin want with robbing a bank?'

'Who said anything about Calvin? It's his son, Stuart.'

This made no more sense to McLaughlan than the idea of Swift senior pulling the job. This time, he said, 'If Stuart wants money, all he has to do is tap his pa.'

'He's got a drug problem,' said Ash.

If Stuart Swift had a drug problem, it was news to McLaughlan, but in a voice that sounded frankly incredulous, Ash added, 'I've heard he's been stealin' from the old man.'

Silly boy, thought McLaughlan. There was a certain type of person you didn't steal from, not even if you happened to be their only, much-loved son, and Calvin fell very much into that category. Nobody ripped him off and got away with it. Doubtless, people had tried it in the past, which was why Serious Crimes had a vested interest in keeping an eye on him, because people who crossed him tended to disappear. Some had done so of their own volition. Others had not. But rumour was one thing. Finding a body and pinning a murder on Calvin was another.

'Who else is involved?' said McLaughlan.

'Carl Fischer,' said Ash.

McLaughlan had never heard of him.

'The driver is a mate of Fischer's – bloke by the name of Leach.'

McLaughlan had never heard of Leach, either, but that wasn't his problem. It wasn't his job to have heard of every villain in London, and nor was it his job to decide what should be done on the strength of the information: he was merely required to brief his immediate superior, and it would then be up to Orme to decide what action, if any, to take.

Orme might decide that Ash was either lying or had been misinformed, in which case, Flying Squad would do little more than ensure that an ARV was close to the bank when the job was tipped to go down. On the other hand, he might decide that a full-scale op was justified.

McLaughlan demanded details relating to the way in which the armoured van would be attacked, and considered them carefully. Then, taking care to sound fairly noncommittal, he said, 'I'll have a word with the guv'nor.'

'Suit yourself,' said Ash, who drifted off to search through other displays.

McLaughlan watched him go, then left the store. It had grown dark in the past ten minutes, and Oxford Street was heaving with people who were staring into the face of a British winter. Most looked resigned to it. All looked cold.

The traffic was moving slowly, and as he made for the tube, McLaughlan thought about what Ash had just divulged. If Orme acted on the information only to find it was dud, they would all look stupid. More than that, operations on even a fairly small scale cost money, and Orme would be expected to account for what had prompted him to spend precious resources on an op that had proved a total waste of time. Therefore, it was in all their interests to determine whether the information was solid, and in this case, with the robbery fairly imminent, they could only rely on an analysis of the information and hope they got it right.

Trouble was, informants often lied. You could never really tell whether they were telling the truth, the partial truth, or – to use a phrase coined by Doheny – *an out-and-out porker*. Ash might be short of money, and provided he didn't do it too often and lose McLaughlan's trust, passing dud information was always good for a few quid. But already, on this occasion, McLaughlan was willing to state that, in his view, the information was probably totally sound.

Orme would want to know what made him think so, and McLaughlan would point out that coppers and villains alike shared certain things in common: if your only son is doing drugs, you'll usually try anything to stop him. In Calvin's case, that meant making it difficult for Stuart to get his hands on any money. Conversely, if you're a user, you'll do anything to get your hands on money, and to someone of Stuart's background, armed robbery would seem the natural solution to the irritating problem of lack of funds. He would know precisely what the risks were, and how to go about it. All he needed was the guts to go through with the job.

Whether he had the guts, McLaughlan couldn't say, but in the circumstances, and knowing what he did about the family, he was prepared to advise Orme that in his opinion, come Monday, Stuart would most likely be found in front of a branch of the Midland. He would be holding a sawn-off shotgun to the head of a terrified guard, and he would be threatening to blow his head from Islington to Richmond. *It won't even fucking bounce!*

The guard would do the sensible thing: he would give him whatever money there was to be had. Even so, if Stuart was anything like his pa, he'd shoot him anyway.

But nobody was going to find out whether Stuart was as vicious as the old man, because this would be his first armed robbery—

—and McLaughlan was in no doubt that Orme would make it his last.

Chapter Two

McLaughlan stood only feet from the window, which was slightly open despite the rain, which found the two-inch gap and spattered in. It ran off the sill in a cold, steady stream and dripped down the back of a radiator, streaking the wall and soaking into the carpet.

Checking the weather had been the first thing he'd done after waking that morning. He had pulled back the curtains and welcomed the heavy rain because he had known it might reduce the number of people on the street at the time that the robbery, then six hours away, was scheduled to go down.

Claire had remained wrapped in the duvet, her only concession to wakefulness to push her hair off her face and out of her eyes. She had watched him dress in near darkness, his desire not to disturb her greater than his need to see what he was doing, and if his air of preoccupation had warned her that a job of some kind was imminent, she had known better than to ask him about it.

He had gone down uncarpeted stairs and into a kitchen where the cat, remarkably dry, had pushed its way through the cat flap and demanded food. He fed it, and the cat pushed off, back to whatever secret second home it had found for itself, a home where, McLaughlan suspected, it would be fed again.

In the knowledge that he would eat at the station later, he had made do with coffee, but he took tea up to Claire, then walked into Ocky's room.

His son was deeply asleep, as McLaughlan had known he would be, and McLaughlan, who had never slept well, not even as a four-year-old, envied him his long unbroken nights.

His room was like no room that McLaughlan had ever slept in as a child. Its walls were textured in blues and greens, the colours bold and strong. It was a far cry from the windowless closet where he and Tam had slept when staying with Iris, and it was also as different again from their room in Islington. There, the walls had been mushroom, and that had been appropriate because damp had often resulted in fungi springing up to discolour the plaster. His mother had scraped the mould away with a knife, had slapped a coat of emulsion on the discoloured patch of wall, had promised that one day, some day, they'd have a better house.

McLaughlan couldn't remember at what point he had realised they would never have a better house. He only remembered swearing to himself that if ever he had a son, he would provide him with something better than a damp patch of wall to stare at from his bed.

He had gone back in to Claire, who was now sitting up and reaching for the tea he'd put by her bed. She hadn't asked what time he would be back, and he had left without saying goodbye – there being something about saying goodbye that smacked of a man suspecting he might not make it home.

She knew. She understood. He wasn't the only cop to harbour superstitions. Some wouldn't walk under ladders, whilst others wore their equivalent of the good old rabbit's paw. McLaughlan wore the crucifix, and refused to kiss his wife, or say goodbye. 'I'll see you later,' he'd said, and then he had left the house for a briefing at Tower Bridge station.

The briefing had started at 6 a.m., and it had taken place in the kind of room that put McLaughlan in mind of a classroom in an underfunded school. The floor wasn't as clean as it might have been, and the walls could have done with a lick of paint to liven the yellowing cream.

Tables that normally served as desks had been pushed up against the walls, their surfaces hidden by weapons, and plastic chairs had been dragged into rows so that McLaughlan and the rest of the team could sit facing Leonard Orme. He had stood with his immense back to an even broader whiteboard where, on a map of the roads surrounding the bank, the positions from which his men would keep surveillance had been marked up in red.

He pulled a screen down in front of the whiteboard and photographs of the robbers had been projected on to it. Without exception, every man in the room knew who Calvin was, and a fair percentage were already acquainted with Stuart. Even so, Orme indicated one of the photos and said, 'Calvin Swift's son, Stuart. Twenty-two years old. Smack habit. Four convictions – three for burglary, one for possession of a class A drug.'

To McLaughlan's eye, the emaciated Stuart looked as

though he had needed a fix when the photograph was taken. No wonder Pa was worried about him. Stuart was in a bad way.

A second photo appeared on the screen: 'The driver. Leach. Late forties. Married, with young kids, apparently.'

'What's his form?' said Doheny.

'Burglary, car theft, and receiving,' said Orme, who indicated the third and final photo: 'Carl Fischer. Ten years older than Stuart. Numerous convictions, the most serious for armed robbery. Two convictions for assaulting a former girlfriend.'

McLaughlan took stock of details relating not only to the men's criminal records but to their physical characteristics, because once those balaclavas were on, the only way he would be able to distinguish one robber from another would be by their physique.

It often proved useful to know which individual was which, if at all possible, not least because it gave some idea of how that individual might react when they found themselves surrounded by armed police. One look at Leach's puffy-eyed, fat little face told McLaughlan he was stocky and unfit. Most armed robbers kept themselves fit. Their freedom could depend on them being able to put in the odd turn of speed, but Leach didn't look capable. McLaughlan doubted therefore that he would put up much of a fight, but Fischer – if his record was anything to go by – might. Stuart, on the other hand, wasn't known to be violent, but if he was high, he might do something stupid. It was worth knowing.

Orme had imparted the information that Stuart was currently living at an address in Islington, close to the bank. Fischer was living with some woman in Romford, and Vincent Leach lived in Elstree with his missus.

They were quite spread out, thought McLaughlan. Not that it made any difference. Now that police knew where they were currently living, it would be possible to keep them under surveillance from the moment they left their homes to the moment they attempted to pull the robbery.

Orme had gone on to ask whether anyone had any questions, and after satisfying himself that they all knew where they were at, he had brought something to the attention of every man present: Calvin Swift was something of a legend in his own time, his career having been one in which violence was the order of the day. He had shot, stabbed, slashed and coshed his way through two generations of bank managers, security guards and members of the public, and word had it that he still ran protection rackets. Once, his victims had been the owners of small businesses in and around the East End. Nowadays, they were the owners of larger concerns located in leafy business parks in and around Essex. Yet a combination of the best possible barristers plus a policy of terrorising anyone who thought themselves brave enough to testify against him had ensured that he had spent a total of only twelve years in prison. His brother, Ray, took advantage of Calvin's reputation, but he was the lesser of the two evils.

He pointed out that families such as the Swifts were nothing unusual. Savage and dysfunctional, some hid beneath a veneer of gentility and sophistication. Their kids attended private schools. They lived in desirable areas. It made no difference. Three minutes into a conversation with

27

any of them, you knew where they'd come from, and you knew what they were.

Barbarians.

'Don't ever forget what you're dealing with,' said Orme. 'But remember, irrespective of Calvin's view of himself, Stuart isn't the son of God. He's merely the son of another sad fuck who thinks he's above the law – so let's put him straight.'

We'll put him straight, thought McLaughlan, provided he shows, and now, as he recalled what Orme had said, he saw a Securicor van turn into the road. But he also saw something else, a flash of silver high above the heads of people who were threading their way down the road. They walked with bodies slightly bent against the rain, their clothes as drab and damp as the walls of the buildings they passed. Many simply kept walking, but some took refuge in places such as the shop beneath the flat, waiting for the rain to ease, unaware that all around in the windows and doorways and cars, armed men were touching the glossy barrels of guns, a thin film of oil on their fingers. They kept their eyes fixed on the armoured vehicle, and as it pulled up at the bank, McLaughlan slipped out of the room with Doheny.

Within seconds, they were down the stairs that led to the back of the shop, and then they ran down an alley that opened out on to the pavement opposite the Midland.

They stood in the rain with their backs to the brickwork, waiting for the getaway vehicle to pull up in front of the van. Once the robbers had the guards at gunpoint, armed police would converge on them from every conceivable direction, and when that happened, McLaughlan knew from experience that anything might be expected of the civilians closest to the action. Some might crumple and cower on the pavement. Others might turn and run. But unless the police were unlucky enough to come up against a 'hero', most would do nothing other than stand stock still, rigid with shock, which suited McLaughlan fine. He didn't need any heroes, and he didn't need anyone collapsing on him, but if anything untoward happened, there were men among the team who were trained to take care of whatever might arise from that eventuality. The rest would concern themselves solely with the robbers.

The doors to the back of the van began to open. Two guards climbed out, the first carrying a metal cash case, the second closing the doors, and because it was police policy never to tell anyone – be it an individual, a security firm or a bank – that they had been targeted by robbers, the guards were unaware of what was going on around them. To have warned them would have been to run the risk of their getting edgy and behaving in a way that might have put their lives in even greater danger.

The guards began to walk towards the bank, but there was still no sign of a getaway vehicle, and McLaughlan now got worried. If the robbers didn't show, the sense of anticlimax after so much planning and waiting would be immense. That kind of scenario did nothing for the nerves, and even less for morale. But just at the point when he became convinced that the robbers had been warned off, a navy BMW pulled up in front of the van. It hadn't even stopped before the doors opened and the emaciated Stuart and the slightly taller Fischer jumped out, their faces hidden by balaclavas.

Within seconds, they were holding the guards at gunpoint, and from the radio that was strapped to Doheny's belt, an order to attack was given by Orme.

McLaughlan and Doheny ran across the road towards the van, and it was then that McLaughlan caught another glimpse of that flash of silver. Moments earlier, it had struck him as something that looked like a moon as it bobbed along the street. He had thought it unimportant, but now its significance registered, and he saw how wrong he'd been.

He also saw something else, something that turned him cold: the men positioned around the scene had left their surveillance points and were running towards the robbers. They, like him, stopped running because they'd seen what he had seen.

The flash of silver came from a globe-shaped balloon. It bobbed above the head of a boy who was three, maybe four years old, and it was attached by a translucent thread to his pink, dimpled hand. As armed police had converged on the scene, he had run up to Stuart Swift, and he was currently pointing up at his gun and asking for a 'go'.

A woman, whom McLaughlan presumed was the boy's mother, came into view. Immediately, she grasped the situation, and she froze. *Good girl*, thought McLaughlan. *Good girl*. But even as he thought it, Swift took the weight of the shotgun with one hand, and with the other, he reached out and grabbed the boy by the shoulder.

Don't do this, thought McLaughlan – the last thing he wanted to see was a child taken hostage – and then he heard a sound he didn't recognise at first. It came from the kid's mother, a pleading, whining paean that didn't sound human. She dropped to her knees, and initially McLaughlan thought she'd passed out, but then she began to crawl along the pavement towards her son.

Orme appeared out of nowhere and called out, 'Stay where you are!' But she carried on regardless, and McLaughlan was afraid that if she made a grab for her child, it might just be enough to tip the balance. He suddenly pictured the aftermath if Swift started blasting away with that sawn-off, and because he had to act quickly, McLaughlan did the only thing he could think of: he called out to Swift, and as he did so, he began to lower his weapon. 'You're out of here – just leave the kid,' but all he saw was a flicker of fear in Swift's eyes. It unnerved McLaughlan because he knew as well as the next man that a frightened armed robber was more of a danger to himself and everyone around him than any cold-blooded killer. Consequently, McLaughlan had no idea what his reaction was likely to be.

Whatever it might have been, nobody was ever going to know, because what happened next was something that was beyond McLaughlan's worst nightmare.

The child made a grab for the gun.

And Swift pulled the trigger.

Chapter Three

It was raining, and the fact of it seemed appropriate to Jarvis, who stood among a crowd to watch as a funeral cortège drew up outside a pub in the East End. Most of the vehicles comprising it were crammed with ageing members of the criminal fraternity, people Jarvis had come up against in the sixties.

Some of the men were showing their age now, a combination of lengthy prison sentences plus the punishment their bodies had taken from tobacco and alcohol having made their mark, whilst the women who had stuck by their men seemed, to Jarvis's eye, to have fared little better, most having grown what Jarvis would have described as *blowzy* in late middle-age.

It was hard to equate what these women had become with the glamorous girls who had sung and stripped and danced at the many clubs where they'd met their husbands. More often than not, their men had been the owners of those establishments, and if they had been purchased from the proceeds of robberies, protection rackets, prostitution and porn, then ultimately they had become fronts for money-laundering operations.

Some were still going strong thirty years down the road, unaffected by factors such as interest rates, changes in government and assessments from an over-zealous Inland Revenue – factors that had an unfavourable bearing on similar, but 'straight' small businesses, and all had been patronised by the likes of the late Tommy Carter, whose funeral was currently taking place.

As per a time-honoured East End tradition, the hearse was pulled by two black horses, the plumes that sprouted between their ears lending an air of pantomime to the occasion, the coffin hidden by wreaths, the words *Dad* and *Tommy* spelt out in red carnations.

Jarvis had known Tommy Carter, but despite having once had the pleasure of helping to put him away, he was there to pay his respects along with some of his fellow officers who had also known the deceased from way-back-when.

The news that he had died peacefully in his sleep had amused and even exasperated some, but Jarvis couldn't find it within himself to wish Tommy ill. Wherever he was, assuming there was an afterlife, Tommy would be working out a way to crack some safe, and he wouldn't much bother who the safe belonged to – God or the devil, it would all be the same to him. Jarvis only hoped that purgatory had better security than Parkhurst.

Tommy had been most active at a time when there was still an air of romance associated with the act of dropping through a roof to blast a safe, but although he had been born and bred alongside some of the most vicious criminals active in the sixties, Tommy, who didn't have a violent bone in his body, had stuck to what he knew best. It was an art, with him: you could always tell when a job had been done by Tommy – the holes he blasted were always perfectly round and perfectly *so*.

In short, Jarvis had liked him, which was why he was in the crowd that had gathered outside Tommy's local when the hearse had paused on its way to the crematorium.

He didn't wear a hat as a rule, but he had worn one today, and he doffed it as the horses drew to a halt. He still knew most of the people in that crowd. Some were the sons and daughters of robbers like Tommy Carter. Others were neighbours and associates, but most of the villains among them were wearing the type of imported suit that made him feel ill-dressed. There were Pearly Kings and Queens, and Tommy would have liked that, Jarvis reflected. It was all a bit of a show, a bit of the old East End, what a man of Tommy's background would have called 'a bloody good send-off'. Better than I'll get, at any rate, thought Jarvis as the men now raised their glasses. 'Tommy Carter,' came the toast, and Jarvis raised his glass.

'Tommy Carter,' he echoed.

As he drank to Tommy's memory, Jarvis thought back to a time when he had come to this same pub for a quiet word with him. Several weeks had passed since Tam disappeared, and as it was common knowledge that Tommy and George were occasional drinking partners, Jarvis thought it worth asking whether Tommy had heard anything of interest.

'George's son is missing,' he said.

Tommy, his hair slicked back in the style of the time, had let him buy him a drink. 'I did hear something,' he admitted.

'What did you hear?'

'He went off lookin' for George. He never came back.'
Tommy stopped right there, and looked a little nervous
as he added: 'Maybe he found him.'

The way he said it told Jarvis all he needed to know
about Tommy's opinion of George. He was ruthless,
violent, and more than capable of turning on his own flesh
and blood if he felt it necessary. 'Thanks, Tommy,' he said,
and that afternoon he had a word with his guv'nor, Don
Hunter.

Though six years Jarvis's junior, Hunter had already
achieved the rank of DCI, but he had respect for Jarvis
who, like himself, was the good old-fashioned East End
type of copper.

It was 1968, and out on the streets of London, people not
much younger than Hunter were exhorting one another to
wear a flower in their hair if they happened to be going to
San Francisco, but Hunter had shown Jarvis into an office
where the in-trays, out-trays, chairs, carpets and walls
were depressingly grey, not only in shade but design.
No flowers. And not much hair, either, not on Hunter,
at any rate, who blamed his premature baldness on the
nature of his work.

'Remember me telling you that George's eldest took
his kid brother to Glasgow then buggered off?'

'What about it?' said Hunter.

'He hasn't come back.'

If anyone else had brought that fact to his attention,
Hunter might have questioned whether, in view of the
lad's age and background, it might be a little early to
start to worry unduly. Instead, he thought it over as
Jarvis added: 'That lad hasn't just left home. Something's
happened to him.'

'Wasn't he in Glasgow during the storm?'

'He wasn't hit by a storm,' said Jarvis, who was confident that Hunter would know what he was driving at. Six weeks before Christmas, two armed men had attempted to pull a robbery on one of Ladbrokes' betting shops. The bookie who ran the outlet was himself something of a villain, and he had made a statement to the effect that he recognised one of the robbers as George McLaughlan. It was therefore fairly safe to assume that his associate was a Glaswegian who went by the name of Crackerjack, because he and George were a team. Eric and Ernie. Laurel and Hardy. *Pinky and bloody Perky!*

To say that the robbery had gone wrong was something of an understatement: the bookie had come out of the back of the shop with a Thompson sub-machine gun kept as a souvenir from the Second World War, and had let rip with it. He swore that his only intention had been to defend himself and his staff – after all, the robbers were carrying shotguns. He therefore intended to plead self-defence when it came to court, and it *would* go to court, thought Jarvis, because somehow, in the chaos that ensued, one of the robbers was shot.

Police had arrived to find the betting shop looking more like a butcher's than a bookie's, and nobody, thought Jarvis – *nobody* – walked away from that degree of blood loss.

He had put all hospitals on the alert, but, so far, none had informed him that they had a patient who had been admitted with gunshot wounds. Crackerjack had to be lying up somewhere. Either that, or Crackerjack was dead.

'I'm wondering,' said Jarvis, 'whether Tam knew something about that robbery.'

'And if he did?' said Hunter.

'What if he was trying to blackmail his dad into giving some money to his mother?'

'His dad's hardly likely to have topped him,' said Hunter. 'Not even George would eat his own kids.'

Jarvis refrained from commenting. In his opinion, George was capable of just about anything. Born and bred in the Gorbals, he had served his apprenticeship with one of the most notorious Glasgow gangs of the sixties before greed and naked ambition had sent him south. Once in London, he had quickly earned a name for himself as the type of Glaswegian heavy who could make himself useful to firms who were fighting over territory once ruled by the Richardsons and Krays. And even if Jarvis gave him the benefit of the doubt, it was always possible that one of his associates might have done something to silence Tam if it looked as though he might be about to cause them a problem.

'What do you want to do?' said Hunter.

'I think I should go back to Glasgow and talk to Iris again. If it turns out she's not worried about Tam, I think we can assume she's seen him since he put Robbie on the train.'

'And if she hasn't?'

'Then I think we ought to take his disappearance a little more seriously.'

Hunter gave that a moment's thought before finally saying, 'You'd better get yourself down to the Gorbals then.'

It was much what Jarvis had hoped he might say.

Hunter added: 'You'll be wanting back-up – I'll see that you get it.'

'Don't bother,' said Jarvis. 'I'm safer without it.'

If it had been anyone other than Jarvis, Hunter would have tried to talk some sense into him, but if Jarvis didn't want back-up, there had to be a reason, so Hunter left him to it. 'Up to you,' he said.

When first he saw the Gorbals district of Glasgow, Jarvis had found it impossible to imagine that this had once been an elegant suburb, the red sandstone tenements home to wealthy industrialists, the literati, the chattering classes. Since the turn of the century it had sunk in status to become the insanitary domain of poor immigrants, many of them Irish, and although a programme of slum clearance had been put in place by the late 1960s, enough of the tenements remained to explain why politicians had long claimed that the Gorbals was the worst, the most notorious slum in Europe.

He entered the tenement building where George's mother lived, walked up the stairs to the landing where, to his knowledge, she'd spent her entire married life, and hammered on the door.

Iris opened the door to him and, once again, Jarvis was struck by the size of the woman. Most of the Gorbals inhabitants were undernourished and puny, which made clan McLaughlan seem all the more remarkable for their sheer physical strength.

It occurred to Jarvis that anyone who knew Iris and then happened to clap eyes on George would have known that she was his mother. Where else could George have got those massive shoulders, those tremendous forearms?

She wasn't a fat woman by any standards, but she was *big*, and as was so often the case when Jarvis saw women of her type, he couldn't begin to imagine her as a child. It seemed to him that there couldn't have been anything remotely soft about her, that even in the cradle she wouldn't have smiled, that somehow she would have seen what the future held in store, and would have kept her thoughts, along with her smiles, to herself.

The door from the landing opened straight into a room where the sofa and chairs had their backs to a galley kitchen. Nothing much about it had changed since Jarvis had first seen it, other than that, a few months back, it had smelt much the same as every other room in a tenement of this type – a mixture of damp walls, filthy lavatories and cooked food. The whole had been overlaiden with paraffin oil that was failing to keep the vermin back from the cupboards and walls and skirting. Now, the smell was lost in the intense stink of human sweat gone stale. It should have served as a warning, but it didn't because Jarvis was ignorant of what it signified.

He scanned it afresh, taking in details that had escaped him before and allowing his eyes to rest on a series of badly framed photographs. They had lined the furthest wall, some depicting a younger George, but the majority of his brother, Jimmy 'Nau' hans'.

Both men had been amateur boxers, but only Jimmy had been talented enough to earn the belts he was wearing when the photos had been taken. Consequently, there was something very terrible about the way in which, in each of those photos, Jimmy had thrust his gloves forward as if to illustrate, for future reference, that there had once been a time when there were hands on the end of what were now stumps.

There were no photos of Iris's husband. What little Jarvis knew about him had come from Elsa who had told him that George's father had been sent to one of the labour camps back in the thirties. He had died there, leaving Iris to raise their sons as best she could.

He also knew, courtesy of Elsa, that Iris had convictions for prostitution, but that had been twenty years ago, and it was difficult to imagine that the woman now standing before him could ever have been attractive enough to entice a purblind water-rat to pay her for sex. She wore her former profession like stigmata, as if every sordid sexual encounter had left on her face some memento by way of a line to remind her of whatever act she had been obliged to perform in order to feed her boys. She'd been a good mother, Jarvis knew that, though some would have argued otherwise. She had fed them, and kept them, and fought for them, and word had it that she was the only living person George and Jimmy respected. That had to count for something, in Jarvis's view – though his views were often out of kilter with those of people who believed they could somehow make the world as neat, as clean, as perfect, as one of Tommy Carter's little holes.

She said, 'I thought I'd seen the back o' you, Mr Jarvis,' and as she spoke, she glanced at the door that led to a small bedroom.

Jarvis grew slightly nervous then, though he couldn't quite put his finger on why. Maybe it was something in her look, or maybe it was the noise from the tenement as a whole – the footsteps of somebody tearing down the echoing concrete stairs, the flush of the lavatory on the landing, the whining, persistent cry of a very young child. A man and woman were arguing somewhere in the building, their voices loud but their broad Glaswegian accents making it impossible for him to determine what all the shouting was about. Their voices drifted up to him in a room where one of the windows had no glass and was patched with tape. And yet, despite the draught that seeped through the gaping repair, the room still stank.

'I said, I thought I'd seen the back o' you.'

She stole another look in the direction of the bedroom, and this, plus the fact that she'd raised her voice unnecessarily, indicated to Jarvis that she might be trying to sound some kind of warning. It was then that it occurred to him that George might be in there, and as the possibility dawned on him, it also dawned on him that maybe it hadn't, after all, been wise to go there alone.

He should have known there was always the chance that George might be around, though he'd thought it unlikely on the grounds that George would suspect the police to be keeping the place under twenty-four-hour surveillance in case he happened to turn up. But if he *was* there, Jarvis reasoned, the wisest thing would be to do nothing to antagonise him. George wasn't Tommy Carter. He wouldn't come quietly. In fact, he wouldn't come at all. Jarvis knew that if he tried to arrest him, George would laugh in his face, and tell him to fuck off home. Jarvis, if he had any sense, would oblige. And yet, he couldn't bring himself to lose face by backing off. 'George,' he said. 'If you're in there, I'm alone, and I don't have a gun.'

There wasn't a sound from that room, but Jarvis was now so certain that George was in there, he walked towards the door, knocked on it, and said, 'You know me, George, and I've never lied to you. I've told you I'm alone and unarmed, and it's the truth, so I'm coming in.'

Iris spoke a soft and genuine warning: 'I wouldn't go in there if I was you, Mr Jarvis.'

Jarvis lifted a latch more in keeping with the latch on a lavatory door and walked into darkness, for the room was no bigger than a closet and had no window. His lower legs banged against a bed pulled down from the wall, but there was nothing to see other than the bed itself with its metal frame and the walls closing in all around it. And then a shape rose up from the floor, a shape that roared as it lunged for him and sent him reeling back through the door and into the room where Iris was still standing.

It took a good few seconds for Jarvis to realise who was attacking him, and the knowledge that Jimmy had him pinned to the wall with those ragged, naked stumps was worse than finding himself staring down the barrel of a shotgun.

He had heard tell that Jimmy would have no truck with a prosthesis of any kind, and that he took no pains to conceal those terrible stumps. But nothing he had ever heard had in any way prepared him for what they might look like, for such had been the ferocity with which the hands had been savaged, he needed further surgery to neaten what was left.

Whether he'd ever been offered that surgery, Jarvis didn't know; he only knew that those stumps were more appalling in reality than anything he could have conjured from imagination, the skin mottled and purple, the scarring thick and red. And it wasn't just the stumps, it was the smell of the man, for the stench that accompanied Jimmy was worse than anything that seeped up from the bins in the courtyard below. But sickened though he was, Jarvis felt a stab of compassion for the man. How could he wash when he had no hands with which to wash himself? What did he do in a tenement with no bath, no shower? Did his mother wash him from time to time, grown man though he was?

Jarvis had no answer to these questions; he had only the smell to make him suspect that, along with his hands, Jimmy had lost all trace of his own dignity as a human being. Not only did he stink, but his hair was down his back as though it hadn't been cut these ten years past. And maybe it hadn't, thought Jarvis. Maybe, with the loss of his hands, Jimmy had seen enough of blades of any description or design.

Through yellowing, stinking teeth, he said, 'She's an old woman, y' bastard – whaddya want tae come botherin' her fer?' and Jarvis tried to explain that he was there because of Tam.

Jimmy wasn't convinced. He raised the longer of his two ragged stumps, his arm a long, thin stick, and it occurred to Jarvis that, judging from the photos hanging on the wall, the sheer weight of muscle that had once been on the bone would, when Jimmy was whole, have been enough to crush the skull of a horse. Now, the muscles were wasted, and as if suddenly aware that he no longer had the strength to kill him, Jimmy gave it up, pushing him away, breathing heavily, as if the exertion had been too much for him. He looked to Iris for some lead with regard to what she wanted him to do, but Iris merely lit a Senior Service, holding it in hands so big, so *masculine*, it was difficult to imagine that, at any time in her life, some man had slipped a ring on to one of those fingers. She put it to Jimmy's mouth and he drew on it before she took it away and held it for him. 'You said somethin' about Tam,' she said to Jarvis, who replied, 'He's been gone for nearly two months. Elsa's getting worried.'

Jimmy came out with a noncommittal, 'He's a grown lad,' but Jarvis battled on: 'I came to find out whether anyone else in the family was worried.'

'And if we were,' said Iris, 'what then?'

'Then I'd ask you to report him missing, and I'll make sure Strathclyde, as well as the Met, take a serious look at where he might be.'

Even as he said it, Jarvis reminded himself that people like these had such an ingrained distrust of all forms of authority that it didn't sound much of an offer. For a start, they wouldn't believe the police would bother to look for any missing member of their family, and second, they would believe that even if the police did look, it would only be to suit their own purposes. Trouble was, thought Jarvis, their distrust wasn't entirely unfounded. If the police took steps to find Tam, it would be with a view to ensuring that once they got their hands on him, they could squeeze him for whatever he might know about the part his father had played in the job on the betting shop. And Jarvis could hardly blame anyone for that: he'd done his share of squeezing Tam and Robbie for information. *Did Tam find your dad, Robbie? How come he didn't come back with you on the train?*

Jimmy took another pull on the Senior Service, burning it down to a mere half-inch with the strength of his inhalation, and as Iris extinguished what was left of it by crushing it in her fingers, she made a rare admission: 'I'm worried,' she said.

Jarvis already knew that. He had picked up on it when Iris had reminded him that he'd mentioned Tam at all. Now, he caught a flicker of alarm as he said, 'What was he wearing the day he and Robbie left here for the station?'

Even as he said it, he regretted it, because it sounded far too like the type of question that was asked when the police suspected that someone had come to harm.

'I cannae remember exactly.'

'Try,' said Jarvis, gently, and Jimmy jumped in with 'She said she cannae remember.'

Iris fended Jimmy off with, 'Give it a rest, will ye, Jimmy?' and, hesitantly, she then confirmed much of what Elsa had told him.

'Did he give any indication of where he might be going after putting Robbie on the train?'

'Not a word,' said Iris.

'Do you think he might have gone to look for his father?'

Iris considered the possibility as if it had never occurred to her before, which could only have meant that Elsa had said nothing, and that Tam hadn't told her what had brought him to Glasgow. 'Aye,' she finally conceded. 'Ah suppose it's always possible.'

'Would he know where to find him?' said Jarvis.

Iris was wary now. 'Maybe,' she admitted.

Jarvis, who knew damn well that Iris could get hold of George if the need should arise, hadn't pressed her for more. There was no point. 'Elsa is considering reporting Tam as missing,' he said.

'He's a grown lad,' Jimmy repeated, and Jarvis had

replied that being a grown lad was hardly any insurance against coming to harm.

He had left them with that thought, and had gone to Glasgow Central to ask members of staff whether anyone recalled seeing a lad of about sixteen standing on the platform with a lad of about nine.

He hadn't held any hope whatsoever that, out of the thousands of people who must have passed through in the past two months, someone would remember either of them, but he'd been wrong: a woman who ran the depressingly inadequate buffet had remembered a boy who fitted Robbie's description, a lad who had walked into the comparative warmth of a bar where pale, milky coffee and warm, amber whisky were sold in equal quantities, a bar where the tables were low and scratched, the windows high and dirty.

Jarvis had said, 'How come you remember him?' and he had learned that Robbie had asked if there were sandwiches left from the day before because if there were, and if they were stale, could he buy one cheap?

The woman had made him a sandwich, had given him a Coke to go with it, and had let him sit in the warmth until the London train arrived.

'Why?'

'He only had this thinnish jumper. It was bliddy freezin'. But it wasn't just the fact that it was bliddy freezin', he looked terrified tae me – Ah reckoned he'd been frightened by the storm.'

He might have been terrified, thought Jarvis. But it wasn't the storm that had frightened him. He said, 'Was anyone with him – an older lad, maybe?'

She indicated windows that hadn't been washed in

weeks. They gave out on to the platform, making the outside world seem even filthier than it was. 'Ah watched him board the train,' she said. 'He was definitely alone.'

No big brother to see him off, thought Jarvis – because after they left Iris something had happened to Tam. The question was, why was Robbie refusing to tell anyone what that 'something' was?

The obvious, the only, answer was that he had to be protecting someone, and a child was hardly likely to protect his brother's killer, unless, of course, the killer was his father.

He put this to Hunter, who told him he was allowing his imagination to get the better of him. He insisted once again that not even George McLaughlan would eat his own kids.

But that, thought Jarvis, had been before the remains of a lad had been found down the docks.

A sound that hadn't been common in the sixties but was now a part of everyday life in the city pulled his mind from the past, and Jarvis lifted his eyes skyward to where a police helicopter chopped its way through the clouds. Some of the people standing beside him would no doubt presume that Tommy Carter's funeral was being captured for posterity. Or perhaps the police were filming the crowd in the hope of catching sight of those who were wanted for some misdemeanour.

Jarvis knew better. Something's going down, he thought, and by watching the line of flight, he deduced that the helicopter was heading towards North London. He watched it disappear, the sound of its engine blotted out by the rumble of the cortège, the clop of hoofs as the horses began to walk down the Mile End Road.

Chapter Four

Two shots were fired at Swift the instant his gun went off, and the denim of his jeans darkened as blood began to saturate the material. But Swift didn't move, and he still kept his grip on the child. He has to be high, thought McLaughlan. He doesn't even know he's been shot.

Like everyone else, McLaughlan dived for cover, and as he scrambled behind the nearest car, he saw a teenage girl, her skinny legs like sea-snakes in tights striped red and yellow. Moments earlier, she had been crossing the road as if heading for the bank, but as soon as the shooting started, she just stood there, a target for any passing bullet.

She started to laugh and Doheny broke cover to grab her, pull her down with him, up against the wheels of a car that was parked too close to the armoured van for comfort. She clung to him, shaking with terror, and he made himself a barrier between her and any further shots that might be fired.

But there were only those two shots, and in the silence that followed McLaughlan looked over the bonnet of the car and saw a helicopter coming in from a distance.

Soon it would hover over the bank, and the men inside would keep all units briefed with regard to what was happening on the ground. He also saw something else: Swift now had the gun pressed hard against the neck of the little boy.

Just yards from them, the mother of the child had come to a halt. Still on her hands and knees, she crouched on the pavement, rigid with shock, and she stared at her child as if she couldn't believe he was still alive.

McLaughlan couldn't believe it either. His mother had stopped her wailing, but the boy was crying now. He was covered in blood, and for a moment, McLaughlan thought that maybe they were about to see him die before their eyes, but the blood had come from the wound to Swift's leg.

Swift seemed hardly to notice it. He was looking at Fischer, who had his back to McLaughlan, his gun held low, and Fischer now did something that seemed bizarre to McLaughlan: he let his weapon drop to the ground, then raised a hand as if to ask for silence. As if convinced that he now had everyone's attention, he lowered his hand again, then started to walk very slowly towards the bank.

Once there, he leaned against the wall, his palms flat to the brickwork. It made him look as if he was expecting to be frisked. But then his entire body began to shake.

He was fighting now, fighting to stay on his feet. It was as if he was trying to convince himself that he hadn't been hit, or that if he had, his injuries were nothing he couldn't handle. And then he went down. Not suddenly. Not heavily. But slowly. Sinking to the ground as if his life were being sucked away through a straw.

He rolled on his back, and when the extent of his injuries was revealed, McLaughlan knew he hadn't been killed by police. Fischer had caught the blast from the sawn-off shotgun.

His ribcage hung wide open, the shirt and jumper that had covered it now little more than a bloodied mass of rags. He was wearing a leather jacket, and beneath the clots of blood, the leather shone like the coat of a racehorse, mahogany brown and very highly polished.

He looked incredibly dead, and it wasn't the fact of his guts having spilled from his ribs that gave the impression. The essence of him was gone, and no amount of technology would ever bring him back, get his heart pumping again, breathe some personality into the lifeless face.

The boy was crying hysterically now, and Orme called out to Swift, 'Stuart, you're injured.'

Swift didn't take his eyes off Orme to look and see if this was true, or examine the damage. He didn't take the gun off the child, either, and Orme tried again: 'Stuart – look at the blood!'

Swift now looked at the pool that was forming around his feet. It didn't seem to worry him unduly, but it worried the little boy. He lifted his feet, first one, then the other, putting them down gingerly, crying more quietly now.

'You're bleeding to death,' said Orme. 'For fuck's sake – let us help you!'

Swift suddenly slumped to his heels, as if his legs had given way beneath him. The way he did it suggested to McLaughlan that maybe he was already going into shock, but short of him dying on them, it would make no appreciable difference: he still had the gun pressed against the neck of the little boy.

He was looking at the getaway vehicle, which wasn't where it should have been because Leach had panicked, had thrust it into reverse, had sent it speeding backwards and up the kerb to crash into the wall of a building opposite.

Now, Leach was sitting behind the wheel, his arms folded, his head down on his arms, shaking as he sobbed. He wasn't in the same league as his associates – he was just a car thief, and *way*, *way* out of his depth. Being the driver, he couldn't afford to pump himself up with whatever Stuart had used to give himself more bottle, so there was nothing standing between him and the reality of the situation, and he would know, thought McLaughlan, that he wasn't going to walk away from this, that maybe he would end up dead like Fischer. He'd lost it so completely, McLaughlan found himself almost feeling sorry for him. One thing was for sure, thought McLaughlan, even if Swift made it as far as the car, not only was the car undrivable, but Leach was in no fit state to drive anybody anywhere.

With Swift keeping that gun on the child, Orme motioned his men to lower their weapons and back off. He himself had put his weapon down, and now he came out from behind the armoured van. 'Come on, Stuart – this is fucking silly.'

That was about as far as Orme got before Swift, maybe out of fear, maybe out of recognition that it was all over anyway, reared up and swung round on Orme. A shot was fired by police—

—and Swift fell to the ground.

I had no choice, thought McLaughlan. No choice whatsoever.

Unlike Fischer, Swift didn't get the chance to go walkabout. He wasn't about to experience the joys of pressing his hands against a wall whilst trying to convince himself that he wasn't about to die, because the bullet had entered him exactly where McLaughlan had intended it should strike – as far from the child as possible.

Straight between the eyes.

Chapter Five

Back-up vehicles begin to arrive, parking up by the kerb, sending sprays of water on to the pavement, and the rain continues to hammer down as Doheny opens the boot of a 4 x 4. He pulls out sheets of tarpaulin, throws them over the bodies, while others are taking witness statements, cordoning off the road.

You lean with your back to the armoured van, and you watch them doing their job. Soon, paramedics will come, along with teams from Forensic. The press will arrive, and crowds will gather as word gets round that something has gone down.

Nobody asks you to do anything, and you don't offer. They leave you alone because everyone knows that different people react in different ways to shooting someone: some go into a kind of panic, seeking reassurance that they haven't cocked-up, that they aren't about to be tried for unlawful killing. Others just go quiet. It's best to leave them alone.

Orme leads the mother of the child to a waiting ambulance, her blood-smothered son in her arms. She sleep-walks her way towards it, and he clings to her, his hands entwined in her hair. He's looking up at something, the helicopter maybe – but when you lift your face to the rain, you find the chopper gone, that what the kid is looking at is the silver, globe-shaped balloon. The thread has caught on the logo of the bank. It hangs there like a banner – a ragged flag of war.

Swift's body is being loaded into a van. It isn't all that different from the one he was trying to rob. Orme sees what you're looking at. 'Let's get you out of here.'

'Not now,' you tell him. 'Not yet. I need a few minutes, a walk, just down the road and back – just to get it together.'

You think he's about to refuse you, but all he does is give the nod to Doheny. 'Go with him,' he says. 'Then get him down to the station.'

You'd rather be alone, but if there has to be someone, you're glad it's Doheny. A man of few words at the best of times, he won't ask stupid questions.

He walks down the road with you, and stands with you when you stop in front of the house. He doesn't know what you're looking at, but fuck only knows what could be going through your mind at a time like this, so he doesn't ask. And you've suddenly got this straight-on view of the house where you used to live. The curtains look expensive – nothing like the curtains of your childhood, that's for sure.

You don't intend to stay there – you want to see it, that's all. You want to see just how much it's changed.

A woman walks out of the house. Her clothes are simple and chic. She has to have money, and money isn't something you could ever have imagined coming to this part of London. But here it is, money, as though the past has been erased from the memory of the area – as if the things that happened here couldn't have taken place.

But they did take place. Thirty years ago, your father carried a dying man through that glossy front door. His blood had stained the paintwork to such an extent that the only way to remove it was to strip the door to the wood. He lifted the bloodstained carpet in the hall, and dumped it in a backstreet down by the market. And when the coppers came, you stuck together, like families do, and denied he was ever there.

You reach for the crucifix, finding it solid and warm against your neck, a constant reminder that Jarvis believed there was something about it, that maybe it was blessed, and that maybe it could therefore keep the person who wore it safe.

You've never believed it was blessed. And as for keeping you safe – you, of all people, have evidence to the contrary: putting his faith in that cross was the last thing Tam ever did, and it failed him completely.

'Better be getting back,' said Doheny, and you turn with the intention of obliging. But you sink to your heels, your hands to your head, because any minute now, you could black out—

Doheny hails a passing patrol as if it were a taxi, gets you into it, and jumps in the back beside you. 'Tower Bridge,' he says. He doesn't ask what's going on in your mind. You're so fucking grateful you could kiss him. You don't want to tell him you're scared.

Of all the villains whose son you could have shot, it had to be Swift.

You're as good as dead if he finds out who you are.

Chapter Six

By the time Orme returned to the station, Leach was in custody, and he went down to the cells to take a look at him. He was still bawling his eyes out, his hands flat to a wall in a parody of the stance that Fischer had taken when dying.

Orme had yet to come across anyone who felt particularly happy about the prospect of being charged with attempted armed robbery, but even so, in his view, Leach seemed to be making a bit of a meal of it. His belt and shoelaces had already been taken off him, along with the fleece-lined jacket that he'd worn during the robbery, and he was shaking, though with cold or shock, Orme couldn't say. 'Get him a blanket,' he said, and the custody sergeant obliged.

Leach seemed almost pathetically grateful for the blanket. He wrapped it around himself, lay down on the bunk and closed his eyes. But, despite his exhaustion, sleep refused to come. It was no surprise. For weeks, Leach hadn't slept properly. Whenever he drifted off, he saw himself wading around inside a septic tank. It was the old-fashioned, brick-sided kind that was sunk into the ground, and Leach had no idea how long it was since it had last been emptied. He only knew it was 10 foot x 10 foot in diameter, that a metal sheet covered it at ground level, that the sheet had been covered by turf to conceal the tank completely, and that once the sheet was pulled away from it, the stink of human waste was indescribable.

It wasn't full. That was the only good part about it. Shortly after buying the place, Calvin had had the house replumbed and the lavatories emptied into a modern sewage system. The tank was therefore no more than a third full, and it was possible to stand in it up to your thighs.

'Dig down,' said Calvin.

'Please, Mr Swift, don't make me do this.'

'I wouldn't like to have to introduce you to Budgie,' said Calvin, and although Leach wasn't sure who or what Budgie was, he did as he was told. He plunged his hands around the tank until he found an object the size and shape of a football.

The look on Leach's face told Calvin that he'd located the desired object, and Calvin said, 'Good. Now bring it up.'

Bringing that thing to the surface was the worst thing Leach had ever done. *Oh, God. Dear God.* He'd had to let it go. And he'd shook his head like a stupefied mule when Calvin had told him to bring it up again.

Fischer had been drafted in to help him at that point, and between them, they had brought to the surface something that had lain in the tank for years.

Calvin had forced them to move it to a resting-place that had already been searched by the police. And after the job was over not only had he made them clean out the septic tank (make a nice little sunken garden, that will), he and Ray had held guns to their heads, had told them never to breathe a word of what they'd found.

Leach curled up on the bunk, the blanket wrapped around him. What Calvin had sworn to do to him if he talked was worse than anything Orme could throw his way: 'I don't want to have to ask you to do this job again, Vinny, but if ever I catch wind that you've shot your mouth off, you'll find yourself diggin' around for your wife an' kids.'

Orme, who didn't have time to worry about Leach for the moment, decided to leave him sobbing into his blanket. His most pressing job was to have a quick word with McLaughlan, then get himself down to Berkshire and break the news to Calvin Swift that his son had been shot dead. It wasn't a job he was particularly looking forward to, but it was one that needed doing before Calvin heard of what had happened via other sources.

He found McLaughlan back in the room where the briefing had taken place. He took him into an office for a quiet word, and asked how he was feeling.

'Fine,' said McLaughlan.

Orme suddenly realised he could hardly have been expected to say anything else in the circumstances. Any admission to feeling even slightly shaken might be construed as weakness. 'You don't have to put it on for me,' said Orme.

'I'm fine,' repeated McLaughlan, who thought back to the reception he'd got when he followed Doheny into the briefing room. Every man in it had surged forward, had crowded around him, had told him he was a lucky bastard – that they wished they'd had the chance to bury Swift. They were right behind him. 'Don't worry about the press. Don't worry about the inquiry. Don't worry about anything, my son – you're a fucking hero.'

They were doing exactly what he would have done if the man behind the gun had been one of them. They were giving him their support. All of them.

All, that is, except one.

He had stood by the row of tables that the weapons were laid out on early that morning, and he had said, 'Somebody pull a chair for the walking corpse.'

Whether he knew it or not, he was paying homage to Calvin Swift's reputation for exacting revenge. He might as well have said, 'If someone can hammer a nine-inch nail into the head of a former girlfriend, there's no telling what he might do to the man who shot his son.'

Doheny had grabbed the offender by the throat and McLaughlan had soothed the situation, had made out that he wasn't fazed by the reference to Calvin's predilection for revenge, or his knack of staying out of jail.

The girlfriend had lived. McLaughlan had seen her mother pushing her down the Old Kent Road in a wheelchair. Her eyes were a little vacant, but you wouldn't have known that part of her brain was cream. She'd seemed happy enough to McLaughlan, waving to passing cars, distributing cheerful greetings to anyone who happened to be within shouting distance.

'You worried about Swift?' said Orme.

'No,' said McLaughlan, and Orme's lack of reaction called him a liar.

'Let me tell you something . . .'

McLaughlan knew exactly what Orme was going to say: that London produced more than its fair share of villains who became legends in their own time, that much of what was attributed to them was apocryphal.

There was nothing apocryphal about Calvin's reputation, thought McLaughlan. Burglary. Armed robbery. Murder. But, apart from one lengthy prison sentence for armed robbery, when had he ever been dealt with? When had anything actually been proved against him? And what hope was there when witnesses and grasses either disappeared, blew their own evidence apart, or claimed to have been mistaken with regard to what they thought they had seen or heard?

'Want me to put armed men on your house for a while?'

'Why don't you paint a target on my head while you're at it?'

Orme didn't know what to say other than to remind McLaughlan that Swift was unlikely to find out the identity of the man who pulled the trigger on his son. He said, 'I'm on my way to break the news to Calvin. We may end up bringing him back to the station – depends on how it goes.'

McLaughlan understood the subtext. He had to remain at the station in case officers more senior than Orme wanted to talk to him. It might, however, be an idea to melt into the background if Calvin was about to be brought in. The man was uncanny. It was like he could look at you and know if you'd done him damage.

He stopped himself from thinking along those lines and concentrated instead on persuading himself that Orme was right: that much of what was attributed to

Calvin Swift was apocryphal. He couldn't be responsible for half of what people attributed to him and stay out of jail.

On the other hand, thought McLaughlan, when you knew how to terrify people it was amazing what you could get away with.

He thought of the girl being wheeled down the Old Kent Road.

Apocryphal or not, he intended to watch his back.

It was eighteen months since Orme had last seen Calvin. They had spoken, Orme walking up to him in a club that should have known better than to make a couple of villains like the Swift brothers members.

Calvin, Orme had said.

Leonardo! said Calvin, who had long been in the habit of embellishing Orme's Christian name by way of insult. He had expected Orme to go away, but Orme had joined his party, albeit briefly, buying drinks for Calvin, his brother Ray, and a couple of women whom neither had introduced.

By drawing Calvin into conversation, Orme had learned nothing other than that Calvin appeared to have been taking elocution lessons. He would never rid himself of his East End accent completely, but he had softened it, and his grammar had improved out of all recognition. Orme had had a hard job hiding his amusement: 'Come again, Calvin. What was that you said?'

Just for a moment it had looked as though Ray had taken sufficient offence to get physical about it. He had risen, very slowly, from his chair, and Calvin had put out a hand to calm him down. 'All right, Ray, Mr Orme's just having a bit of a joke at our expense. We enjoy a bit of a joke. Isn't that right, Mr Orme?'

'I've long had you down as a joker,' Orme admitted gravely, and Ray, who hadn't been able to trust himself to keep his notorious temper, had taken himself outside for a breath of air.

Like Ray, Calvin had been wearing a suit that was clearly tailor-made. Dark grey, well cut and immaculately pressed, it marked him out as a *somebody*, and for that reason alone, Calvin would no doubt consider it to have been worth every penny of whatever it had cost him. Orme would never aspire to a suit like that, but then again, neither would he ever wear his hair as long as Calvin, and he certainly wouldn't tie it back in a rubber band. Silken and grey, that hair had shone with expensive grooming, and yet, in Orme's view, a pony-tail on a man of fifty-six always conveyed the impression that the person wearing it was probably a villain and Calvin was no exception: seen from face-on, he looked like a business tycoon; seen from the side, he looked like the killer many believed him to be.

The accidental meeting had taken place shortly after Calvin and Ray had bought a large country property in Berkshire. It was a far cry from their East End origins, and ideal for the kind of family that could best be described as extended.

The brothers had always lived together to Orme's certain knowledge, and over the years they had been joined by various of their relatives. Some, like Stuart, and like Ray's daughter Sherryl, were a permanent fixture, but the mothers of Stuart and Sherryl, along with grandparents, cousins, and anyone who could lay some claim to being even distantly related, had occasionally moved in, before moving on, dying off, or ending up in jail. If Orme's information was correct, these were comparatively quiet times in that the property's only residents were Calvin, Ray and Sherryl.

There was no telling how Calvin might react when told that Stuart was dead, so Orme had taken the precaution of taking three of his men with him, two in a second vehicle. It was the first time any of them had seen the Berkshire property, which turned out to be large, symmetrical, probably early Georgian. It was also very isolated, and Orme was glad he hadn't gone there alone.

He pulled up in front of massive wrought-iron gates. They, like the wall that surrounded the three-acre garden, were modern in design and totally out of keeping with the house. They hung from pillars that comprised part of a twelve-foot, razor-topped wall, and cameras were in evidence, as was a state-of-the-art burglar alarm. You had to laugh, thought Orme.

How much was it worth? he wondered. A million? More? Its tall, elegant windows looked out on to the kind of lawn that Orme was convinced could only exist in a BBC period drama. The almost violent green seemed manufactured, the Regency stripes the result of meticulous rolling. Calvin had clearly kitted himself out with a decent gardener, thought Orme. Maybe he came with the house.

A helicopter stood on a pad way off to the left. It was a fair indication that Ray had to be around somewhere, it being his preferred mode of travel, and the prospect of having to deal with him wasn't one that lifted Orme's heart. It wouldn't make his job any easier, that was for sure. If nothing else, Ray could be guaranteed to do the complete opposite of calming and soothing Calvin – all unavoidable problems could only escalate in his presence.

Orme got out of the car, walked up to the gates and pressed a button on the intercom. Immediately, two large Dobermans were pounding the gates with massive bull-like shoulders, their barking almost drowning out the buzz of the intercom. 'Calvin, it's Leonard Orme,' said Orme, and a slight whirring sound made him look up to see a camera take on anthropomorphic qualities and give him the once-over.

Moments later, the dogs stopped barking as if they'd heard a command inaudible to the human ear. They ran round the side of the house as the gates slid open, and Orme climbed back into the car, then drove it down an immaculately gravelled drive. As he pulled up in front of the house, the elegant Georgian door swung wide and Calvin stood at the entrance. He smiled, as if seeing Orme were an unexpected pleasure. 'Leonardo!' he said. 'What's all this?'

'Can we go inside, Calvin?'

'Inside, Leonard? What would you want to go inside my house for?'

'We need to talk,' said Orme. 'I'd rather we talked inside.'

'What do we need to talk about?'

'Inside,' said Orme.

And Calvin let them in.

The room he guided them into came as a shock to Orme. He hadn't known what to expect, but he hadn't been prepared for a room that was large, light and clean, a room in which the floor was of a highly polished maple.

Abstract works of art hung on the bone-white walls, and Orme wondered who had chosen them. Not Calvin. Not a chance, he thought, though he didn't know what made him think so. He supposed it was conceivable that Calvin might have learned a thing or two about art when in prison, but then again, if Orme's memory of what lay on his record was correct, he had shown no interest whatsoever in art. Rather, he had developed a deep and abiding interest in law, which he had studied with a view to quoting passages verbatim at whatever judge he might come up against in the future.

Calvin was clearly asking himself why Orme had appeared on his doorstep accompanied by three of his men, but, still sounding relaxed, he said, 'Expecting trouble, Leonard?'

'Calvin,' said Orme, 'Stuart tried to pull a bank job this morning.'

Calvin looked at him as if he might be having him on. 'Stuart?' he said, and his grammar slipped, the accent suddenly thick as he said, 'I don't know nothin' about no bank.' He looked at the men with him, as if considering whether this was some kind of wind-up. 'What's goin' on?'

'He was shot,' said Orme, and just for a moment, Calvin looked like any other parent in the face of bad news – as if he didn't believe what he'd just been told.

'He was killed,' said Orme. 'So was Carl.'

Light streamed in through a window curtained in ivory silk. There was no design to the silk, no discernible pattern, just the gentlest of movements in a breeze that didn't exist. Calvin stilled the softly moving fabric by resting his hand on it.

'Do you hear me, Calvin – hear what I just said?'

Calvin was playing with the curtain. Strange, thought Orme. He had expected violence, or an outburst of rage at the least. But Calvin was stroking the fabric as if it were a dog, a sweeping down of the palm, a comforting gesture. Controlled.

'Calvin?'

'I want to see him,' he said.

Right now, thought Orme, Stuart was lying on a slab with what was left of his brains in a glass bowl. 'That wouldn't be advisable,' said Orme, who was reluctant to say any more in case he inadvertently brought it to Calvin's attention that Stuart would need the services of an expert embalmer before any of his family got to see him. Pathologists were not renowned for their expertise with wax. Someone would have to fill the hole made by the bullet, and the tissues surrounding the entry wound would need the skill of an artist if they were to give the appearance of there having been no injury inflicted on the deceased.

The sound of someone approaching drew Orme's eye to the door, and Ray appeared, a ballpoint pen in his hand. The minute he saw Orme, he didn't waste energy pretending to courtesy. He compressed the end of the pen, the *snick* of the nib contracting preceding the inevitable: 'What the fuck's all this?'

'Stuart's been shot,' said Calvin, and he said it very quietly, his hand on the pale silk curtain.

It wasn't often, thought Orme, that you saw someone

truly stripped of the ability to react to what they'd been told. Ray, who was notorious for acting and reacting in an instant on the slightest provocation, stood as if nailed to the floor. It was, however, a temporary paralysis: seconds later, he lunged for Orme, stabbing at his eyes with the ballpoint pen.

It took some considerable effort for Orme's men to pull him off, and as Ray was pinned to the ground, he yelled something animal – something that Orme didn't catch.

The noise brought Ray's daughter, Sherryl, running into the room. For a minute, it looked as though she couldn't believe her eyes, and then her father shouted, 'Stuart's dead.'

Like Ray, Sherryl was momentarily rendered incapable of reacting to the news, then she launched herself at the men who were cuffing her father. She was a stick of a girl, but she knew how to put her weight behind a punch. Orme couldn't bring himself to hit her back, but one of his men had no such hesitation. He smacked her in the mouth and sent her reeling, then grabbed her and pinned her arms behind her back.

She started to howl. No tears. Just an outraged cry. Then Calvin told her that Carl was also dead, and she stopped the noise and started to cry for real.

With her split lip, and the blood dripping down a pale blue cashmere jumper, she looked the little-girl-lost. God forbid her brief should take a photograph of that, thought Orme. She'd get them all suspended.

Orme knew her of old, and knew that she spoke with the kind of accent you only got from years of attending a particular kind of private school for girls. She'd had the best of everything all her life. Ponies, sports cars, designer clothing – you name it. Not that it made any difference: Sherryl was her father's daughter, no mistake about that.

He ordered his men to put Ray in the car, then told them to radio for back-up. Once it arrived, Sherryl could follow her father to Tower Bridge, where they would both be charged with assault. They would spend the night in the cells, which, if nothing else, would give them a chance to cool off, and that was no bad thing: Orme wouldn't have put it past Ray to muster up every member of the family he could lay his hands on with a view to firebombing the station if left to his own devices in his current frame of mind.

Even as Ray and Sherryl were led outside, Calvin was calling their brief, Edward Bryce. Orme stood by as he pulled a mobile phone out of his pocket, punched a single key, and got through in an instant.

Not many people kept the number of their brief so readily to hand, thought Orme, but then Calvin made a habit of needing him. This was nothing new.

'Edward,' said Calvin, and the accent was pristine again. 'We've got company – *Leonard Orme.*'

None of your Leonardo now, thought Orme, who, at any other time, would have welcomed the sudden show of respect, the realisation that none of this was a game. Calvin listened to something Bryce said in response, then broke in: 'Stuart's dead.'

He had managed to say the words without his voice betraying what it had cost him, but the expression on his face had been a different matter. Edward Bryce, currently comfortably ensconced in chambers, wasn't standing in the room with Calvin. He therefore wouldn't know that, on forming the words, Calvin's face had been contorted by a spasm of grief. 'Ray and Sherryl are being taken to—' He turned to Orme for confirmation:

'Tower Bridge,' said Orme.

'Tower Bridge,' said Calvin. 'Can you be there?'

Orme calculated that Bryce would be at Tower Bridge long before he got Ray and Sherryl back to the station. They had to travel from Berkshire. Bryce had to nip across town. And once he got there, thought Orme, he wouldn't waste time. He would gather information relating to what had happened, and he would already be drafting an application to court requesting Ray and Sherryl's release on bail. It was a job that any solicitor could do, but Calvin didn't deal with mere solicitors any more: Bryce was a barrister, and this job would be beneath him. However, so long as Calvin was footing the bills, Orme very much doubted that Bryce would turn him down.

Calvin had ended the call and was searching through his pockets for his car keys. Once he found them, he stared at them as if he couldn't quite work out what they were for.

'Where are you off to?' said Orme. He had never seen Calvin like this, but, then, it wasn't every day a man was told his son had been shot dead by armed police.

'I'd best get down the station – Ray might need me.'

It looked very much to Orme as though it was Calvin who needed Ray, and he didn't want him driving in that state. 'I'll give you a lift,' he said.

Chapter Seven

Orme got back to the station to the news that Bryce had been there for over an hour. He had kicked off by demanding details of the shooting, and when these were denied him, he had demanded a meeting with one of Orme's superiors. When this was also denied him, he had threatened to make an announcement to the press, but Doheny had held him at bay with the news that Orme was on his way, and that the minute he got there, Bryce would be the very first person he saw.

Orme wasn't surprised to hear that Bryce had threatened to use his influence with the press. And unfortunately, thought Orme, he *did* have influence. He seemed, in fact, incapable of uttering two syllables without it making headline news, largely because his propensity for defending villains of the calibre of the Swifts had brought him to public notice some years ago.

The press had clutched him to their collective bosom from the word go, loving him for the fact that he was ostensibly *establishment* yet clearly devoid of respect for establishment values, and Orme could imagine the content of any announcement he might make: 'My client, a valued member of the community, a contributor to numerous charities, was, earlier today, devastated to learn of the death of his nephew, Stuart, an innocent bystander caught up on the periphery of a bank raid and shot by armed police in a case of mistaken identity.'

'Where is he now?' said Orme.

'I put him in one of the interview rooms and left a couple of ours in there with him – told them to make sure he stayed there.'

'Good,' said Orme, adding, 'Where's McLaughlan?'

'He's being looked after,' said Doheny, and Orme knew McLaughlan was in safe hands. The rest of the squad would close ranks around him, protect him, calm him down, keep the curious, the vicious, and the plain bloody stupid off his back. Doheny added: 'Where's Calvin?'

'He wanted to come down on Ray's account, so I brought him in. Couldn't think what else to do with him.'

He followed Doheny to the interview room where, earlier, Doheny had left Bryce in the capable hands of a couple of DCs from Flying Squad. He had told them not to let him out of that room – not even if it meant breaking his legs, because Doheny knew that, given the chance, Bryce would be all over that station like a thin film of oil. Somehow he would get his fingers into files that contained sensitive information, or he would home in on the young, the bent or the plain stupid, and extract from them the kind of material that kept him at the top of his profession.

Doheny now opened the door to find Bryce standing by the window. It gave out on to a plain brick wall, and the room itself was less than welcoming, its paintwork a match for the yellowing cream of the walls of the briefing room.

Bryce didn't turn to face the door when it was opened, yet he seemed to know that Orme was there. 'You took your time,' he said.

He was, as Orme well knew, in the habit of wearing black outside court as well as in: the suit, the shoes, the overcoat that he'd slung on the back of a chair – all were black. But the cufflinks were solid gold, a family crest too intricate, too small for Orme to determine the motto stamped on the precious metal.

No matter, thought Orme. Whatever the motto might be, chances were it had its basis in honesty and truth, and neither of those virtues held the slightest meaning for Bryce.

His privileged background was such that Orme couldn't imagine he had ever wanted for much. He wanted for something now: 'If you've got any sense, you won't press charges.'

'They assaulted me and my men.'

'In the light of what they'd just been told, I think a court is likely to view their behaviour sympathetically.'

'I won't let it go at a caution,' said Orme, and because he was leaving Bryce in no doubt that this was non-negotiable, Bryce left it, and said, 'I think you should be aware – I've been engaged to represent Leach. I've already spoken to him.'

Orme looked at Doheny, who gave a barely perceptible shake of the head as if to say it was news to him.

'Who's paying?' said Orme.

'That's between me and my client.'

It had to be Calvin, thought Orme, who couldn't understand it: neither of the Swifts would engage Bryce to represent someone unless they had something to gain. Stuart was dead, so it wasn't as though they could pressure Leach to take the rap and reduce any sentence that might have been given to Stuart. And they certainly wouldn't be doing it purely for Leach's benefit – what was he to them? He said, 'I'm just about to question him,' and Bryce replied, 'Good. Let's get on with it, shall we?'

Orme had Leach brought up from the cells and put in an interview room where he allowed him his jacket and gave him a cigarette. He was taping the interview in the presence of the same Flying Squad officers who had kept Bryce contained until his return from Berkshire, but he quickly discovered that Leach wasn't about to give them any trouble: neither was he about to say a word against Stuart or Carl, preferring, for reasons that were totally lost on Orme, to claim that he had planned the robberies, and that he had conned Stuart and Carl into participating.

Fear of the Swifts had to be behind the stand he was taking, thought Orme, but he still couldn't see the point of it. He put it to Leach that Stuart had suggested the robbery, that Fischer had planned it, and that they had picked him out as the driver because they knew him, and he was a convenient choice.

Leach denied it.

'Where did you first meet Stuart?'

'Calvin had some work done on a house he used to own. I was working for the building firm he hired to do the work.'

76

'What kind of work were you doing?'

Leach recalled what it had been like to reach down into the filth of that septic tank to pull up something that had been rotting there for years, and he heard again the warning: *If you breathe a word to a soul . . .* He said: 'Just casual labouring stuff.'

'And how did you come to meet Carl?'

'He was working for the same firm as me.'

Orme supposed he ought to have been impressed that Leach and Fischer had at least got a job, though he suspected that, like many villains who ended up working for building firms after coming out of prison, they had been motivated by the opportunity to weigh up which properties were ripe for a good robbing a few weeks down the road. 'What kind of work was it?'

'Maintenance, mostly.'

It sounded feasible. 'Okay,' said Orme. 'So there you were, working at "El Pondarosa", and along comes Stuart, and he says, "Do you really want to spend the rest of your natural working your bollocks off for the minimum wage? Pull this job with me, and I'll see you right."'

'I told you,' said Leach. 'It wasn't Stuart's idea. I planned the job, and I talked the other two into pulling it with me.'

'Do me a favour, Vinny. You couldn't plan a bloody Tupperware party.'

'I'm telling you, Mr Orme, I planned the job.'

'And I expect you persuaded Calvin to front the money for the expenses.'

'What expenses?'

Orme shook his head as if saddened by Leach's lack of basic knowledge with regard to how these things were done. 'Armed robberies cost money, Vinny. Think of the expenses. Clothes. Coshes. Cars. The occasional Wimpyburger. Somebody has to front it. I say it was Calvin.'

The suggestion that Calvin had been involved in the planning of the robbery agitated Leach: 'You're gonna get me killed!'

'Calm down, Vinny, nobody's going to kill you.'

'Calvin had nothing to do with it.'

'I say he did—'

'Besides, he wouldn't have dealings with Carl. Ray had made it plain he wasn't welcome.'

'Why?'

'He was screwing Sherryl – Ray didn't like it.'

Orme only had to think back to Sherryl's reaction to the news that Fischer had been shot dead to know it had to be true. Leach added: 'Ray warned him off.'

'And what did Carl have to say to that?'

'Not a lot,' admitted Leach.

I'll bet, thought Orme, who knew that, under normal circumstances, Fischer wouldn't have been the kind of man who frightened easily. One word from Ray, however, had shown him the door. 'Did he ever attempt to see Sherryl again?'

'Not so far as I know.'

Wise man, thought Orme. Not that it had made any difference in the long run. Fischer had avoided dying at the hands of an irate Ray Swift, only to die at the hands of his nephew. He said, 'I think I can see how you got involved in this, Vinny.'

'How do you mean?'

Orme, who badly wanted Leach to make a statement

78

to the effect that Stuart had planned the robbery, if only because it would look good during the inquiry into his death, replied, 'Stuart was an addict. He needed money. He persuaded you and Carl to take part in the robbery, which he planned.'

Again, Leach denied it.

'Why are you doing this, Vinny? What do you think you have to gain by it?'

'Just telling it like it is.'

Orme couldn't work it out, but he tried to get it through to Leach that if he carried on like that in front of a judge, he would find himself looking at an even longer sentence than the one he was undoubtedly going to get in any event, which was the only point at which Bryce intervened: 'Bullying my client isn't likely to endear a court to your cause.'

Orme was reminded that the tape might be played in court, and that what he was saying might be construed as unacceptable. But he didn't like to see Leach digging an even deeper hole for himself than was necessary, purely in order to give the Swift family an advantage of some sort, so he tried to get the message across in a different way. 'You married?' he said, knowing that he was.

'Yes.'

'What's your wife called?'

'Moira.'

'Did Moira know what you were up to this morning?'

No response from Leach, though Bryce looked as though he might jump in again at any moment.

'Does she know where you are right now?'

The look on Leach's face said that Moira was in for a shock and, as if talking to a child, a note of mild exasperation in his voice, Orme said, 'What are we going to do with you, Vinny?'

'How do you mean?'

'You're just a car thief, really – at least, you were. Now you've gone and done something very bloody stupid, and you're going to lose your wife and kids, you realise? They won't even know who you are by the time you get out.'

That started him bawling his eyes out again, and Orme switched off the tape before Bryce's objections could be recorded for posterity. He had intended to wait until Leach calmed down with a view to continuing to question him, but he quickly realised that wasn't going to happen: Leach was losing control of himself, crying and sobbing and pleading with Bryce to protect him.

Orme couldn't quite work out what his problem was: 'What are you scared of, Vinny? Carl's dead. So's Stuart. Whatever you tell us about them, they can't touch you now.' But Leach wasn't hearing him, and at the point when he leaped from his chair and threw himself at the door, Orme – who, as a rule, was a firm believer in leaving villains to ponder the seriousness of their situation – gave an order that, for him, was uncharacteristic: 'Take him back to the cells,' he said. 'Get him a doctor. Tell the doctor to give him a sedative.'

Chapter Eight

Claire McLaughlan had listened to the lunchtime news on Capital Radio. The attempted robbery had been reported, but names of the two dead men hadn't yet been released. It hadn't even been stated whether those who had been killed were police or robbers.

The rituals that Robbie had carried out before leaving the house that morning hadn't been lost on Claire, and she suspected he had been a member of one of the teams involved. She had therefore spent the afternoon waiting for him to call because at times like these he usually let her know he was okay. But there hadn't been a call, and Claire, who knew how the police went about breaking bad news, was beginning to grow afraid.

She had long lived with the knowledge that, one day, an unmarked police car might draw up outside the house, that one of her husband's colleagues might knock on the door, and that she would open it to find him standing there with a female officer. He would say *Claire*, and she would know by his tone of voice that something was wrong. He would ask if they could come in, and she would let them into the house without a word.

She imagined that, if ever that day came, Ocky would be playing on the carpet. The female officer would pick him up and take him out of the room, and then the news would be broken that her husband was injured or dead.

She knew these things because she had been told that this was the way it was done. And the first bad signs were a phone call, or the arrival of a car.

Sometimes the call or the car arrived within minutes of a woman's husband having been shot and rushed to a hospital, and whichever hospital it was, it would be one where there was a surgeon who had trained in a place where war or gang warfare was rife. This surgeon would have experience of how to treat horrendous gunshot wounds. And the wounds from the type of hardware used by villains today often were horrendous. It didn't much matter that they had been inflicted on a London street rather than in some alley in Beirut; they ripped a man apart just the same.

Her way of coping was to convince herself that, whatever the operation, it would always go down as planned and that Robbie would therefore be safe, even though she knew that, statistically, this wasn't possible. There had to be occasions when things went badly wrong.

Ocky was sitting on the couch, playing with some toy, and an unfamiliar car pulled into the drive. Claire didn't see it, but she heard it pull up, and she knew from the sound of the engine that it wasn't their car.

Walking across that room to look out of the window was like wading through treacle. She didn't know how long it took her to get from the couch to the window, or why, when she got there, she avoided looking at the car. It was there all right, dark and sleek, a powerful, unmarked saloon. She saw it the minute she opened the blinds, but then she averted her eyes and focused on the houses standing opposite.

The traffic that sometimes cut through this road during rush-hour had subsided. Now the road seemed quieter, restoring this part of London to some semblance of normality. This was what they had fought and saved and planned for – not a police house, but a decent house of their own in a decent road in a decent part of London. The dream had come true four months ago, and if the house had been old, unmodernised and totally devoid of heating, what did it matter? This was the house they had wanted, the house with a garden, one they had felt was suitable for a small and growing family.

Now what? thought Claire. What do I do with all this if he's dead? What do I tell Ocky if we end up in a flat somewhere, and he doesn't have a father, and we don't have that much money? How will I ever get over losing him?

She dragged her eyes from the houses and looked at the car. Doheny climbed out of it, leaving whoever was with him to get out by themselves. And, suddenly, Claire couldn't stand it. She wasn't having some officer taking Ocky upstairs and out of the way. She didn't know what to do, and she fumbled with the blind, wondering whether, if she didn't go to the door, Doheny would go away.

He wouldn't. She knew that. She would have to go to the door.

The downstairs rooms currently echoed for lack of carpets, and when Claire turned the television off, Ocky wailed in protest. She scooped him up from the couch and carried him to the front door, Ocky clinging to her and closing his eyes against the strength of the bulb that lit the porch.

'Claire,' said Doheny, and it was just as she had imagined it might be, only Robbie was standing in the drive as if he wasn't really sure if this was home.

The relief was overwhelming, and yet she couldn't move. Part of her wanted to run to him, but the greater part, the part that lived with an all-too-familiar anger, kept her in the porch. *If he only knew what it does to me every time I switch on the news, or see a squad car slow as it passes the house—*

Ocky reached out for his father, Claire passing him over as he and Doheny walked into the house and through to the living room.

Doheny stood in front of a fireplace that currently didn't exist. Behind the plasterboard there was a massive hole in the wall. One day, there would be a surround, a grate, a fire. Right now, there was nothing, and the room seemed bare and cold. Even so, Doheny said, 'You've done a lot to the place since Marie and I last saw it.'

If, by a lot, he meant that they had put back one of the walls that a previous owner had removed, restoring the house to its original proportions and giving each of the downstairs rooms some kind of focal point, then Claire supposed he was right. But there was still a lot needed doing. The floorboards had yet to be polished up, just as the wallpaper, largely woodchip, needed stripping down.

The furniture was good. Very few pieces, but carefully chosen. 'We've run out of money,' she said, simply. 'It'll have to stay as it is until we've saved.'

'Took us years,' said Doheny, kindly, but Claire couldn't imagine that Doheny's house had ever been anything other than warm and comfortable. This was currently little more than a shell, a place that she hoped would one day be a home, its only finished room now the one that was Ocky's.

'Way past this guy's bedtime,' said McLaughlan, adding, 'I'll take him up.'

The minute he disappeared, Doheny followed Claire into a kitchen where cutlery and crockery were stored in cardboard boxes on the floor. There wasn't a unit in sight, just an old gas cooker, a newish, second-hand fridge, and a washing-machine, and she found herself gabbling that they had ripped the kitchen out, that it hadn't been fit for use, that she was embarrassed to let him see the place like this. 'I wasn't expecting any-one,' she explained. But when did you ever expect that knock at the door? And how could you know, when it came, how you would react? If Doheny had been there to tell her that Robbie had been killed, would she have cared that the kitchen was a mess? 'Drink?' she offered.

'Not for me,' said Doheny. 'You go ahead.'

He knew, she thought, that she had feared the worst when she saw the car.

She poured herself a drink and he told her what had happened. He didn't give the details, and Claire was glad about that. She didn't want the details. She didn't want to know how near her husband had come to being shot.

'Where's our car?' she said, and her voice had a slightly hysterical edge, as if she might be about to start berating him with remarks such as 'Why does he keep putting himself in dangerous situations? He's married now. We've got a son. Why can't he just get a desk job?'

'Claire,' said Doheny, softly, her tears having taken him by surprise as much as they did her. He reached for a roll of kitchen towel, tore a piece away and handed it to her, waiting until she got herself under control.

'How will it affect him – killing someone, I mean?'

'Hard to say,' said Doheny. 'But from what I know of him, I can't see him being the kind to let it get to him.'

Claire, who felt she knew Robbie rather better than Doheny did, made no comment. He sometimes disappeared for days to places in his head that not even she had been invited to visit. These were places with doors that were not only closed but firmly bolted, and questions such as 'What do you mean, you used to have a brother? Where is he? How do you mean he disappeared? Where do you think he is?' went unanswered.

She saw him to the door, and before he left, Doheny wrote his home number down on a scrap of paper, handed it to her, and said, 'Any problems, give me a call.'

Ocky was lying in bed, turning a small toy tractor round in his fingers, McLaughlan smoothing the duvet over him. Claire walked into the bedroom. 'You okay?'

He gave a nod, but didn't look at her, and that was much as she had expected by way of a response. Whatever he was feeling, she knew he wouldn't show it. He kept his thoughts, his feelings, to himself, along with his past.

The blues and greens of the wall were lit by a night-light, the shade a carousel that projected a galaxy of stars on the dark blue ceiling. She watched as Robbie adjusted the shade a fraction, then bent across Ocky's bed to retrieve the fallen tractor. He returned it to his son with hands so strong they could have crushed the toy as if it were foil. But he didn't look at Claire, and he didn't speak, and because she knew him well enough to know it was pointless to try to draw him out of himself, she kissed her son goodnight and left him to it.

He was frightened of being alone in the room with the galaxy of stars, for despite the soothing blues and greens, the room housed any number of places where *Boogey* might be hiding – *Boogey* – who might drag him out of bed and into the night. Mummy and Daddy would look for him, but they would never find him, because *Boogey* had killed him, and eaten him, and buried his bones in a pit filled with goo!

McLaughlan settled him down again and stayed with him a while, sitting on the edge of his bed, and holding his hand until Ocky drifted quietly into sleep. He had never had an imaginary Boogeyman to fear – his *Boogey* had been real enough when Jimmy had come down to London, Iris having sent him down, claiming she couldn't cope and needed a break.

At the time, McLaughlan had resented her for it, but in adulthood, he could well understand why Iris might need a break. She had done everything for Jimmy from necessity, and whenever it got too much for her and she landed him on their doorstep, George had taken over where Iris left off, dressing him, feeding him, lighting his smokes, wiping his backside, keeping him quiet with whisky and those strange, sad women that he brought to the house 'tae see tae Jimmy's needs'.

Elsa had threatened time and again to leave if Jimmy came, but George had known she had neither the money nor the courage to stand up to him, so the smell and the ranting and wailing had come down from Glasgow to stay with the family, sometimes for weeks on end.

McLaughlan had dreaded not only Jimmy's visits but the very mention of his name. Those stumps of his were worse than any nightmare Ocky could dream up. And it wasn't just the stumps: Jimmy had sensed his fear of him, had resented it, had come after him because of it. And the *way* he'd come after him: it made McLaughlan's skin crawl even now. It had been a game, according to Jimmy – just a harmless game – one in which he pretended to be a zombie, stretching out his arms as if he were dead and *feeling* for him. And when he found him, hiding under the stairs or under his bed, he gave him a hug, which was why, whenever he heard that Jimmy was on his way, McLaughlan had begged his parents not to leave him alone with him.

He was told that it wasn't right to run away from people, just because they were disfigured in some way, and his mother had read him stories to illustrate the suffering of some monsters. But in those stories the monsters hadn't staggered drunkenly into the bedroom of a child in the dead of night, falling on to the bed to slap those stumps around, searching with fingers that didn't exist for a face that was flat to the mattress. McLaughlan had hated Jimmy. He'd wished he would die, and yet, perversely, he had also hoped that Jimmy would live for ever, for then he could never turn into the ghoul that would be so much worse than the living, breathing horror of a man.

Please, God, don't let him find me. I'll be good for the rest of my life if only you don't let him find me.

Chapter Nine

He stayed by the bed long after his son had fallen asleep, turning the metal tractor in his hands, and thinking back to what had taken place that afternoon.

By the time Doheny got him back to the station, word was already out about the shooting, and a lot of people had wanted to talk to him. Some wanted to speak to him from necessity, but there had also been those who were asking out of curiosity: *What does it feel like to kill someone, McLaughlan?*

He had found that out in the moment that he sank to his heels in front of his former home, but he had known better than to admit to what he felt. Some would construe it as shock. Most would construe it as weakness, a warning that perhaps he would prove to be one of those people who couldn't hack what they'd done. 'Who'd have thought McLaughlan would be the type to crack?' He wasn't about to crack, not if he could help it, but by the time Doheny had got him back to the station, he felt as though he didn't belong to himself, as if the commands passed from his brain to his body had to obtain permission from some third party before they had any chance of reaching the nerves and muscles.

Doheny, who had hands-on experience of the scenario that unfolded after a copper had shot someone dead, had reassured him that his senior officers would be backing up his actions, but reminded him that there would automatically be an investigation to establish whether his actions had been justified. It was an investigation that would be carried out either by the Complaints Investigation Branch, or by an outside force. Until such time as it became obvious that he was totally in the clear, he would be suspended from firearms operations, though not from duty, as to suspend a man in his position from duty would make him appear in some way culpable in the eyes of the media and the public. Did he understand?

McLaughlan had understood. He had seen other men go through the procedure, so the thought of what lay ahead didn't worry him as such. What worried him was the feeling he had that everything around him was slowing down. It was normal, he knew that. There was always a big build-up to that kind of police operation, and the job itself usually went down at high speed. Therefore, the painstaking procedures that invariably followed were always an anticlimax, as if even the simplest tasks took a lifetime to perform.

It was acknowledged that men in his position tended to do inexplicable things after killing someone. Some went straight to their senior officers and resigned. Others lashed out at their colleagues, blaming them for not having done something that might have prevented the shooting. Worst of all were cases in which coppers took it out on their wives and kids, and Doheny had said that he hoped McLaughlan wouldn't find himself making that mistake. He had gone on to say that if he should need to talk to someone, he could talk to him, for although there were counselling programmes in place for men in his position, there was also a deep suspicion that anyone seen to be making use of them would be regarded as weak. Sometimes all someone needed was the knowledge that they could turn to 'one of their own' in total confidence. No written reports to land on the desk of some senior officer who'd never had to deal with anything more traumatic than having the dog put down. No one making a study of your struggle to come to terms with what you'd done.

He had suggested that McLaughlan should leave his car at the station and let him give him a lift home later – even if it meant hanging around for a while until he was free of the procedural aftermath of the morning's operation. 'No point surviving having a sawn-off waved in your face only to die from wrapping the car round a lamp-post because your mind is elsewhere.'

McLaughlan had been able to see the sense in what he was saying, but now that Doheny was gone, he wanted to talk to Claire, if only to admit to her what he hadn't been able to admit to Doheny: that as he had sunk to his heels in front of the house, he had been engulfed by a feeling of total isolation. It was almost as though a plastic bubble had formed around him. He could see out. People could see in. He could make out what they were saying by studying the shapes made by their lips as they spoke the words. But the words meant nothing. And it wasn't the first time McLaughlan had felt this way: for months after Tam's disappearance, people like Jarvis had twisted their mouths into shapes that made up the words 'What happened to Tam?'

He had understood the question. He had even known the answer. But he hadn't been able to speak. And now, when he reached out to Ocky and touched his sleeping face, he couldn't feel the surface of his skin. It was as if the nerves had been stripped from his fingers, as if he were feeling the face of his child through the film of that same plastic bubble.

Claire came in and spoke to him. 'Are you coming down?'

He watched the words being formed. He even heard them. But they didn't connect.

'What's wrong?'

He shook his head and followed her down the stairs.

Chapter Ten

Bryce had spent an entire morning in court. During that time, he had been obliged to admit to a magistrate that, no matter the mitigating circumstances, it was not acceptable for a person to attempt to assault a police officer by stabbing him in the eye with a ballpoint pen. But he trusted that the magistrate would show compassion when deciding the appropriate sentence, as his clients regretted their behaviour and wished to make it known that they had apologised to the officers concerned.

Sherryl's lip had been swollen and purple. She still wore the cashmere jumper and knee-length skirt that she'd worn the day before and, like Ray in his superbly tailored suit, she looked decent, middle-class and badly wronged.

After weighing them up, and considering the circumstances that had provoked the attack, the magistrate chose to be lenient. Sherryl was sentenced to forty hours' community service, and Ray to sixty.

They'd got off lightly.

Not that they'd shown much gratitude. There were times when Bryce was convinced that Ray had no grasp of what law was, much less how it worked. He certainly had no grasp of what Bryce could and couldn't achieve: he was a barrister, not a magician. Father and daughter were lucky not to have been jailed.

Half an hour later, Vincent Leach had appeared in a very different court, before a very different judge. He had answered, 'Yes,' when asked his name, and 'Guilty,' to the charge of attempted robbery. He had then been remanded.

Once he was taken down to the cells, Bryce had gone to see him, finding him recovered from the sedatives administered the night before, but subdued and deeply depressed. He, like Ray, exhibited a tendency to regard Bryce as some kind of magician, and Bryce didn't know whether to be irritated or touched by the man's faith in his ability to extract him somehow from the inevitability of a lengthy prison sentence. Unlike Ray and Sherryl, however, Leach was deeply grateful that Bryce was representing him at all. He was also bewildered, because he shared Orme's inability to see what the Swifts had to gain by paying for his legal representation.

Initially, Bryce had also been puzzled by the request that he should represent Leach. It was only after speaking to Ray at length that he had understood what the Swifts wanted from Leach by way of return.

He entered the cells beneath the court and asked Leach a very simple question: 'The man who shot Stuart, what did he look like?'

Leach just shook his head. 'How the fuck would I know?'

Bryce gave him a look that told him he would be wise to rack his brains.

Leach started thinking hard, reliving events that, due to the medication, could almost have happened decades ago. 'Stuart had a gun on the kid,' he said. 'Orme came out from behind the armoured van. Tried to reason with him. Stuart swung round on him, raised the gun like he was going to shoot him. I heard a shot, and Stuart fell down, and—'

Speaking very slowly, as if to an imbecile, Bryce said, 'Who fired the shot that killed Stuart?'

'I don't fucking know!'

Exasperated, Bryce replied, 'I don't expect you to know his name and address, just tell me what he looked like.'

Leach closed his eyes as if doing so might help him to remember. 'I was in the car,' he said. 'Carl and Stuart were dead—'

Bryce was losing patience. 'Don't waste my time, Vinny.'

'Gimme a minute,' he said.

Bryce gave him a minute, and Leach started to speak, but he spoke slowly. 'All I remember . . .'

'All you remember is – what?' said Bryce.

'He was tall. Very tall. After the shooting, he went to stand by the van. Orme spoke to him, but mostly people left him alone. That was it for me. They came and got me out the car and next thing I knew they were cuffing me. I couldn't see nothing more.'

'What do you mean by tall?' said Bryce.

'Taller even than Orme.'

Orme, as Bryce well knew, was six foot two, and there couldn't be that many Flying Squad officers taller than that. 'Anything else?' he said.

'That's it. That's all I remember.'

It wasn't a lot, but at least it narrowed the field, thought Bryce, who knew that somewhere there would be a report relating to the operation. In it, the men who had been part of the teams Orme had used would be named, and all Bryce had to do was match one of those names to a man who was taller than any of his colleagues.

He wasn't entitled to access the report, but information flowed two ways between police and villains. Provided the money was right, Bryce would get his hands on it one way or another, and once he did so, matching the name of the man who shot Stuart to the description Leach had given would be a mere matter of observation.

'You've done very well,' he said. 'Let's hope, for your sake, you've got it right.'

Chapter Eleven

Jarvis had never married. No one to blame but himself, he knew that well enough: at a critical point in his life, he had made a bad decision, and he was paying for it now. No one to share his retirement with. No daughter to come round and tell him that, at his time of life, he ought to be taking it easy – or, at the very least, *behaving* himself, getting to bed at a reasonable hour, minding where he went at night, and who he associated with, not to mention the danger of some middle-aged predatory woman moving in on him to bleed him of his assets, such as they were.

In looking around his flat, he couldn't imagine any woman of higher social status than a bag-lady deeming it worth the trouble. Not that he was complaining. It suited him well enough. Purpose-built in the late 1960s, the flat was in a three-storey block positioned at a junction in Crouch End. His bedroom backed on to one of the two main roads, but that was all right – at least he could lie in bed and listen to passing cars, the sound of people shouting as they left the pubs at closing, the wail of sirens that sometimes kept him awake deep into the night.

On retiring from the force, he had considered moving out of town, but he had been born and bred in London, had spent all but twelve years of his life there, and he hadn't been able to see himself sitting at some window, staring out at a patch of village green. The countryside was all very well in its place, but life – real life – happened here. He couldn't imagine what it would be like to live in a place where the local village fête made front-page news. When you were getting on, you liked your morning paper, and you liked to find there was something in it worth reading.

That morning's paper had reported the attempted robbery and the deaths of two of the robbers. Such news reports were hardly uncommon, yet they never failed to touch a nerve in Jarvis. They were the one thing guaranteed to make him dwell on the past, not so much because he had been a senior police officer but because, as he had gradually realised over the years, he was destined to spend the rest of his life incapable of reading or hearing about a robbery without it bringing Elsa sharply to mind.

Usually he had the past under some kind of control, and memories of Elsa were vaporised at the touch of a mental button, but articles of this nature caused his mental defence mechanism to malfunction. This, in turn, filled him with all manner of regrets, which he tried to push aside by focusing on the subtext to the article. It was written in such a way as to suggest that the police had behaved in a manner that could only be regarded as cavalier, and he had to read it twice before it hit home that Swift had been holding a gun to the neck of a very young child.

Once he realised this, Jarvis, who had known some of his fellow officers do some fairly despicable things, doubted that even the press expected the public to feel any sympathy towards the men who had been killed, but it gave an edge to the story. It gave the story *legs*. For weeks to come, columns would be devoted to the views of so-called firearms experts, preferably those who were in some way anti-police. Slowly but surely they would publicly dissect what little information they had managed to glean with regard to what had happened, and they would then make it known that the police had cocked up badly. They should have done this. They should have done that. They certainly shouldn't have done whatever they did.

None of the senior officers involved in the operation would be allowed to explain, much less defend their actions. And the Met's wall of silence would be construed as guilt, as culpability, as yet another example of unacceptable police behaviour.

He turned his attention from the more sensational elements of the story and started reading between the lines: in itself, the mere fact that Flying Squad had been lying in wait implied that the robbers had been grassed. He wondered who the informant had been and what he was thinking right now. Whoever he was, Jarvis wouldn't want to be him if the families and associates of the dead men discovered his identity – and talking of identities, thought Jarvis, once the IDs of the robbers were known, they wouldn't have stood a chance.

Like most people, coppers and villains alike, Jarvis despised informants, but there was no getting away from the fact that they were a very valuable asset to the force. They could also be a positive liability, as he had discovered when an informant had told him where he could find what was left of Tam McLaughlan. The man had heard on the grapevine that Tam had been murdered, and his body dumped in a disused warehouse in Glasgow.

Jarvis had used dogs to help him find the body. It hadn't been difficult. The minute their handlers had unleashed them, they raced into the depths of a red-brick warehouse where, a century earlier, tons of grain had been stored in huge metal silos.

The silos were rusted through, many of them looking like gigantic tin cans that were collapsing in on themselves, and the body had been dragged into one of them through the chute that dispensed the grain into smaller containers for shipping purposes.

The deceased was dressed in the kind of clothes that began to confirm Jarvis's worst fears. They appeared to be a match for the jeans and jumper Elsa had described, but beyond that, it wasn't possible to identify the remains. The body's vital organs had turned to liquid, and the skin containing that liquid had swollen and burst. But it hadn't been a natural process of decomposition that had caused a minor explosion in the chest cavity, thought Jarvis. Whoever he was, this lad, his chest had been blown apart by the blast from a shotgun.

Jarvis had suspected that Tam was dead, but that hadn't made it any easier to face up to the possibility that this might be all that remained of him. He'd liked him. He'd bought him matches and glue and had watched as he repaired the hull of his ship. He couldn't bear to think he'd come to this; nor could he bear to think of what it was going to do to Elsa.

In the absence of dental records, Hunter had suggested he should ask Elsa to look at the clothing, and even now, Jarvis could remember how hard it had been to ask that of her. She hadn't seen him for a while, and yet, when she opened the door to him, it didn't seem to occur to her that he might be bringing bad news. Not even the fact that there was a female officer with him had rung an alarm bell. She had just let him into the room at the back, and the first thing Jarvis had seen was those paper chains. Easter had come and gone, yet she hadn't taken them down. The colours had faded completely now, and every link was greyish.

Robbie had started lashing out at the paper chains, his mother shouting out at him to leave them alone. But Robbie had known why Jarvis was there, even if Elsa didn't, and Elsa had started screaming at him to 'Leave the bloody things!'

He had run to her in a way Jarvis had longed to do, had put his arms around her as if he could protect her, and Elsa had started panicking. 'Don't ask me to look at him, I couldn't. Oh, God – where's George?'

Jarvis had reassured her it was only the clothes he wanted her to see, that nobody was asking her to try to identify the body. And then he had said something stupid: 'Nothing much to identify in that regard, I'm afraid.'

She'd started to cry then, and Jarvis had thought, You stupid man, you stupid, *stupid* man.

He had taken them both to the station because Robbie had refused to be left behind with the female officer. It wasn't so much the fear of being left, it was more that he had wanted to take care of his mother.

He had wanted to be the one to try to identify the clothes, but he was a mere child – and much though Jarvis would have done anything to spare Elsa, he couldn't allow it. So Robbie had sat outside the room where the clothes had been spread out on a table. And Elsa had entered the room with Jarvis beside her.

'Just take your time. No hurry. And no need to touch – unless you want to.'

He had seen other people grab the clothes of a loved one, press them to their faces, not caring that the stench of death was upon them. But Elsa did nothing of the kind. She just walked out of the room and grabbed hold of Robbie, held him very close. 'They're not his clothes.'

Jarvis had taken them home, and all the while his anger had been mounting. Where was George when she needed him? How could he leave her to struggle along with no money, no support of any kind?

He'd never known the house to be anything other than drab, and they'd walked in from the station to find it cold. Jarvis had flicked a switch on the electric fire, but none of the elements had obliged and he realised the meter had run out.

'How are you off for cash?' he'd said, and she'd admitted there was nothing in the house. No food. No money. Not even for the meter.

Jarvis had plied the meter with what small change he'd had, and then he had gone down to the Spar to buy some food. He had returned with bread and milk, and slices of oak-smoked ham, and Robbie had devoured it as if he hadn't eaten in a month. He had fallen asleep on the couch a short while later, and Jarvis had carried him up to bed, had undressed him, had tucked him in.

Nowadays, thought Jarvis, you wouldn't dare undress a lad of ten if you were a grown man. In those days, things were different. People thought nothing of it. It hadn't even occurred to him not to wipe his face and hands with a flannel, to help him into pyjamas. The lad had hardly noticed he'd been so tired, though at one point, he'd said, 'Where's my dad?' Bloody good question, thought Jarvis, who had now spent the best part of three months looking for him, and was fast becoming the butt of Hunter's sarcasm. 'I know you fancy his missus, Mike, but you haven't done him in, have you?'

He had gone downstairs to find Elsa standing in the kitchen, tears streaming down her face, and Jarvis had put his arms around her – to comfort her, or so he had tried to convince himself at the time.

And then she had told him that, over the weeks, she'd been thinking about something. 'That crucifix,' she said. 'The one that Robbie brought back from Glasgow.'

'What about it?'

'It didn't strike me as odd that Robbie should have it, but the more I think about it . . .'

Jarvis wasn't sure what she was getting at until she added, 'It's not stolen. George's father gave it to George when he made his first communion. George gave it to Tam, and Tam would have passed it on to a son of his own. So for Tam to have given it to Robbie means something. It means he must have known that something was about to happen to him.'

'You can't be sure of that.'

'He's *dead*, Mike.'

'Don't say it. Don't even let yourself think it.'

They had stayed like that for what seemed a very long time, Elsa resting her head on his shoulder, Jarvis with his arms around her waist. And when she had asked him not to leave her, he had tried to persuade himself that he couldn't allow this to happen. Any copper known to be associating with the wife of a villain would lose his job. And yet he had held her even closer. 'I'm not going anywhere,' said Jarvis, and even as she led him to the bedroom where, for lack of a wardrobe, George's clothes had lain in a heap on a brown, basketweave ottoman, Jarvis decided he wanted her for himself. He made up his mind to fight for her, to do whatever it took to get her away from George. He would be a good father to Robbie. Whatever the effort, the sacrifice, he would treat him as his own. For Elsa, Jarvis would train himself to forget that Robbie was the son of George McLaughlan, and Robbie would love him. He would see what he had done for them, and he would come to regard him as more of a father than George had ever been.

He had it all worked out, and in the hours that followed, George McLaughlan hadn't existed for Jarvis. He had existed for Elsa, though. As always, George was never far from her thoughts: 'He mustn't find us like this.'

'You leave George to me,' said Jarvis. 'I can handle George.'

'You don't know him.'

'I can handle George,' repeated Jarvis.

Chapter Twelve

Edward Bryce had a particular taste in women. Those he was attracted to tended to be of a type who could wear the classic Chanel suit exceptionally well – the jacket with its simple lines, and the skirt above the knee.

Margaret Hastie was the complete opposite of his ideal. She sat across the table from him in a restaurant that was almost as famous for its lighting as for its food, one that, like Bryce, was completely out of her class. She looked rather nervous sitting there, as if she felt out of place, and her discomfiture wasn't entirely without foundation: her navy blue suit, like her mid-length hair, was cheaply and poorly cut.

In a voice that owed its thinness to inadequate cheek-bones, she reminded him that she had to be back at the office by three, and Bryce paid the bill, then led her outside to a waiting taxi.

They climbed into it, and Bryce gave the address of his flat in Kensington, where, a very short while later, he stood in front of a mirror that dutifully reported on Margaret Hastie's buttocks. It told him they had once been high and firm, but that at some point in her early forties, they had given up all hope of maintaining their position. There was very little fat to them. They hung like the breasts of a starving woman, the skin falling in folds towards her outer thigh, one buttock drooping slightly more than the other.

He sat her on the bed, and as she watched him undress, she wore the kind of expression he had come to associate with those among the accused who were uncertain of a favourable outcome to their predicament. 'You do love me, Eddie?'

He put a finger to her lips. His hands were elegant and tanned, and she kissed them, saying, 'I don't know what I'd do if you let me down.'

'I'll never let you down, Maggie. What makes you think I'd ever let you down?'

She didn't answer but, then, she didn't have to. They had talked through her insecurities more times than Bryce cared to remember. The age difference worried her – at forty-seven, she was nine years older than Bryce – and she was certainly no beauty. She had no assets to speak of, so what did he see in her when he could have his pick of so many young, lovely, middle-class, well-educated professional women?

He reminded her of something he had told her many times – that he preferred women who were mature, intelligent and interesting, women with character, women who had *done* something with their lives. Younger women were pretty, but silly. He didn't *like* silly women. But nor did he like ball-breaking, smart-mouthed, career-minded women, or Daddy's girls who were petulant, spoiled and inexperienced in every department of life.

He also reminded her that when people were in love,

they sometimes couldn't imagine what their partner saw in them. He often wondered what *she* saw in *him*. But what did it matter what either of them wondered? They loved each other; they had a future. That was all that mattered.

There were, of course, times when, no matter how much he reassured her, nagging doubts got the better of her; times when she felt she needed absolute proof of his love. Absolute proof could only be obtained through marriage, but for the moment, she would settle for his agreement to her moving into the flat. Bryce had therefore proposed to her some weeks ago, and had furnished her with a ring that he told her had belonged to his late mother. He had expected these gestures of intent to assuage her fears, but, if anything, Maggie had grown more insistent of late. 'It's a lovely flat, Eddie, but it needs a woman's touch.'

He'd reminded her that she'd lose her job if anyone found out that her husband-to-be was a high-profile barrister.

'Why?'

'They'd realise there was a possibility that you might tell me things you shouldn't, so I'd rather you didn't tell anyone we were involved.'

'I'll pack the job in. I'd planned to in any case after we were married. Looking after you, entertaining your friends – that'll be a full-time job in itself.'

'All in good time, Maggie. I've various commitments to get out of the way before we tie the knot.'

He didn't undress completely. Often, she liked him to keep his shirt on. She liked the feel of the cotton against her skin, liked also the contrast between his tan and the crisp, sharp whiteness of the material. Sometimes she would feel for him through the cotton; the sensation reminding Bryce of what it was like to be goosed by his mother's elderly Labrador.

As always, she was hungry for him. But now came the difficult bit: his talents were many and varied, but he lacked the creative ability to manufacture sexual fantasies vivid enough to drown out the sound of her voice or the haunted look of a woman intelligent enough to know, deep down, that something wasn't right.

Generally speaking, he managed well enough provided she didn't speak. The instant she opened her mouth to say, 'Oh, yes, oh, yes, it's good,' whatever alluring sophisticate he imagined himself to be screwing evaporated, and left him back in Maggie's scraggy arms. This angered him, but what angered him more was the danger that women like Maggie posed to national security. Countless government offices were staffed by unmarried women of a certain age, and it hadn't been unheard of for enemy agents to enter into a pseudo marriage ceremony with them to obtain information. These women had once had their fair share of looks, and they'd once attracted men into their lives with relative ease. Their last major relationships tended to have come to an end when they were in their early forties. There had usually been a few sexual relationships since then, but none with men who wanted to settle for a woman who was middle-aged, lonely, and quite obviously desperate to get married.

He kept his erection long enough to ensure that Maggie was satisfied, then slid away from her with it still intact. He couldn't abide condoms, and he had more sense than to ejaculate inside her: somehow, he couldn't stand the thought of her taking part of him with her back to the office, or to that dreadful little one-bed flat in Camden Town. Besides, he didn't trust her. She was desperate enough to fall pregnant, and her insistence that she'd gone through the menopause had failed, completely, to convince him.

'I'd better be getting back. They'll think I've been bloody kidnapped.'

It occurred to Bryce that if ever Maggie's employers so much as suspected she'd been kidnapped, the entire staff would declare a public holiday. Not that she was hated: it was more that she was considered the office dragon. Women sniggered behind her back. Men took the piss with impunity. And Maggie was no fool. She knew what people thought of her. 'I'm only doing my job, Eddie. Anyone would think I'm hard on the staff for the sake of it, but it's important to get things right.'

Bryce could only agree that it was *very* important for Maggie to get things right: she worked for New Scotland Yard in a civilian capacity, where she was trusted to collate and archive sensitive information.

He glanced surreptitiously at a brown canvas shoulder-bag that lay at the foot of the bed. It was easily large enough to hide the leather, zip-around document case that she had taken out of the office when she left to meet him for lunch.

'I nearly forgot,' said Bryce. 'Did you manage to get your hands on that report?'

Margaret Hastie was struggling into her skirt. Her blouse was on and buttoned, her tights pulled over her knickers. She slipped her feet into flat-soled shoes, bent down and picked up the bag. She took the document case out of it and handed it to him. 'You'll get me bloody shot.'

Bryce almost longed to tell her that the contents of the document file might well get somebody shot, but that unless, for some reason, she suddenly started to show a propensity for shouting her mouth off, the person on the receiving end of a bullet wouldn't be her. 'What would I do without you?' he said, and in a moment of rare insight, she replied, 'You'd be all right – you'd find someone else to do your dirty work.'

Similar remarks were usually met with a protest, but on this occasion, Bryce let it go. There were times when he simply couldn't be arsed.

She was sensitive to the absence of reassurance, and she finished dressing in silence, but before they left the bedroom, she turned on him, her eyes like dark grey pebbles: 'If anyone ever gets their hands on that report, they'll know who gave it you.'

'Has anyone ever found anything you've passed to me?'

'No,' she admitted.

'So relax,' said Bryce.

He guided her into the living room, called her a taxi, then made her a cup of tea. As she drank it, she started to talk about some woman at the office who was getting married in summer. Bryce had long ago perfected the art of switching off, but when the words 'Corfu' and 'second time round for both of them' bit through his defences, he wandered into the front room to escape her.

She followed, and he felt his senses assailed by such phrases as 'cost of catering, these days', and 'four months gone, and she's kiddin' herself if she thinks it doesn't show'.

Self-discipline plus years of training enabled him to control an urge to scream, and he nodded and smiled as she told him about the dress, the firm providing the cars, the little church in Hammersmith, the advantage of white crockery over kitchenware with a lemon trim that went with the linen place mats. And then a black cab pulled up in front of the flat, and Maggie trailed reluctantly to the door. She was sorry to go. She was *always* sorry to go.

'When will I see you again?'

'How about dinner. Friday. Usual place?'

She agreed. She always agreed. And he would cancel. He always cancelled. He would give her enough to keep her on a string until such time as he found someone to replace her. But he suspected he was stuck with her for quite some time to come, because women in Maggie's position were few and far between. He wondered whether she realised the uniqueness of her position, or her potential power. 'Either you marry me, Eddie, or I'll start to divulge the secret of your string of professional successes.'

If that ever happened, Bryce would have to call on a favour from a friend. It didn't much matter which friend. A barrister of his ilk tended to collect the type of friend who could deal with the Maggies of this world on a fairly permanent basis, should the need for drastic action ever arise.

He saw her out of the flat, and watched her make for the taxi, her skirt clinging to her legs as she walked into the wind. She strode out rapidly in her flat-heeled shoes, her head bent heavily, one shoulder lower than the other, as if borne down by the weight of the canvas bag.

She gave him a smile and a wave, then climbed into the taxi. He watched it pull away—

And then he was free!

He took a shower, threw on a tracksuit, then took the document case into his study. He sat with it at his writing desk, drew out the papers, and started to read them.

Each of the pages bore the emblem of the Metropolitan Police, and the warning that the report was highly confidential. He found the fact that it had been stamped *Top Secret* endearing. It was so quintessentially British, so trusting, it brought a lump to his throat. And as he read it, he reminded himself that, by stealing the report and passing it to him, Maggie, who had signed the Secrecy Act, had committed an act of treason. If caught, she would be jailed, and jailed for a very long time, for acts of treason were invariably severely dealt with, even when committed by a person of previous good character. But that was fair enough, for the potential danger to Maggie was nothing by comparison with the danger to the person most likely to suffer as a result of the information she had placed in his possession.

He scanned the pages and learned that Orme had used two teams of Flying Squad officers. All had been armed. He also learned that, during the attempted robbery, shots had been fired by three of Orme's men, but that Fischer had died from multiple injuries sustained when he caught the blast from the sawn-off shot gun fired by Swift.

Two shots had been fired by two different men in the moments after Fischer had been shot dead. One bullet had lodged in the wall of the bank. The other had severed an artery in Swift's leg.

Bryce read on and learned that Orme had put down his weapon and had started to try to reason with Swift in the hope that he would (a) release the child, and (b) let the police get him the medical help that he clearly urgently needed.

Swift had responded by whipping the gun away from the neck of the child and aiming it at Orme. An officer called McLaughlan had reacted instantly, shooting Swift dead.

The name McLaughlan rang a bell with Bryce. He turned to the beginning of the report and found another name – that of Gerald Ash, the grass who had tipped off police with regard to the impending robbery.

According to the report. Ash was a known informant. Over the years, he had divulged a considerable amount of information to the police, and he had a number of contacts. On this occasion, the contact he had used was none other than McLaughlan, the very man who had subsequently shot Swift dead.

Gerald Ash, thought Bryce. He'd never heard of him, but he was willing to bet that Calvin and Ray knew who he was. What they did when they discovered what he had done was a matter for them. Like McLaughlan, Ash would have to take his chances, thought Bryce, and knowing Calvin as he did, he didn't rate those chances very highly.

Chapter Thirteen

Commuters were accustomed to sitting in traffic that had come to a standstill on the M4, but it was unusual for cars to have been brought to a halt as early as 6 a.m.

They had been stopped by police after a motorist had dialled 999 from his mobile. Emergency services had relayed the information to Traffic, and they, in turn, had contacted a patrol: 'You'd better take a look at one of the bridges – the caller isn't sure what he saw, but he sounded a bit distraught.'

It had taken the nearest motorway patrol a mere six minutes to get to the bridge in question, and because, during those minutes, the sky had lightened perceptibly, they saw what the motorist had seen rather more clearly than he had.

They also saw something else: cars that had previously been travelling at high speed were suddenly slowing dangerously, the drivers flashing their lights, gesturing to one another and pointing at the bridge. Any minute now, thought one of the uniforms, there's going to be a bloody awful accident.

He started the siren, and cars in all three lanes slowed

to a crawl, then came to a halt. Within seconds, there was a tailback of half a mile.

With the traffic at a standstill, the uniforms got out of their patrol and walked towards the bridge. They weren't alone. The sound of car doors slamming, of people walking towards the bridge, was dominant now. But nobody spoke. People put their hands to their mouths, then turned away, some scrambling on to the grassy verge that flanked the hard shoulder, and retching into the bushes.

A woman jumped out of her car and ran down the carriageway. She was trying to get as far from the bridge as possible, and because he was frightened that, ultimately, she might run smack into traffic, one of the uniforms went after her, catching her easily, but failing to calm her down. She shook her head violently, as if to rid herself of what she had seen. 'You're all right, love. You're all right . . .'

His colleague returned to the vehicle to radio for back-up. It was going to take more than one patrol to close the motorway and put out cones that would guide the oncoming traffic into a filter. Back-up wasn't all he requested, however: 'You'd better inform the Murder Squad,' he said.

A pension book found on the victim provided the Murder Squad's Detective Inspector Tarpey with a name: Gerald Ash. It also provided him with Ash's date of birth and address.

The police computer divulged that Ash was an old villain turned grass, that his contact was a Flying Squad officer called McLaughlan, and that Orme was McLaughlan's senior officer.

Tarpey had initially attempted to contact McLaughlan, but had found that he was on leave, so he contacted Orme instead.

An hour later, Orme arrived to find that screens had been erected around the bridge. Traffic had been diverted, and both carriageways were empty.

He stood alongside Tarpey in the central reservation, staring up at the bridge, or rather, at Ash, and he came to the conclusion that, at first glance, people could be forgiven for thinking he had hanged himself. Clearly, that wasn't true. In order for someone to hang themselves, or to be hanged, for that matter, they had to be in possession of a neck. Ash no longer had a neck to speak of. He had lost it, along with the head that had formerly been attached to it. And yet his body was swinging from a rope attached to the bridge.

'What's holding him there?' said Orme, and as if to oblige, the body spun slowly to reveal that a meat hook had been driven into Ash's back. He hung like a side of beef, his clothes so drenched with blood it was barely possible to recognise his raincoat as ever having been fawn. A piece of cardboard had been pinned to his coat, and the word 'Grass' had been printed on it in block capitals. 'Who wanted him dead?' said Tarpey, and Orme was reminded that just because Ash had tipped police off about the bank job, it didn't necessarily mean that this was down to Swift. He said: 'Ash has been the mouth behind quite a few convictions, but if I were you, I'd start with Calvin Swift – Ash grassed Stuart.'

The name Swift had an interesting effect on Tarpey. Stuart had been buried at Tower Hamlets two days ago, and due to the nature of his death and the notoriety of his family, TV and press had covered his funeral. Orme guessed that Tarpey had seen it on the news.

The sight of Stuart's coffin being lowered into the ground by six known gangland figures had all the ingredients of good drama, particularly when complemented by the sight of Calvin Swift standing by the grave in a jet black suit, a vicuna overcoat draped round his shoulders. It was raining, yet he wore shades.

Ray and Sherryl dressed equally dramatically, and that was what it was, thought Orme – a touch of *The Godfather II*. Calvin had known the media would be there, and he wanted to come across as a big-time villain whose son had been murdered by police.

It was precisely the kind of news feature that kept the ratings high, and two television programmes were shown that evening: one relating to gangland families of the sixties, and one concentrating on what had become of some of London's old villains.

There was the suggestion that most had done well for themselves, that some had even gone straight, *wink wink*. Orme knew differently. At best, the majority ended up living on income support, scrounging drinks from younger villains, boring them to death with tales of 'what we did in the sixties', the way that some men talked about the war. Some were destined to die in jail having spent up to half their lives inside for a series of crimes that were hardly worth the bother, and a small proportion would end up like two of the great train robbers, Edwards and Wilson, the former found hanging in a garage, the latter shot dead at his home in Spain.

The pathologist asked some of Tarpey's men to haul

the body up so that he could lay it on the bridge and make a cursory examination. They were doing this with obvious reluctance, and Orme didn't blame them. Any minute now, one of them would have the unenviable task of wrapping his arms around Ash's chest and hauling him over the rails, which would mean that the mess of bloody flesh that was all that was left of his neck would be right in that man's face.

He noticed that Ash had stuffed cardboard into the soles of his shoes, and it occurred to Orme that none of the villains depicted on the programmes shown on the day of the funerals had lifted their feet to the cameras. Pity, thought Orme. It would have been more of a deterrent than the policy of zero tolerance currently being considered by the government.

In seeing him like this, it was hard for Orme to believe that there had once been a time when Ash was considered dangerous. He didn't look dangerous now, thought Orme. He hadn't looked dangerous for years. Nevertheless, Ash had been precisely the kind of villain that researchers might have tried to locate for their programmes, because, on the surface of things, there was still a certain glamour to having made it to the status of a category A prisoner, the men who had once been regarded a danger to the public. But Orme knew well enough that when Ash's body was taken to the mortuary to be stripped of the clothes he had died in, the pathologist's assistant would find that his undergarments were soiled and worn. His pants would be in holes, or maybe even patched. Like Ash himself, they would be filthy and falling apart. A man without scruples or friends, Ash had died impoverished and a victim to murder. Stick that in front of your cameras, thought Orme. Let them see what men like Ash, and the women they marry, amount to in the end.

He had thought it best not to bother the pathologist until he had finished his initial examination of Ash's body, but once he appeared to have done so, Orme and Tarpey approached him. 'I know it's early days,' said Orme, 'but as soon as you can let me have a cause of death . . .'

The pathologist surprised him by replying, 'I can tell you now. Cause of death was hanging.'

Orme looked uncertain, but he wasn't about to point out that the victim had no head. The pathologist added: 'When a person is hanged very violently, there is always the potential for decapitation.'

Orme was left to wonder what he had meant by a violent hanging. He couldn't imagine a man to be hanged in any way that wasn't violent. He hoped that Ash's head would be located before some old dear found it wrapped in a bin-bag and dumped at the bottom of her garden. With luck, it would be weighted down and rotting in the Thames, or dealt with in some way that meant some innocent person would be spared nightmares for months, maybe years to come. Tarpey said, 'Do you happen to know his widow?'

Orme confirmed that he had in fact met her on occasion, that it was never a particularly pleasant experience, but that if Tarpey thought she would take the news of Ash's death better from him, he was willing to be the one to break it.

'I'll take it from there,' said Tarpey. 'And, it goes without saying, I'll keep you informed of developments.'

Orme was reminded that Ash's murder was Tarpey's

investigation. Frankly, thought Orme, he was welcome to it. Anyone who had the task of trying to pin anything on the Swifts would have their work cut out.

Hilda Ash knew that the men on her doorstep were police the instant she saw them. 'What's he done?' she said, sounding as though, whatever it was, she was already resigned to it, along with whatever the consequences might be.

'It's not what you think,' said Orme, but she stood there, weighing them up, as if asking herself what gave them the right to imagine they knew what she thought.

She had to be in her seventies, thought Orme, who sometimes wondered how these old birds managed to stick a lifetime of being married to a villain. She was the small, tough, stringy type, her mouth a scarlet slash in a face powdered to the texture of crushed velvet.

She let them in with the comment, 'I thought he had more sense at his age,' and Orme reassured her it was nothing like that, and please could they come in?

She let them into a room where Orme suspected she and Gerald Ash had spent most of their time. Two bars of an electric fire glowed within feet of a couple of wing-backed chairs upholstered in Dralon, an old West Highland terrier sleeping on one of the chairs.

She didn't invite them to sit, and she didn't ask what they wanted. She just waited for one of them to tell her why they were there.

Normally, Orme had a particular method of breaking bad news, but now that he was attempting to do so in circumstances such as these, he realised that the success of his technique was rather dependent on the co-operation of the person to whom the news was being broken. Normally, people were instantly worried when police arrived on their doorstep. They asked a series of questions that usually began and ended with 'What's wrong – has something happened?' This then gave the officer concerned the chance to break the news that something had indeed happened, and to take it from there. Hilda Ash, however, had grown so hardened to the phenomenon of visits from the police that she displayed all the characteristics of an overworked magistrate. 'Get on with it,' she said. 'I haven't got all day.'

'Mrs Ash,' said Orme, 'does the name Calvin Swift mean anything to you?'

The snort was one of pure derision. 'Yes,' she said, but she offered no further information, and it was left to Orme to ask why.

'Come wi' me,' she said, and they followed her through to a kitchen. 'Take a good look round,' she said. 'What do you think of *that*?'

If Orme was expecting Tarpey to spot something untoward – something that had escaped him – he was disappointed. 'It's a very nice kitchen,' he said, hopefully.

'No, it bloody isn't.'

She dug the heel of her shoe into one of the floor tiles. 'Look at them,' she said, and Orme looked down. They were perfectly ordinary floor tiles, patterned in green and white. He was about to say so when he noticed something. The pattern was out of synch. He mentioned it, still not knowing whether this was what he was supposed to have picked up on, and Hilda Ash gave a grunt of approval, then opened a cupboard door and invited him to try to close it.

Orme attempted to close it and found that the door was slightly warped, as if laminate had been applied over unseasoned wood. Whatever the case, it wouldn't close, and she said, 'Four thousand quid we paid for this kitchen.'

At any other time, Orme might have asked how Gerald Ash had managed to get his hands on four thousand quid, but he didn't bother. For all he knew, he might have had it stashed from a job pulled years ago. Hilda continued: 'We told him we weren't satisfied with the work.'

Orme suddenly realised what she was trying to tell him: the Swift brothers owned legitimate business concerns that laundered stolen money. One of those businesses was obviously a kitchen replacement firm.

'It wasn't Calvin who put the kitchen in,' said Mrs Ash. 'It was someone who worked for him. Anyway, he came and had a look at it himself, and he agreed it wasn't right, so he said he'd give us part of the money back.'

Orme suddenly had a feeling he knew why Gerald Ash had grassed Stuart Swift. The phrase 'never steal from a thief' came sharply to mind. 'And did he?'

'Did he buggery,' she said. 'It's been two years, and not a soddin' penny. Bloody villain.'

Orme had to smile at that one, and then he recalled the purpose of his visit. 'And what did Gerald have to say about that?'

Hilda Ash's eyes began to glint with a suggestion of the steel that had seen her through a lifetime of prison widowship. At least, thought Orme, she'd be well prepared to cope with the real thing. 'Nobody takes the piss out of us,' she said. 'By the time you get to our age, you know that if you wait long enough, the chance to get your own back always comes.'

It had come, thought Orme, when Ash had heard on the grapevine that Calvin's son was planning to pull a job on Securicor. Orme took a chance: 'Hilda,' he said, 'let's put our cards on the table. Gerald had a few good friends in the force.'

Knowing instantly that Orme was referring to her husband's penchant for informing when the need for money arose, Hilda Ash leaped to his defence. 'Gerald wasn't no grass.'

'He's dead,' said Orme, bluntly. 'Early this morning, his body was found hanging from a bridge on a motorway near Heathrow.'

The crushed velvet cheeks faded from crimson to cream, and Orme led her through to the room where the dog continued to sleep, unaware that for once his mistress was glad of a copper's arm to lean on. Orme said, 'Did Gerald mention anything about the attempted robbery that happened a week or so back?'

He didn't tell her which robbery, not wanting to lead her in any way, and Hilda Ash replied, 'He told me Calvin's son had been shot by police.'

'Do you think he might have talked about it to anyone else?'

She was very badly shaken, and Orme had to give her a moment. 'It's very unlikely,' she said. 'He was always so careful.'

Orme couldn't imagine him to have been anything else. Anything less would have been tantamount to suicide. He said, 'Do you happen to know where Gerald went, or who he might have spoken to last night?'

Hilda shook her head. 'I haven't seen him in days.'

Orme couldn't hide his surprise. She picked up on it and said, 'Fifty-five years we've been married, and right from the word go he's done as he pleased.' The scarlet slash had almost disappeared in the pinch of her lips. '"You'll see me when you see me." That's what he used to say.' She was crying now and Orme was uttering platitudes of a kind that coppers in his position invariably uttered. Gerald Ash had been a vicious piece of work, a violent criminal, a dangerous man. The world would be a better place for his passing, but he wasn't about to say so to his widow.

Chapter Fourteen

McLaughlan had been on leave since shooting Swift, and Orme, who had tried to phone him earlier to give him the news of Ash's death, now tried his number again.

It was Claire who answered, and when Orme asked to speak to McLaughlan, she told him he was visiting family up north.

'How is he?' said Orme.

'Fine,' she said, and that was all he got from her. He had never found Claire easy. He had the feeling she wasn't behind McLaughlan with regard to his choice of career. It wasn't unusual. Wives and girlfriends tended to worry, and as their concern was totally justified, Orme wasn't about to start trying to reassure them – there might come a day when he found himself obliged to retract whatever reassurances he had given. *I'm sorry to have to inform you* . . .

'Ask him to give me a ring,' he said.

'Sure,' said Claire, and Orme came away with the feeling that he was the last person she had wanted to hear from just then. That, however, was McLaughlan's problem. He wasn't about to start advising his men with regard to how best to handle the women in their lives: he had enough on his plate advising them how best they might manage to stay alive long enough to collect a pension.

The telephone was reproduction, something Claire had picked up in the BT shop on the high street. She liked the weight of the receiver, the art-deco design, the fact that she couldn't decide if it was ugly.

She replaced the receiver and turned to Robbie, finding that Ocky was sitting quietly beside him, holding his hand. 'Daddy doesn't feel very well.'

Claire wasn't sure whether 'Daddy' was ill, or just plain angry. She only knew that he had barely spoken a word to her, or to Ocky, since the day he shot Stuart Swift. She had given up asking him what was wrong, just as she had given up trying to touch him. When she tried to put her arms around him, he pulled away. And it wasn't so much that he pulled away as his body language, his silences, the way he walked out of whatever room she walked into – all these things were shouting the same message: *You don't understand what I'm going through.*

Every night since the shooting, he had lain beside her, cold, unresponsive and wakeful, but she could handle what he was doing to her. What she couldn't deal with was what it was doing to Ocky. 'Why doesn't Daddy like me any more?'

'Daddy loves you, sweetheart – he just isn't feeling very happy right now.'

'Why not?'

'He's had a problem at work.'

'Is somebody being nasty to him?'

'He's sort of being nasty to himself.'

'Why?'

I only wish I knew, thought Claire.

He had spent most of the past week lying on the bed, staring up at the ceiling, not speaking, not moving, not even reacting when either she or Ocky entered the bedroom. He wasn't eating, but neither was he drinking, and that, in its way, was something to be grateful for, she supposed. Not that he had ever been much of a drinker. She knew he had once had an uncle who was an alcoholic. He'd had some sort of disability – she wasn't sure what. She only knew that it wasn't hereditary but had resulted from some kind of injury to the hands. Robbie had never said exactly what the injury was but, then, he never really talked about his family. She knew he was estranged from his father, and also from a stepfather figure who had more or less brought him up. And that was about as much as she knew, other than that the idea of ending up anything like the alcoholic uncle had terrified him enough to turn him off the thought of drink altogether. Whatever the case, he rarely drank, and shooting Stuart Swift hadn't changed that, though it seemed to have changed almost everything else about him.

That morning, Ocky had slopped milk on the kitchen floor and Robbie had hit the roof. 'For God's sake, Claire, why don't you keep him under some kind of control?'

The tears hadn't come immediately, but later she had found Ocky in his bedroom, curled up in a corner with his favourite toy. His sobs had been noiseless and deep, and it had been that, rather than anything Robbie had said or done to her personally since the shooting, that had made her snap. She had picked Ocky up and had run out to the car with him, and Robbie had come out of the house to persuade her back with apologies and promises that he'd make an effort, get help if he needed it. She'd relented, but already she was beginning to regret it.

'That was Orme.'

'I gathered.'

'I told him you'd gone up north.'

'I heard.'

'He wants you to give him a ring.'

'I can't.'

She sat down beside him as cautiously as if he were an invalid, as if the slightest movement might send a spasm of agony shooting through his body. 'You can't avoid him for ever. You're due back on duty in another couple of days.'

'I'm not going in,' he said, in a tone of voice that suggested he'd made up his mind.

The media make euphemistic references to the state that Ash was found in. His widow was 'advised' not to attempt to identify the body, just as your mother was 'advised' not to attempt to identify the body found in the warehouse. You still carry an image of the way she walked out of that room – the way she grabbed you, the way she broke down as she said, 'They're not his clothes.'

Claire is having a go at you: 'Why won't you tell me what's wrong?' And there's nothing you want more than to tell her the truth, to admit you're the son of a convicted armed robber, to describe Tam's last moments and tell her how he died. And then to talk about Jarvis, who brought to your life the only stability you ever knew as a kid. But you wonder what her reaction would be.

Maybe she'd ask the obvious: 'What made Jarvis leave?' It's a question you doubt you'll ever be able to answer. All you know is that Jarvis found a tin, that something about it caused him to walk away.

You tore the lid off that tin and looked inside, but all it contained was library tickets, birth and vaccination certificates – a photo of Tam making his first holy communion at a church in Glasgow. That was it. There was nothing in that tin to cause a man to give up on the family he had made his own – not so far as you could see – but Jarvis never came back.

Months later, you traced him to a flat in London and you turned up on his doorstep. But Jarvis said he didn't want you there. 'No hard feelings, Robbie, it's nothing you've done . . .' You felt he owed you more. You wanted an explanation. You never got one.

How do you explain these things to someone whose background is so far removed from your own? Claire would want to know more. She'd want to know why shooting Swift has brought it back to you. But it hasn't brought it back – it never went away. Somehow, you developed techniques that helped you deal with it, that's all. Shooting Swift kicked the legs from beneath those techniques, left you stranded back in the plastic bubble. She won't understand that the bubble isn't a metaphor, that it's real, that you can touch it, that you can feel yourself to be contained within it, but that you can't break free of it. But you long to take the gigantic leap and tell her about your past.

She wants to know what you mean by saying you're not going in. You tell her you mean exactly what you said – you're not going back.

Ocky puts his arms around your neck. He asks the question

133

Claire doesn't dare to ask: 'Does that mean you won't be a policeman any more?'

You fight the urge to crush him close, and you tell him you don't know, you just don't know.

Chapter Fifteen

Tommy Carter was the kind of villain that even a hardened copper couldn't help liking. You'd arrest him because he'd given you no choice – he'd pulled a job so beautiful, so neat, you knew it had to be him. So you'd go down the pub and you'd buy him a pint and you'd tell him you were every bit as sorry about it as he was but you were going to have to nick him. Tommy was always a gentleman about it. 'Sorry to put you to the trouble, Mr Jarvis, but you know how it is . . .'

Ash, on the other hand, was devoid of any redeeming characteristic, and the manner of his passing had been enough to guarantee that his death made the headlines. On reading those headlines, Jarvis thought it small wonder he had been murdered. He was vicious. He was a liar. He was a grass. And now he was dead.

Ironically, Jarvis had last seen him at Tommy's funeral. Prior to that, he hadn't seen him in – he didn't know how many years. They hadn't spoken, although Ash had seen Jarvis looking in his direction, because the expression of contempt on Ash's face had indicated to Jarvis that he wouldn't exactly welcome a word of greeting.

Jarvis had left him to it. Pity, really, thought Jarvis. It would have been so easy for either of them to walk up to the other, to put the past behind them, but Ash wasn't the kind to put the past behind him, Jarvis knew that. Ash was the type who bore a grudge, and bided his time until a situation arose that enabled him to redress the balance, exact revenge, restore his slighted honour. Maybe that was what had got him killed in the end.

There was some suggestion that whoever had murdered Ash had done so to send a message to other informants. It reminded Jarvis that, thirty years ago, a similar assumption had been made over an equally brutal murder.

It had occurred at a gym in Bolan Street, close to the heart of the Gorbals. The name now conjured an image of office blocks, a complex with a job club, a well-woman clinic, but Bolan Street had once been very different. No one with any sense went near the place – with the exception of drug-dealers, prostitutes, villains, and people like Eoin Kerr, sixteen years old, but with the physical build of a youngster half his age.

Bolan Street had been in the kind of darkness you only got in a road where every streetlight had been smashed, and Kerr, who had later made a statement to Strathclyde, had wisely averted his eyes from the shadows of a dozen derelict doorways, and the few scrubby trees that stood dying of the cold.

Despite the time of morning – 6 a.m. – people stood in the doorways or gathered beneath the trees. Some were homeless. Others were women who worked the pitches abandoned for the night by the better class of whore. But Kerr was afraid of neither the homeless nor the whores:

he feared only the dealers, and what they might do if they thought he'd seen something he shouldn't.

There wouldn't be much he could do to defend himself for, even by Gorbals standards, he lacked height. He stood only four foot seven, and there was precious little muscle on his skinny body.

His head was slightly egg-shaped, as if his mother had been obliged to redesign the dimensions of his skull at a moment's notice in order to squeeze him through a pelvic girdle the width of a wishbone, and his skull was all the more ugly for the stiff, reddish stubble that passed for hair.

A less determined boy might have resigned himself to a lifetime of being tormented by his peers. But Kerr had long ago begged the trainer for a key so that he could work out at the gym at an hour when nobody would be around to taunt him.

He had fitted the key to the lock, and had found that the door to the gym was already open. This, however, was nothing new apparently: consequently, he thought little of it. He opened the door, pushing it wide and finding that, as usual, it opened into darkness.

He was used to feeling his way to the wall where the light switch was set, the gym having once been accessed from Cumberland Street, but when he flicked the switch, no lights came on.

Again, he thought nothing of it for, often as not, the trainer didn't get round to paying the various bills, so his only reaction had been to feel for a switch that he knew would activate an emergency lighting system. How this system worked, he had no idea; he only knew that it worked off some kind of battery.

The light that was shed was barely enough to see by. The shadows it cast distorted what lay before him so that, at first, he couldn't believe what he was seeing. And then he realised there was nothing wrong with the lights, or with his eyesight: it was more that what lay before him was something he didn't want to believe was there.

A chair lay on its side in front of a glass trophy cabinet, the cabinet itself defaced with something that had turned the glass opaque.

A man lay on the floor some yards from the chair, and even though his injuries were such that identification, in the ordinary sense, was impossible, Kerr knew well enough who he was. In death, as in life, the man was a monster. Jimmy McLaughlan, thought Kerr.

News of Jimmy's murder had come in from Strathclyde, and within an hour of hearing about it, Jarvis had gone to break the news to Elsa. They'd been seeing one another for almost a year by then, and during that time, Elsa had had her good days and her bad days over Tam.

Few people realised what it was like for the relatives of a missing person, thought Jarvis. Their emotions were all over the place, not just for weeks or months, but for years on end. Finding out what had happened to their loved one became an obsession. There hadn't been a day since he and Elsa had become involved that she hadn't talked about where Tam could be or what he might be doing.

Those were the good days.

On bad days, Robbie would let him into the house and he'd find it a shambles. Elsa would be upstairs, lying on the bed, her eyes wide open, unblinking. The number of times his heart had been in his mouth – she'd looked like a suicide – and he'd shaken her by the shoulder to make her move.

She'd moved all right: she'd risen up from the bed like someone possessed, screaming that he knew Tam was dead but was keeping it from her to stop her going mad. It wasn't always easy to divest her of this notion, not least because he was in fact convinced that Tam was dead. 'Even if I wanted to, I couldn't keep something like that from you, Elsa. Nobody could.' And yet, thought Jarvis, that wasn't exactly true either: he had a suspicion that Tam's death was precisely what Robbie was keeping from all of them, and once or twice, Jarvis had confronted him outright: 'What do you say, Robbie? Is your mother right?'

Strange, thought Jarvis, that a boy so young could look so old, so crushed, and yet say nothing. And it wasn't so much that he would say nothing with regard to what had happened to Tam, as that he barely spoke a word at all.

On more than one occasion, Jarvis had said to Elsa, 'He never says much. A lad of his age, it's not normal . . .'

Elsa had too many emotional problems of her own to deal with to take on somebody else's, even if the somebody else happened to be her one remaining son. Consequently, she was totally out of touch with the oddness of Robbie's behaviour. 'He's always been quiet.'

Jarvis remembered the chatty, cheeky kid he used to be, and disagreed. He had only gone quiet after Tam went missing, and that was what bothered Jarvis.

He would usually manage to calm Elsa down, but it was never easy. Even less easy to deal with were periods of almost suicidal depression that not even medication seemed to alleviate, countered by periods of almost manic optimism after she managed to draw confidence from the fact that the clothes she'd been asked to identify weren't Tam's. She saw it as an omen. Tam was all right. Tam would drift home in his own good time. He'd probably done something stupid – like gone down the docks and stowed away. 'He's probably in Australia by now.'

Jarvis had wanted nothing more than to believe that Tam was up to his neck in eucalyptus trees, but he doubted it. In his opinion, Tam was dead. Robbie knew it, and George was somehow involved. Therefore, the best that could be hoped for was that George would shortly be caught, that he would confess to what had happened to Tam, and that once he was safely in jail, Elsa could file for divorce.

In the meantime, Jarvis, who couldn't risk his job by moving in with Elsa, had done what he could to make sure she was well looked after. He gave her money for food, paid the rent and utilities, and had made the house as secure as possible, not so much because he wouldn't have put it past George to break in if she refused him access, but because he was frightened of the house being broken into by a burglar. He had fitted every window with a security bolt, and the doors to the front and back had such an array of deadlocks that it often took Elsa thirty seconds or so to let him in.

On the day he went to break the news that Jimmy had been murdered, it had taken Elsa longer than her usual thirty seconds: it had been a couple of minutes, Elsa having lost the key to one of the deadlocks.

If not for the fact that he'd tried to phone before calling but had found the line constantly engaged, Jarvis might have thought she wasn't there. His repeated knocking had gone unanswered, and he had ended up looking through a window into the kitchen. He had seen her, almost as if she were hiding in the recess that passed for a larder, and he'd felt a fool – he didn't know why – as though she might have been trying to avoid him.

She had opened the door, behaving as if he'd somehow managed to catch her off-guard. 'You don't usually just drop in.'

'You've been on the phone for an hour!'

'I was talking to a friend.'

'Didn't you hear me knocking?'

'I had the radio on.'

The radio was still blaring out from the kitchen. Jarvis turned it off, and advised her to sit down, adding that he had some bad news. *The look on her face!* Just for a moment, Elsa had seemed terrified, and it had suddenly occurred to him that she thought he was going to tell her George was dead. When Jarvis had said it was Jimmy and not George, she hadn't been able to hide that she was relieved. Not that Jarvis had expected her to be upset: Elsa had been repulsed by Jimmy, so he wasn't expecting tears and he didn't get any. But she hadn't been completely unmoved by his death and, to Jarvis's surprise, she had talked, for the first time ever, about what he had been like in the old days. 'You'd have liked him, Mike – he was a good laugh, Jimmy. Good-looking, too, though I know you'd never believe it.'

It hadn't been the maudlin, regretful reminiscing of someone who wished they'd done more for the deceased when they were alive. This was the recollection of a genuine liking for someone, the memory of some of the good times they'd had. Jarvis had been touched. And then she had gone and spoiled it all by mentioning George in a way that made him almost choke with jealousy: 'George will go to pieces when he hears.'

She had been going to say something else, but had thought better of it. Not that it mattered: Jarvis had known well enough what she'd been about to say – that she wished she could be there for George at a time like this.

It had led to the first real argument they'd ever had. Jarvis had told her to piss off back to George if she was so worried about him, and Elsa had tried to reason with him: 'What's so bad about showing a little compassion? Jimmy was his brother. George isn't inhuman, he does have feelings.'

'Pity he doesn't extend his concern to you and Robbie.'

'He cares, in his way.'

'Like fuck he does!'

He'd stormed out of the house with Elsa telling him not to bother coming back. But, of course, he had gone back. He'd gone back within the hour to apologise, and to admit that he'd been jealous.

The trouble was, any mention of George was always guaranteed to send his blood pressure through the roof. He couldn't get away from him, that was the problem. Whenever he was with Elsa, George's name always cropped up in conversation. 'Where do you think he is, Mike?'

If only I knew, thought Jarvis. And as if that wasn't bad enough, Hunter had started to taunt him with odd little comments that got right up his nose: 'You have to hand it to him, he's a piece of work. No wonder

142

you can't find him, Mike – he's too fucking clever for you.'

Jarvis had been all too painfully aware that George was running rings round him, just as he was aware that Elsa was right: George was going to be gutted when he heard about Jimmy—

—which meant there was always the chance of using Jimmy's death as the bait that would finally trap him.

Jarvis arrived in Glasgow to find that a frost the texture of glass had settled on the city. He walked from Central Station to the gym in Bolan Street to find that it had been cordoned off since morning.

Jarvis walked up to the cordon to introduce himself to Whalley, the detective assigned to head up the murder investigation, and Whalley had given him what Jarvis later described to Hunter as the *north–south* stare – a look born of suspicion of anyone who happened to be from an outside force and, worse still, *an English fucker tae boot*! He wasn't about to make Jarvis's life any more difficult than it was, but nor was he about to welcome him to Glasgow with open arms. 'This is nothing Strathclyde cannae handle, Mr Jarvis.'

'I didn't come to offer advice. I came to ask for it,' said Jarvis. He held out his hand, and if there was more reserve than enthusiasm behind Whalley's acceptance of the handshake, then at least it took some of the edge from his voice.

Whalley had introduced him to his men. Most had been born and bred in the Gorbals, and some had known Jimmy McLaughlan when he was thought of as a fighter, not a monster. Consequently, there had been a sense of outrage hanging in the air, and anger in Whalley's voice as he described the scene that had greeted the lad who found the body.

The gym was housed in a small, abandoned factory surrounded by jerry-built housing. Flakes of asbestos hung down from a roof, and the electrics looked almost criminally dangerous. It was cold in there, and it stank – a putrid, festering stench that Jarvis could barely stand. It occurred to him even as he walked in that if nobody had mentioned who the victim was, he would have known it was Jimmy.

He fought the urge to put a hand to his mouth and averted his eyes from a bloodstain that marked out a Machiavellian map on one of the walls. Above his head ran girders that had once supported machinery of some kind. Now they took the weight of six heavy bags, each divided from the other by a mere few feet. Old-fashioned weights stood in one corner, and in an opposite corner, a skipping rope lay in snake-like coils on the filthy wooden floor.

According to Whalley, Jimmy had been in the habit of sleeping at the gym, and Jarvis had said he couldn't imagine that Jimmy, or anyone else for that matter, would want to sleep in a place as cold and uncomfortable – not when they had a bed of their own to go to, albeit a shakedown bed in a condemned Gorbals tenement.

'It wasnae by choice,' said Whalley, who went on to explain that Jimmy drank himself to a stupor most nights. None of the local landlords was willing to let him drink inside their pubs. Most would only serve him if he went round to the back where they gave him free drinks – provided he stayed there.

It was bribery, thought Jarvis, but you couldn't blame a landlord for that. The minute Jimmy walked into a pub, everyone in it was almost guaranteed to walk out into the sweet, fresh air, and away from the beast, the monster, that the former local hero had become. Slipping Jimmy free drinks to keep him out of the way must have seemed a small price to pay on the whole.

Whalley went on to explain that, sometimes, Jimmy drank himself senseless, and that since no one had any intention of 'leaving him tae freeze tae death', some of his former friends would take it upon themselves to get him out of the cold. Few could be bothered to carry him up to the tenements, but the gym was close to some of the pubs, and Jimmy had a key. It was often the case that someone would find it in one of his pockets, shove him inside, and toss it in after him.

'So the trainer let him use the place as some kind of emergency doss-house?' said Jarvis.

Whalley replied that Jimmy had precious few places of refuge left to him, but that so far as his former trainer was concerned, he was always welcome. 'Ye have tae understand,' said Whalley, 'Jimmy put his trainer on the map. He was a champion, the first he ever trained.'

He was also a heavyweight, a true contender, potentially one of the greats, thought Jarvis, and it was to his former trainer's credit that he hadn't forgotten what Jimmy had once represented.

A chair lay on the floor, the wooden back scarred by shotgun pellets. Jarvis was struck by its similarity to the chair that Jack Profumo's mistress, Christine Keeler, had been sitting on when her photograph had appeared on the front page of *The Times* a few years earlier. There were many such chairs around at that time, their feminine curves and narrow waists seeming somehow appropriate to someone of Keeler's calling, but not to that of a boxer.

Jimmy had been shot from behind, and the blast had toppled him over, along with the chair. The floor, the walls, the trophy cabinet, all had been smothered with blood, and just as Jarvis was wondering why his killer had made him sit facing the cabinet, Whalley said, 'I reckon his killer wanted those newspaper cuttings tae be the last thing he saw.'

Jarvis was more interested in the chair than in any assumption Whalley might have made with regard to the clippings. There was a chalk mark around it, and a further chalk mark showing where Jimmy's body had been found. The body had long been taken away to the morgue, but the chair remained, and Forensic experts were examining the area of floor it had stood on.

Here, the blood had dried into blackened pools, and further splashes had almost completely obliterated the contents of the trophy cabinet. It was nailed into the wall and housed small pewter trophies, photographs, and newspaper clippings, many of which featured Jimmy.

In studying them, Jarvis realised that, in his heyday, Jimmy had been as near perfect a specimen as any man could ever hope to be. His neck alone had been broader than Jarvis's head, and even from those newspaper clips, you got a sense of the sheer power of the man.

'Ah think this is a revenge killing,' said Whalley. 'It has the look o' the kind o' thing someone might do tae an informant, though I find it hard tae believe Jimmy would grass anyone.'

Jarvis also found it hard to believe. Besides, Jimmy would have had to have done someone some serious damage to warrant it coming to this, and if that had been the case, one of Strathclyde's officers would have come forward by now to let Whalley know that Jimmy was his informant, and that he had grassed a particular villain, if only so that Whalley could determine who might have had a motive for murdering him.

The severity of the punishment meted out to informants was usually determined by the degree of damage they had done to the offended party. Most Glaswegian informants were punished with a razor slash that ran from mouth to cheekbone, but some were murdered, and when that happened, they were invariably murdered brutally. In that regard, Jimmy's murder certainly fitted the picture.

They had graduated to the topic of George McLaughlan, with Jarvis revealing his true motivation for being there: 'I need your help,' he admitted, and Whalley had seemed to warm to him properly then. Jarvis might be English, and he might be from an outside force, but he wasn't your average ignorant English bastard, after all.

'What with?'

'George is bound to surface. He may even turn up at the funeral.'

'Ah doubt that,' said Whalley. 'He's not that fuckin' stupid.'

George wasn't stupid at all, thought Jarvis. That was just the trouble. 'Maybe not,' he admitted. 'But he's bound to turn up somewhere, sometime, around the time of Jimmy's funeral.'

'You want us tae watch Iris's place, is that it?'

'I'll watch it with you,' said Jarvis. 'And I'll wait.'

'You might have a long wait,' said Whalley. 'George is a clever bastard.'

Jarvis, who had suffered quite enough of people telling him what a clever bastard George McLaughlan was, didn't need to hear it from Whalley as well as from Elsa and Hunter. 'I can wait as long as it takes,' he said.

He returned to London to the news that a story relating to police corruption had broken in *The Times*. It claimed that certain detectives within the Met were taking money in exchange for dropping charges, for being lenient with evidence offered in court, and for allowing a criminal to work unhindered.

As a result, a former chief constable of Cumberland had been appointed by the Home Office to investigate the allegations of corruption, and in the months that followed, a number of Jarvis's colleagues became the subject of media attention. Some would ultimately find themselves in the dock of the Old Bailey, and among them would be Hunter, who was caught taking bribes from some of the major players of the day.

During the course of the inquiry into Hunter's activities, something came to light that terrified Jarvis: it had long been suspected that someone was tipping George off whenever the Met or Strathclyde discovered his whereabouts, but the news that George's contact was none other than Hunter came as a total shock. Jarvis couldn't believe it. He didn't *want* to believe it, and not just because he had liked and trusted Hunter: he had long had the feeling that Hunter was on to him with regard to Elsa but had previously put it down to nerves. Now, however, he couldn't help wondering what, if anything, Hunter had said to George. Also, Jarvis was well aware that if Hunter should choose to blow him out, he could kiss his career goodbye, but it was concern for Elsa's safety rather than for his job that took him to Hunter's home to ask him a few straight questions.

Hunter had stood in the doorway to the kind of four-bed detached that Jarvis couldn't afford on police pay. His wife, Doreen, had stood in the background, looking a great deal more haggard than Hunter, who merely looked resigned to it all. Her voice had filtered past him, the mouselike plea of a woman at the mercy of her neighbours: 'Who is it, Don? Tell them to go away.'

'Get back in the house,' said Hunter, and because she obeyed him instantly, she didn't hear when he went on: 'It's only a colleague of mine, or should I say a *former* colleague?' He knew full well he was going to prison, thought Jarvis, and before he could say why he was there, Hunter said, 'I suppose you've come to spit in my face?'

'No,' said Jarvis, quietly, adding: 'Can I come in for a minute?'

'Prefer that you didn't,' said Hunter. 'I'm right off coppers just now.'

Jarvis wasn't about to leave without getting what he came for. 'There's something I have to know.'

'Don't tell me, you want to know why I did it?'

'No,' said Jarvis, who knew why he'd done it – why *anyone* would do it. When a villain waved a good deal of money under your nose, it could be very hard to say no. Bills had a habit of mounting up. Wives liked their little holiday from the drudgery of the suburbs. Kids always needed something or other – clothes, a new pair of shoes, money for the school trip to some godforsaken alp. He decided not to piss around trying to find out how much, if anything, Hunter knew. The look on Hunter's face – the one suggesting that Jarvis was no better than he was – told him all he needed to know on that score, and he came straight to the point.

'I need to know if you've told George about me and Elsa.'

If Jarvis needed reminding that George would be anything but amused by the news that someone was screwing his wife, he got it in Hunter's incredulous, 'I wouldn't do that to you, Mike – I wouldn't want it on my conscience.'

Jarvis hadn't known what to say. He'd felt awkward, standing there, Hunter at the door, and him hopping from foot to foot on the welcome mat. He had felt a bloody fool. Hunter had added, 'Listen, Mike, I'm the last person anyone should be taking advice from right now, but that aside, I'm telling you – cut it out.'

'George doesn't frighten me.'

'Then what you doin' standing on my doorstep lookin' as though you could do with a blood transfusion?'

'I need to be prepared, that's all.'

'You're out of your mind,' said Hunter. 'Nothing – and I mean *nothing* – is going to help any of you when George finds out. And he will.'

'You haven't told him, then.'

'Not a word,' said Hunter. 'It'd be like making myself an accessory to murder.'

That was all that Jarvis had wanted to hear. 'Good luck,' he said to Hunter.

Hunter had snorted with laughter. 'Luck?' he said. 'You're the one who needs the luck. I'll get prison. But I'll come out, and I'll carry on with my life. But you, my son, are living on borrowed time.'

Chapter Sixteen

A short while after Orme had phoned, Claire walked into the living room to find Robbie standing well back from one of the windows. He didn't turn to look at her when she walked in, and he didn't respond when she asked if something was wrong.

She asked him again, and this time, he replied, 'We're being watched.'

For one split second, Claire believed him; and then she looked past the few square feet of paving beyond the window. The road with its pedestrians, its cars, contained only people and vehicles that were moving. Nobody hanging around or staring out from one of the houses opposite. Nothing she felt might warrant investigation.

The sound of toys, some large, some small, being spilled from a large cardboard box in the room above seemed almost abstract, as if the textured silence that had swamped the house since the shooting were the norm. It was followed by the sound of Ocky coming down the stairs taking a step at a time, the cautious descent of a child who had been taught to take it slowly.

Claire, who was also taking it slowly, walked towards the window with the intention of asking what, precisely, had led him to believe they were being watched, but she didn't get that far: in two gigantic strides, McLaughlan had crossed the room, had grabbed her by the arm, had pulled her to the floor.

She gasped and rolled free of him as Ocky appeared in the doorway. Instantly he realised that there was something strange about the parental tableau before him, and he said, in a small and enquiring voice, 'Mummy?'

Claire, numb with shock, shook her head at McLaughlan. 'Please,' she said. 'Don't do this.'

'They might be armed.'

She had heard of this kind of thing happening to others. Young men. Strong men. Men like her husband who found themselves incapable of living with the fact that they had ended the life of another human being. A tangible threat would be preferable to the alternative, so she crawled to a corner of the room, stood up, and stared out at the houses, the road beyond.

She was willing the threat into being, but there was no one. Nobody standing opposite or anywhere in view. Just a few people walking, a few cars passing. Nothing out of the ordinary. Nothing that could be construed as any kind of threat.

Ocky started to cry – the automatic response of a child faced with the possibility that the most important adults in his life were frightened of something.

He ran to her, and she scooped him up, then rested him on her hip. 'It's okay, Ocky, everything's okay,' and McLaughlan tried to reassure them by pointing out that whoever was doing the watching wanted him, not them.

A part of Claire wanted to tell him that she wasn't afraid of some imaginary gunman, that she knew full well there was nobody there, that what terrified her was that he suddenly bore no resemblance to the calm, balanced person she knew him to be. But because she had no idea what someone in his state of mind might do, and because she was afraid that if she said the wrong thing he might turn violent, she said nothing.

'I have to go out,' he said. 'You understand? Don't open the door to anyone. *Anyone!*'

Claire was dumb with shock.

'Promise me?' said McLaughlan, and Claire, who would have promised him anything right then, gave a nod. 'And don't close the blinds – I don't want them to know I know they're there.'

These were the words of a madman, of someone who had lost their grip on reality, thought Claire. And then he left. No goodbye. No explanation with regard to where he was going. He just walked out.

She watched him back the car out of the drive, and once it had disappeared from view, she ran to the phone and dialled Doheny's number. She caught him at home, the comforting sound of family life filtering through from the background.

Doheny's world came across as normal, well-rounded, chaotic, and he slowed her down with a calmness that rubbed off: 'Start again. Take it from the top.'

She told him what had happened, and found herself justifying her anxiety by adding, 'If he really thought he was being watched, surely the sensible thing would have been to turn to you or Orme. He didn't, because deep down he knows there's nobody out there. Why would he go out if he thought there was? It doesn't make sense.'

Doheny couldn't argue with that. He stood by the telephone with his youngest child fishing with fingers both light and deft for the keys that were deep in his pocket. For a boy of six, he showed an almost extraordinary talent for pickpocketry, and a different father might have had considerable expectations of his future.

Doheny retrieved the car keys and clipped him round the ear with more affection than exasperation. 'What do you want me to do?'

That was a point: Claire hadn't thought that far ahead. 'I don't know,' she admitted.

'Have you thought what the possible consequences might be if you tell Orme?'

She hadn't had time to think beyond the fact that she was worried, that she wanted advice. The possibility that there might be unfavourable repercussions to having asked for that advice hadn't occurred to her. It occurred to her now, as Doheny said he hoped she would think carefully before she contacted Orme. He added, 'It isn't uncommon for people to feel they're being watched when they're under this kind of stress.'

'He frightened me—'

'Claire,' said Doheny, 'if you tell Orme what you've just told me, he'll take action. He won't have a choice. And that will put into motion a chain of events that not even Orme can stop. You're talking about doing something that could get Robbie kicked out of Flying Squad, maybe even the force.'

'You weren't here – you don't know what he—'

'Plenty of men go through this kind of reaction after a shooting.'

She said again, 'I'm frightened.'

'I can understand that,' said Doheny, 'but maybe, even now, he's asking himself how he could ever have imagined he was being watched, and maybe he's panicking in case you've already said something to someone.' He added that he had known men do far worse things than tell their wives they thought somebody was watching them. He'd seen wives beaten up, abused, accused of infidelity. Claire was getting off lightly. 'Give him a chance,' he said. 'These are early days. Don't blow him out.'

'But—'

'He'll never forgive you, Claire.'

She was fighting conflicting emotions: the greater part of her wanted to phone Orme, but Doheny's warning hadn't gone unheard. What if she was wrong? What if Doheny was right and Robbie came back, full of apologies, the crisis over, never to be repeated? Wasn't it a little premature to do something that might humiliate him, damage his career, wreck their marriage?

'If you want,' said Doheny, 'I could talk to Orme myself.'

'No,' said Claire. 'Let's just see what happens.'

She brought the call to an end and replaced the receiver. Out in the road, a car slowed down, then passed the house. In her current frame of mind it was all too easy to imagine that the passenger had been staring at the house as the car cruised by, and if she could imagine such things, how much easier must it be for Robbie?

Ocky, his face puckered with worry, said, 'Is something wrong with Daddy?'

Claire's every instinct told her *yes*, but Doheny's warning forced her not to heed those instincts. 'No,' she replied. 'Daddy's fine. Daddy's just got a lot on his mind, that's all.'

Chapter Seventeen

The woman behind the counter remembers you. She tells you she never forgets a face, and that you were one of the men who was watching the bank.

She asks what you want and reminds you that she already gave a statement to a uniform. She saw it all. The child. The balloon. The shooting. She read in the paper about the man found hanging off a bridge.

She asks if you knew him and you look at her as if to say you know nothing – you don't even know who the fuck you are any more. She senses something about you – there's something not quite right. You see her working it out for herself. But she thinks that if you're a copper it must be okay.

You're using the shop as means of finding out if you were followed, but you don't tell her that. You browse a little, as if the fruit on the state-of-the-art displays is a source of fascination, but it's not the fruit you're looking at, it's the people on the street. Most of them are walking past, but some are hanging around, and you try to recall if you've seen their faces before.

The woman behind the counter has stopped asking questions. She's trying not to let you know she's got her eye on you, and she's longing for another customer to walk in, though she doesn't know what's frightening her; she only knows she's frightened.

You pick an apple out of a display. You hand it to her, and you pay for it, and you bite it as you walk out on to the street. It tastes like parchment. The skin has been waxed to enhance the red, but the flesh is juiceless. You let it drop to the ground. It's soft. It doesn't roll. It lands with a sickening thud, spreads out like a suicide, and ends up under your feet as you make for the house.

You remind her that a week ago a security van was attacked just up the road. One of the robbers has made a statement relating to the use to which this particular house has been put in the past. You have to check the story out, so would she mind if you made a search of the cellar?

'How do I know you are who you say you are?'

You show her your ID and she doesn't just glance it over, she takes it from your hand, reads the small print, hands it back.

'Well, I'm not sure . . .' She's very coy. She has the eyes of a Turkish whore and she's trying to make them girlish. 'What would my husband think?'

She's going to let you in. You know it. She knows it. But, right now, she's playing this game. It excites her. It makes her morning. She's so fucking bored that winding you up and keeping you cold on the doorstep is a source of amusement.

She stands at the door in an ivory silk kimono, and her voice is almost as polished as the floorboards. 'And, anyway, I thought policemen always went round in pairs, like women, nipping to the loo.'

The contempt behind the comment winds you up. You want to smack her in the mouth, but you're not about to allow her to *deflect you from your goal. She hasn't finished with you yet: 'How do I know I can trust you?'*

She says it in a way that suggests she hopes she's about to discover that you can't be trusted an inch. You don't reply. Whatever you say, she'll weave some sexual innuendo into the words, and sex is the last thing you want to have to think about right now. You reckon she has to be in a state of terminal frustration, that she's probably comparing you to the jerk she married for money. 'I'm really not sure I should let you in at all . . .' But even as she's saying it, she's opening the door. And now she's letting you in because women like her are not only vain but stupid. They think their wealth forms a barrier between them and the more unpleasant aspects of life. You couldn't even hazard a guess at how many women like her end up as murder victims. And she's worse than any hooker: hookers do it for money, women like her are doing it for power.

She stands at the door in a way that makes it impossible for you to walk past without brushing up against her. And beneath the silk kimono her nipples are so hard you can feel them through the leather of your coat. But all you can think about is the size and shape of that hall. It's so familiar to you, yet so very different from the way you remember it. The walls were once bare plaster. Now they are amber and crimson, warm with colour and texture, and you wonder what it took to give the floorboards that patina.

You're cool with her, and it turns her on: she sees you as a predator. But it's very important to her that the danger is an illusion. You just have to look the part. She doesn't know that you are the part, that she couldn't just switch you off like some disturbing documentary. She let you in because she thinks she's a good judge of character. She doesn't have the first fucking clue what's happening in your head, or what it means to you to be *standing here in the hall where Crackerjack spilled his guts out on to a carpet.*

You ask her how long she's lived there and she throws you a gift by telling you her husband bought the property seven months ago. You tell her that one of the robbers had access to the house prior to her living there, that there may be a weapon hidden in the cellar.

'A gun? How very exciting!' The comment is droll, and made all the more so by the affectation of boredom.

She tells you she'd almost forgotten there was a cellar. But you haven't forgotten. You haven't forgotten the number of times you hid down there from Jimmy, or that this was where Crackerjack died from gunshot wounds.

The hinges on the cellar door have been painted over. The paint cracks as you open the door and flakes fall on the polished boards at your feet.

You stand on the topmost step, and reach for the string that used to hang from a light switch set into the ceiling. The string has gone, and she tells you to wait while she fetches you a torch.

You wait, and while you are waiting you tell yourself you were out of your mind to come here, that even now she might be checking you out. But in seconds she comes back with a torch and she holds it a fraction longer than is necessary when passing it to you. She touches your hand as you take it. At any other time, you'd see it as the come-on she intended it to be. Right now you see it as a pain in the arse.

You tell her there's no need for her to stay down in the cellar, but although she backs off, she doesn't leave. She's standing on the wooden steps, the hem of her kimono touching the dirt. You tell her she'll get cold, and she says you can warm her up later. You switch on the torch and shine it around the cellar.

Nothing has changed. That's the first thing you notice. The ground is earth beneath your feet, and the limewashed walls are lit from a window set at pavement height. You walk over to that window and you study the brickwork beneath it. The outside wall is double-skinned, and you know about the cavity between the rows of bricks. You pull out one of the bricks, and then another, and feel for something hidden deep in the cavity. You bring it out. Just touching it reminds you of your father. The last time you saw this gun, it was lying next to Crackerjack, and nothing on God's earth was going to stop the bleeding: 'How bad is it?'

'It's bad.'

'Don't let me go, George.'

'You're not going anywhere.'

The sight of that gun has turned her on. She starts to stroke the barrel, the movement of her fingers suggestive, taunting. She doesn't know the gun might just be loaded, that the man who hid it liked to be prepared for any eventuality, so you keep her fingers well away from the trigger.

There comes a point, as you knew there would, when her fingers slip from the barrel of the gun. Her skin-pink, nylon-fibre nails snag the denim of your jeans. She's searching for a hard-on and because you haven't obliged her, she suggests that maybe you're one of those men with a problem. She starts to laugh, and you grab her, and you press the gun so hard against her neck she starts to whimper. You hold her up, and you tell her you're not police; you'll fuck her if that's what she wants, but only after she's dead.

The dull sound of urine hitting the floor of the cellar makes you release her, and she's stamping her feet as she screams a riverdance of fear. She tells you she'll do anything, but please, please, don't hurt her, and you wonder how many women before her have tried to make a similar bargain.

You've never hit a woman in your life, but you have no choice. You have to stop her screaming, and you whack her across the face. You tell her it's her lucky day. She opened the door to you. She could just as easily have opened the door to a killer.

McLaughlan pulled the navy crew-neck sweater over a bullet-proof vest that was larger and bulkier than that which he generally wore. This vest was older, and less well designed. It didn't matter. So long as it did the job. So long as the other two vests that were lying at his feet also did the job.

He had bought them from a shop that sold decommissioned weapons, sometimes to enthusiasts but mostly to villains, who made a few minor adjustments and got them back on the road.

'Robbie – what are you doing?'

He turned from the image before him to see Claire at the door to the bedroom, Ocky standing beside her like a small, uncertain stranger. He'd seen his daddy dressed in these clothes before, but never with the bullet-proof vest bulky beneath the sweater.

He stooped and picked up the other two vests, held them out to her. 'One is for you. The other is for Ocky.'

'Robbie—'

She was shaking her head, backing away, Ocky looking as if, at any moment, he might cry.

'Put them on,' said McLaughlan. He reached out and grabbed her, pulled her back in the bedroom, and forced her into the vest, ripping at the Velcro fastenings, adjusting them, making it fit. 'We're sleeping together tonight,' he said. 'All in the same bed, the same room.'

And then she saw the gun. She knew nothing about guns. Nothing. But what she did know was this: the police didn't issue officers with sawn-off shotguns. This was a sawn-off shotgun. It was old. It was filthy. It was lying on the bed. She looked at it, but some instinct made her glance away. That same instinct forewarned her that she had to say the right things, make the right moves, that Ocky's life, or her own, or both, might depend on it.

'Ocky,' said McLaughlan, 'come here. Put this on.'

Ocky stayed in the doorway and McLaughlan scooped him up. He laid him on the bed next to the gun and strapped him into the smallest vest the shop had been able to sell him. It buried him, and when Ocky tried to shake his way out of it, Claire began to plead with him: 'Do as your daddy tells you, Ocky – don't argue, baby, don't argue.'

Chapter Eighteen

The realisation that he had last seen Ash at the pub that had been Tommy's local put Jarvis in mind to drop in on the place, so he left the flat and walked it for the exercise.

It was very much in the fashion of pubs like the British Lion and the Elephant and Castle – pubs that were so quintessentially British they almost looked like the kind of place you might find on the Costa del Sol.

In this particular pub, as in so many others, the ceilings and walls were beamed and brassed, and a picture of the Queen hung over the bar.

Over the years, that picture of Her Majesty had smiled on some of the hardest men in British criminal history – patriots to a man – which was why a row of Union Jacks stuck out of a series of holes punched into one of the walls by a spray of bullets.

Rumour had it that a previous owner had arranged for those bullet-holes to be made – good for trade, good for tourists, and good for a laugh with the regulars.

Whether it was true or not, Jarvis couldn't say. There was something random about them, something that spoke of the person who fired the shots having been unaccustomed to handling a firearm, as if it had run away with him and scared him half to death.

It was dark in the pub although outside it was broad grey daylight. The windows were not only frosted but heavily curtained in brown, and the only lighting came from gold-fringed wall-lamps.

He stood in the doorway a moment to take a quick look round. It wasn't always wise to go ploughing into these places: there were plenty of villains like Ash in pubs like this – villains who, like some coppers, had a long memory and an unforgiving nature. He scanned the snug but found that most of the people sitting at the beaten-copper-topped tables were people he had encountered without a problem at Tommy's funeral, so feeling it safe to do so, he walked up to the bar, ordered a draught bitter, and watched his back in a mirror behind the optics. 'Have one yourself,' he said to the barmaid, who put a couple of quid in the Perspex tips box, then turned to serve some other customers.

There were glass shelves next to the optics, and stacked on them were bottles of liqueurs. Of all of them the one that took Jarvis's attention was a bottle of Advocaat. It fascinated him because, to his certain knowledge, that very bottle had stood on those shelves since the pub first opened its doors. Nobody ever drank it. None of the villains, for sure. And none of their girlfriends would touch the stuff. It was probably stuck to the shelf, never having been lifted since the war. In fact, Jarvis could envisage the entire bar and its contents ending up at the British Museum, and the bottle of Advocaat displayed in a glass-domed case all its own.

The barmaid began to clear glasses from the tables, her clothes reminiscent of those that might have been worn in Tommy's day. Something to do with the fashions coming back, Jarvis presumed. Her PVC mini-skirt looked a size too small, the white knee-length boots a size too large, and her eyelids were heavy with shimmering turquoise shadow. She looked about fourteen to Jarvis, who failed to find anything even remotely erotic about her. She moved without any of the grace that had first attracted him to Elsa but, then, some women were born with style. Their backgrounds didn't come into it. Grace Kelly. Lauren Bacall. Rita Hayworth. These had been sensual women. Not one of them had needed to get themselves up in PVC or plaster themselves with makeup to turn a man on. A look had been enough. And the look wasn't always beckoning, either. Sometimes there was a flash of temper behind it, the suggestion that the woman couldn't be tamed.

Elsa's eyes had flashed when Jarvis had told her he didn't want her going to Jimmy's funeral, largely because he wouldn't explain why.

He could have revealed that Iris was under surveillance and that he didn't want Elsa caught up in any trouble if George should show his face, but no matter how much he loved her, he wasn't about to risk blowing his best chance to date of catching George by divulging something that she might let slip to Iris. Consequently, Elsa could see no reason not to go. What's more, she took it into her head to take Robbie with her, and when Jarvis suggested that the funeral of a murder victim was no place for a boy of ten, it had made not the slightest difference. Irrespective of his views, she had gone to Glasgow the day before the funeral, and the night before she left, she asked if he happened to know whether Strathclyde were watching Iris.

It had been very casually put, a question she simply dropped into the conversation, and in an equally casual manner, Jarvis had replied, 'Not to my knowledge.' It had been the first time in the course of their relationship that he had lied to her, and he hadn't felt good about it. But there had been something about the fact that it had taken her so long to open the door to him the day he went to the house to tell her Jimmy was dead – he couldn't shake the idea that George had been in the house. He knew it didn't make sense in that if George believed that Elsa was opening the door to another man he'd hardly have been likely to hide. And where would he have hidden? In the bedroom? In the cellar?

He had always known the house had a cellar. God knows, he and his colleagues had searched it often enough over the years. It was accessed via a door off the kitchen, and the stairs that led down to it were wooden, slightly unsafe.

It was gloomy down there, and the smell of damp was strong enough to make you hold your breath, but you could see well enough: there was a window set at pavement height, one that had once been grilled for security reasons. Somebody – George probably – had ripped away the grille to give himself the option of escaping via that window should the need arise.

In hindsight, Jarvis wished that he'd checked the bedrooms and cellar, but Elsa would have been on to him in an instant: He could just imagine her saying, 'Don't you trust me?'

Jarvis was faced with having to make an admission to himself. He loved Elsa. He saw the best in her. But, all things considered, he didn't trust her an inch. George McLaughlan still had a hold over her – that was how he saw it. Left to herself, Elsa was as trustworthy as the next woman, but George was pressurising her into certain things. He had probably turned up like the proverbial bad penny, and rather than risk antagonising him, Elsa had let him in, had pretended that everything was all right between them. And then Jarvis had arrived, and she'd known how it might look to him, so she'd persuaded George to hide in the cellar with the explanation that some copper was at the door. Even so, when Elsa had said, 'What will you be up to while I'm in Glasgow?' Jarvis replied, 'I haven't really thought about it. Why?'

'Just wondered. You'll be staying in London, though?'

'Where else would I be?'

'Just wondered,' she said again.

The turnout for Jimmy's funeral took everyone by surprise. Glasgow didn't forget its heroes easily, and the sheer volume of people who crowded around the graveside made it easier for Whalley's men to keep an eye open for George.

Jarvis, who had only ever known Jimmy as the monster he became, had later seen photographs taken by some of those men. Iris and Elsa had been easy to pick out, but Robbie was lost in a crowd comprised of people from the gym, the pubs that Jimmy favoured, a rep from the world of professional boxing, and reporters from the local and national press.

George hadn't shown, but there had been other members of the family, people Elsa had mentioned as being related to Iris in one way or another. Some seemed bewildered by the turnout. Others appeared uninterested as if they were wondering why they'd bothered going. They had drifted back to the tenement for a drink, but all had disappeared by 8 p.m.

After the last of the relatives had gone, Jarvis sat beside Whalley in an old Ford Pop that was parked within sight of the tenement. Elsa was still in there, and he wondered how she might feel if she knew that he'd lied to her, that he wasn't in London, but sitting a mere two hundred yards from the room where she and Robbie would shortly be sleeping on that lice-ridden, shakedown bed.

He hated to think of either of them having to cope with the squalor, and hated also to think of them surrounded by armed police. If George turned up, things could get very nasty very quickly.

He calmed himself by telling himself that if George intended to show up to give Iris some support, he'd have done it already. It was a bit late in the day for him to start thinking about providing a shoulder for Iris to cry on. He had left Elsa to do that, just like he had left her to do everything else – from coping with Tam's disappearance to putting bread on the table. And whilst the thought of the way George treated Elsa made him angry, it also pleased him in a sense because it left the way wide open for him to do what George had never done: provide for his wife and family.

He had almost managed to persuade himself that tonight would pass uneventfully when one of Whalley's men made radio contact: *'They're on the move.'*

Whalley asked for clarification and was told that Iris, Elsa, and Robbie had left the tenement building and were walking down the road towards Bolan Street. A short time later, they climbed into a cab that had been parked up a side road, waiting for them.

An unmarked car had followed the cab, which had doubled back on itself a couple of times, darting down side roads, parking in car parks, setting off again. It had taken a good half-hour for the driver to make a five-minute journey, but eventually the police had been led to a guesthouse down by the docks.

All the while the unmarked car had been following the cab, Jarvis had been convincing himself that Elsa hadn't been able to face another night on that shakedown bed and that she had told Iris she wanted to spend the night at a guesthouse with Robbie. He visualised Iris saying, 'I don't want tae be left on ma own,' but he knew this was a fantasy. If Elsa had wanted to spend the night in a guesthouse, Iris would have told her to please herself. She wouldn't have tried to persuade her to stay at her place, and she wouldn't have gone with her, either. The whole scenario – from the fact that they had left the tenement, to the fact that the cab driver had clearly taken precautions against being followed – could mean only one thing: they were going to meet George.

Initially, he had persuaded himself that Elsa wouldn't have agreed to see George of her own volition, that Iris had coerced her on the grounds that Robbie had a right to see his father. And then he faced the facts because he knew it wasn't true.

'You're quiet,' said Whalley.

'A lot on my mind,' replied Jarvis, who realised

Strathclyde now had a tactical problem to solve. For all they knew, George might already be in the guesthouse. On the other hand, he might not. Their only way of finding out would be to speak to the owner and ask if someone fitting George's description was there, but if they did that, and if the owner was a friend of George's, they ran the risk of the owner tipping George off that the place was about to be hit by armed police.

The same thoughts had clearly been going through Whalley's mind, and he said, 'What do you think? Do we go in now or do we wait?'

He'd no sooner said it than George walked straight past the car. He'd approached from behind, and neither Jarvis nor Whalley had seen him coming. The sight of him made Jarvis catch his breath. He wasn't a stranger to George. There'd been many an occasion when Jarvis had seen him face to face over the years. He therefore wasn't surprised by the size of him, or by the way he had come out of nowhere – that was George all over. But in seeing him on what was, essentially, his home territory, Jarvis was struck by just how confident he was. Most people steered well clear of the docks at night, and those who didn't had sense enough to be nervous, to question what they were doing there, and to keep well clear of the place if they possibly could. He walked up the path to the guesthouse, and rang a bell. When the door was opened to him, Whalley said, 'Here we go.'

'What are you planning to do?'

'Go for it, while we know where he is,' said Whalley. He reached for the radio with the intention of giving an order to his men, but Jarvis put out a hand to hold him back. 'Not now,' he said. 'Not yet.' And when Whalley

asked him why not, Jarvis replied with a lie: he told him
that, in his view, it would be unthinkable to allow armed
men to go bursting in there when they knew for a fact
that a ten-year-old kid was inside.

It had been a good excuse, but an excuse had been all
it was: Jarvis hadn't wanted Whalley's men bursting into
that place because, as he sat in that car, he had suddenly
faced up to the fact that Elsa wasn't a pushover. He
hadn't been able to stop her from going to Glasgow,
and Iris wouldn't have been able to force her to go to
the guesthouse for Robbie or anyone else's sake. She had
known that George would be at the guesthouse, and she
had gone there for one reason only: she had wanted to
see him.

He had faced the facts, yet he still desperately wanted
to prove himself wrong, and the only thing that was
going to do that was the sight of George McLaughlan
leaving the guesthouse. If he did that – if he left within
an hour or so, if he didn't spend the night in there with
Elsa – then Jarvis would have something to cling to,
something that would persuade him that Elsa wasn't
still in love with George. He said to Whalley, 'Give
him a chance to see his family, then maybe he'll come
out. It'd be better to hit him on the street than in there
with the chance of shots being fired, especially with his
kid around.'

Whalley had to agree, if only to cover his backside in
the event of Robbie getting caught up in any shooting.
'We'll give him an hour,' he said.

That hour was the longest Jarvis had ever spent. They
were in the worst possible situation for armed police
to be in. There was a kid inside the guesthouse, and

whatever they did, it could turn out to be the wrong thing. If Whalley stormed the place, Robbie might get hurt. If he didn't, the minute George knew they had him surrounded, he might take Robbie hostage. Either way, Robbie might end up dead. George wouldn't be the first villain to use his son to buy himself a ticket. *Not even George would eat his own kids.*

Jarvis wasn't so sure.

He longed for George to walk out of there, and he longed, also, for Elsa to leave with Robbie. Neither happened. He had known that neither would. And when the hour was up, he and Whalley left the car and walked up the path to the guesthouse.

They didn't want George warned by the sound of the bell reverberating through the house, so Whalley knocked fairly quietly, and the owner opened up in the expectation that, at this time of night, the people on the doorstep might be drunks.

Whalley and Jarvis showed their IDs as armed police poured into the guesthouse right behind them. 'Where's the back?' Whalley demanded, and the owner pointed through an archway that led to the kitchens beyond.

Whalley nodded to one of his men who went to open the doors and let more men in that way. Then Whalley showed the guesthouse owner a photograph of George as he added, 'You let this character in here about an hour ago. Which room did he go to?'

The owner made as if to lead them up the stairs, but Whalley stopped him, and asked him just to tell him where it was. 'Rooms three and four,' said the owner. 'They're off the first-floor landing.'

Jarvis mounted the stairs ahead of Whalley and his

men, and he was the one who knocked on the door to room three. The door was opened by Iris, and beyond her, Jarvis saw Robbie in a large double bed. He sat up and blinked, his eyes heavy with sleep, but Jarvis was more concerned by Iris's reaction. The minute she saw the stairwell crammed with Whalley's men, she screamed, 'George – police!'

Even as she shouted the warning, Whalley was giving the nod to two of his men. They rammed the door of the bedroom opposite and knocked it from its hinges, leaving Jarvis with an unimpeded view of the room.

The minute the door was smashed open, George dived off the bed and stooped for something lying on the floor. Instantly Whalley's men had him at gunpoint and he froze. But George wasn't looking at Whalley, or at the guns: he was looking at Jarvis.

Jarvis, however, was looking at Elsa. He barely recognised her, not as she was right then. But, then, he had never before seen her dressed in cheap polyester lingerie, the half-cup bra, the fishnet stockings, the G-string. Whalley's men had to be getting an eyeful. And yet that wasn't what bothered Jarvis so much as what she and George had been doing the minute they rammed the door. It was that alone which caused him to be engulfed by an almost blinding rage, a jealousy so intense he could barely breathe. He hurled himself at George and started to punch him. And George McLaughlan laughed at him. That was the worst thing: he had raised his arms to defend himself – the automatic response of a trained boxer – but he hadn't thumped him back. 'Mike,' he soothed, 'you'll do yourself an injury.' And Whalley's men had grabbed Jarvis, had held him back, while Whalley looked at him with something approaching awe. Nobody he knew would have gone for George McLaughlan with their bare fists. He couldn't even begin to understand what had possessed Jarvis to do it. For the first time since they had met, Jarvis saw respect in Whalley's eyes, and Whalley said, 'We'll take it from here, Mike.' Then he and his men put cuffs on George and led him from the room.

He had gone quietly enough considering, yet the house had seemed filled with noise, most of it made by Iris but some of it coming from Robbie, who was clinging to his gran and begging her to stop the coppers taking his dad.

It wasn't until that moment that Jarvis realised there was more to the saying *blood is thicker than water* than people gave credit for. In all the time he'd known Robbie, he'd never seen him show the slightest sign of affection for his father, but it was there, and as Whalley's men led George downstairs, it wasn't to Jarvis or Elsa that Robbie turned: it was to Iris. 'They've got my dad.'

Jarvis had thought he'd got his anger under control, that using George as a punchbag had got it out of his system, but seeing Robbie crying like that had made his anger resurface in almost as great a force as it had a mere few moments ago. He found himself yelling at Elsa, 'You don't do that!'

'Do what?' said Elsa, and suddenly he was right in her face, screaming his rage, pointing towards Robbie. 'You don't let a lad of ten sleep in the same bed as—'

'Say it. Go on. *Say it!*'

Jarvis fought to get a grip on his temper. He was as close as he'd ever been to hitting a woman, and he inched a little closer as Elsa said, 'You don't let a lad of ten sleep in the same bed as an old whore. That's what you were going to say.' Jarvis didn't deny it, and she added, 'Well, that old whore is his gran. She happens to love him. And that's not what this is about – not if you're honest. You think you can come in here and spout off at me for letting Robbie sleep in the same bed as Iris, but what you really want to do is have a go at me for screwing George.'

'George is a villain.'

'George is my *husband*,' said Elsa. 'You're the other man. You're the one who sneaks around at night, terrified of your superior officers finding out, terrified of George.'

'George doesn't frighten me.'

'If I had a quid for every time I've heard you say that George could retire.'

'Judging from the length of sentence he's likely to get, he just has.'

That hit home. 'Bastard,' she said.

Jarvis replied, 'He was there, at the house, when I broke the news about Jimmy.'

She didn't deny it.

'In the cellar?' said Jarvis.

Again, no answer.

'I thought so.'

She was crying now. Shock, thought Jarvis. And Robbie came in, put his arms around her. They formed a duo of resentment, as if he'd wrecked their lives, and he felt it to be so unfair that he could have throttled her. 'He'll never be any good,' he said. 'You know that, don't you?'

'You leave my mum alone.'

179

'He'll never change,' said Jarvis. 'He'll always be a villain. But if that's what you want . . .'

Even then, if she'd made some sign – the smallest sign, thought Jarvis – he'd have relented. He'd have sat down on the bed with her; he'd have put his arms around her, and he'd have told her he understood, that it couldn't be easy to shake yourself free of the father of your children, not when there was history between you, and not when your kids still loved him. But Elsa had said nothing. Not a word. She sat on the bed and she cried for George, so Jarvis left her to it.

He pushed past Iris who stood on the stairs lighting a Senior Service. The smell of the tobacco seemed to follow him out of the guesthouse, and once outside, he watched as George was led towards a van.

He towered over the men Whalley had cuffed him to and, big though they were, they looked nervous, as if at any moment George might just take off with them, dragging them down the street as he broke free. There wouldn't be much they could do but go with him. At least, that's what it looked like. In reality, not even George would be able to drag two full-grown men more than a few difficult yards. But the reality, and the impression he made, were two different things, and Jarvis could understand why Whalley had taken no chances: as well as the men either side of him, he had put an armed man behind him. George McLaughlan was marched to the van at gunpoint.

Seconds before he was loaded into it he stopped dead, like a horse who had suddenly decided that nothing on God's earth was going to get him into the stalls. Jarvis watched, fascinated, as the men around him froze, but

George's hesitation had been a momentary thing, nothing more than a sudden reluctance to enter a confined space with its darkness, its locks and bolts.

The street was well lit, and Jarvis could see clearly enough to know that the beating he'd tried to give him hadn't left so much as a mark anywhere on his body. He'd have been as well to pick up a pillow and hurl it across the room. No wonder George had laughed at him.

The men either side were tugging as if on the chain that held an elephant, but George didn't budge: he wasn't going in that van until he was good and ready.

He stood his ground long enough to get the message across that, if he'd wanted to, he could have put two-thirds of Whalley's men in hospital before they'd managed to get him under control, and the way he did it made Jarvis face up to something he had never really admitted to himself before: in Elsa's eyes, he was nothing by comparison with George. He was ordinary and, not only that, he was boring. Elsa wanted financial and emotional security, but not as much as she wanted the drama, the sexual excitement that involvement with a man like George invariably guaranteed. No matter that she suffered as a result. No matter that she never knew where the next penny, the next meal, was coming from. No matter that she had one son missing and another so disturbed by whatever had happened to his brother that he could barely speak.

Jarvis walked away.

Chapter Nineteen

Doheny knew all the tricks by which the mind distorted perceptions following a shooting. Whatever the justification for firing the shot, some people were capable of convincing themselves that a man was lying dead because they had panicked, they had misunderstood their instructions, they hadn't listened properly.

The guilt could be overwhelming, and close on the tail of guilt came fear of a disciplinary hearing that would result in them losing their job, being shamed, shunned and ostracised by their colleagues, their family, the press. So they cracked up, broke down, imagined that the people closest to them didn't love them, had never loved them, that their children weren't their own, that their families despised them, that somebody out there was after them, that somebody wanted them dead.

McLaughlan hadn't claimed that anyone wanted him dead, but despite having asked Claire not to let herself be panicked into doing something she might later regret, Doheny was concerned about him. The imagined fear of being followed was but a very short step from the equally imagined, but no less disturbing, idea that somebody out there might be trying to kill you.

There was always the possibility that a good night's sleep had calmed McLaughlan down. On the other hand, there was also the possibility that he had woken up feeling more convinced than ever that someone was after him, so Doheny decided to give Claire a call before he left for the station. If McLaughlan answered the phone, he could suggest they met for a drink. If Claire answered, he could just ask how things were.

He dialled McLaughlan's number, and let the phone ring until it was clear that nobody was there to answer it. He half expected it to cut over into an answering-machine, but it went on ringing, and Doheny replaced the receiver with a view to calling later.

He grabbed his coat and made for the door, but as he did so, he suddenly felt uneasy. He checked the time – just after 8 a.m. McLaughlan wasn't due back on duty for another day, and Claire was a full-time mother.

So where were they?

He ignored the redial, and dialled the number manually – just in case he'd got it wrong the first time. There was no question this time: he'd got it right, and again the phone seemed to ring for a very long time. They had to be out, thought Doheny, although where they could be at this time of morning he couldn't say, unless they hadn't spent the night at home. Maybe they'd gone to friends and stayed over. It was possible.

But unlikely, thought Doheny. When Claire had phoned, she hadn't exactly sounded in the mood for socialising.

It came as a shock when the phone was suddenly answered. Doheny had been about to hang up, with the intention of dropping in on Claire on his way to the station, and the minute he heard her voice he knew there was trouble. 'Claire?' he said.

She whimpered, *'Please – help me!'*

Doheny almost shouted down the receiver: 'Claire?'

'He's got a gun.'

The line went dead, and Doheny stood in the hall. He had often heard the expression 'blood running cold', and he had even thought he'd experienced it often enough. Now he knew that the adrenaline that pumped through him prior to action came nowhere near to producing that effect. For the first time in his life, he knew what it was to feel his blood run cold.

There was no question now with regard to what should be done. He cut the connection at his end, then dialled direct to a phone that was never allowed to go unanswered. The very first ring was cut short by the voice of an operator based at Tower Bridge.

'Get me Orme,' said Doheny.

McLaughlan appeared at her side, the bullet-proof vest now over, rather than under the crew-neck sweater, the filthy sawn-off shotgun in his hand.

Claire had never seen him carry a gun before. Knowing what he did for a job and imagining what he might look like when he carried a gun was one thing: seeing him in the living room, a gun in his hand, was another.

The barrel had been maimed to its present length, leaving the gun unbalanced to the eye, the snout of a pit-bull terrier on the body of a greyhound. It was something of a work of art, its ornate silverwork depicting pheasants rising out of foliage. Now the silver was tarnished to an almost inky blackness, and she suspected that the discoloration on the stock was due to bloodstains.

A gun such as this would once have been regularly cleaned and kept stored in a room with weapons equally well bred. But at some point it had been stolen. She couldn't be sure of that, but it seemed unlikely to Claire that the type of person who would have a vested interest in maiming what had once been a beautiful gun would buy one new for the purpose. This gun had changed hands in a bar, a car-park, a hotel bedroom.

Ocky sat on her hip, his legs wrapped tight round her waist, his arms wrapped tight round her neck. He wasn't a child who normally wanted to be carried everywhere, but some instinct was telling him to stay as close to his mother as he could. He also kept quiet, and he watched his father with wide, intelligent eyes. He didn't even comment on the gun. It was almost as if he knew his mother was terrified of it, and that, therefore, he too should be terrified. He wouldn't even look at it.

'You've taken your vest off.'

'I can't wear it, and carry Ocky.'

'Then put him down.'

'He won't let me.'

McLaughlan walked towards them and Ocky cringed away. 'He's frightened of the gun,' said Claire, and she wondered how she had managed to keep the anxiety out of her voice. Inside she was screaming, but all she could think about was the number of times she'd heard of women surviving, of saving themselves and their children by staying calm.

'I thought I heard the phone.'

'You did.'

'Who was it?'

'Doheny,' said Claire.

'You didn't call me.'

'I thought you said you didn't want to speak to anyone.'

'Doheny is different.'

'What if he told Orme he'd spoken to you after I'd told him only yesterday that you'd gone up north?'

He hadn't thought of that. She watched him take it in, consider it, and finally, accept it.

The room was dark, almost completely so, the blinds having been drawn the night before. Now, with daylight fully established, McLaughlan had decided to keep them drawn for the moment. He pulled one aside the merest fraction, and searched the outside world for something to feed his conviction that somebody was out there. Suddenly Claire couldn't stand it. 'At least we could open the blinds.'

'I want them closed.'

'You said yesterday that you wanted them left open – you didn't want them to know you knew they were there.'

'I've changed my mind.'

There could be no arguing with a man who held a gun in his hand. He used it as a pointer when he indicated the rooms above their heads and said, 'Upstairs.'

'What for?'

'I want you where I can see you.'

'Why?'

'To protect you both.'

Claire walked ahead of him, Ocky on her hip. 'Where are we going, Mummy?'

She didn't know. Front bedroom? Back bedroom? Into the attic?

'Bathroom,' said McLaughlan, and Claire acquiesced as if it were the most normal thing in the world for all three of them to walk inside and bolt the bathroom door.

The pre-war, cast-iron bath stood beside a basin that was coming away from its pedestal. It ran the length of a wall in which a single frosted window, the frame rotten with age, provided a constant draught of freezing air.

It was possibly the coldest room in the house. But it was also the cleanest because Claire had made it so. She had known it would be quite some time before they could afford a new bathroom, so she had scrubbed it, had disinfected it, had made it usable. She had also insisted on one small item of luxury: the old chrome taps had been ripped from the bath and replaced. A bracket above the taps held a shower hose, and Claire had fixed a rail from the ceiling to hold a makeshift curtain.

McLaughlan undressed, stood in the bath and took a shower, but he left the curtain undrawn because he wanted to keep an eye on Claire and Ocky.

They stood as far away from him as they could, and Claire was doing her best to protect Ocky from the constant spray of water, but because McLaughlan hadn't pulled the waterproof curtain, they quickly got soaked.

Ocky was crying now, his voice a mere quiver above the hiss of the water. Despite the water being warm, he was shaking, though mostly with fear.

Claire was also shaking with fear, but doing her best to hide it, and when McLaughlan asked, 'Are you okay?' she smiled, and nodded.

This, thought Claire, is what it's like to have to deal with the mentally ill. They had been inside the bathroom for just under two minutes and yet her views on Care in the Community had undergone a shift. She had previously been of the opinion that people should be forced to take more responsibility for those close to them. Now she was beginning to realise what it must be like to have to deal with bizarre behaviour twenty-four hours a day. No help. No money. And no medal to mark the fact that you had sacrificed the quality of your own life in order to improve the quality of somebody else's.

Her mother had once told her that a woman should never marry a man unless she couldn't believe her luck and, until the shooting, Claire had lived in a constant state of not being able to believe that someone like Robbie could possibly want to marry someone like her. It wasn't so much a lack of self-esteem that made her question her luck so much as a cool appraisal of the facts: he was, by anyone's standards, intelligent and good-looking whereas she, by anyone's standards, was of average appearance, average intelligence and average talents. She had even told him so, as if to prod him out of some fantasy world in which he deemed her to be far more interesting than she actually was and into the real world where, in fact, she was fairly ordinary, but all he had said was: 'There's nothing ordinary about you, Claire. There's never anything ordinary about a woman with integrity, a woman who knows the meaning of the words loyalty and fidelity, a woman who actually enjoys putting others first.'

It had almost seemed too much to demand passion on top of the friendship and security on offer, but in watching him rinse the soap from his hair, his face, his skin, she could remember a time, not so long ago, when they had showered together, when passion, like water, appeared to be on tap.

Now, that passion, that intimacy, seemed but a distant memory. They would never have that again, thought Claire. All trust in him was gone. And in its place only fear, and the suspicion that she had never really known him.

The gun had been propped up next to the taps, the stock resting on the slippery surface of the bath, the barrel pointing towards the ceiling. If it fell – if it went off—

She knew the damage a shotgun could do. Shortly after Robbie had started his firearms training, he had brought home photographs that were circulating among the men. They had been taken at the scene of various incidents, some in the UK, but most in the US, and they depicted people who had been shot with a variety of weapons.

Of all the injuries shown in those photographs, none had been worse than those inflicted at close range by a sawn-off shotgun. She hadn't known it was possible to shoot the face off a man, and she didn't want Ocky to see his father illustrate how it was done.

He turned the shower off and reached for the gun, stepped out of the bath with it and grabbed his sodden clothes. He struggled into them, then gave what seemed like an order, the acoustics of the bathroom making his words seem more a threat than a request: 'Open the door.'

She now allowed Ocky to climb up on to her hip as she drew back the bolt. It was flimsy, the kind of bolt a child could have dislodged without difficulty. But as she opened the door, he held her back. 'I'll go first,' he said. 'Just in case . . .'

Just in case of what? thought Claire. There was nobody there. Nobody in the road, the garden, the house. What was he expecting to find on the landing? Some masked gunman?

She opened the door and McLaughlan stepped out on the landing. And then she saw the gun hauled out of his hand, saw him slammed face down on the hard wooden boards. She heard a voice she recognised as belonging to Doheny, 'Take it easy, McLaughlan,' and over and above his voice, the sound of people running up the stairs.

She stood in the doorway, Ocky on her hip, and now the tears she'd managed, so far, to hold streamed down her face. He didn't say a word. He lay with his stomach pressed to the hard wooden boards, and he just *looked* at her.

She shook her head. 'I'm sorry . . .' and suddenly she was surrounded by people, some of them women, all of them armed. This is what it's like, she thought. This is what it's like to be the wife of a villain, to try to fend for your children, and all around you, men in balaclavas are bursting into the house. And it doesn't matter who they are to the child you've got on your hip – all he knows is that Mummy is crying, the men have guns and they all wear masks. No use telling a child of four that the men are police, that they're on your side, that nobody's trying to kill you.

Ocky was rigid in her arms. So far, he had clung to her, but he hadn't even whimpered. Now he started to scream and the sound of his screaming was more than McLaughlan could stand. He reared up, taking Doheny with him, and it wasn't until that moment that Claire fully realised how powerful he was. He shook off the men who were holding him in a way that seemed almost effortless, and used his shoulders to knock another man down. He was brought down again by several of Orme's men. They pulled him down and kept him pinned him to the floor.

It was Orme who got them off him. Claire hadn't known he was there. She heard his voice and it drew her eyes to the doorway of Ocky's bedroom. He stood there, and in his hand, he held the sawn-off shotgun. 'Let him get up,' he said, and after his men had led McLaughlan downstairs, he tried to put his arm around Claire. She cringed away from the gun and he said, 'It's unloaded,' but that didn't make any difference. She hated the sight of it, hated being anywhere near it, and Orme handed it to one of his men who took it out of her sight. 'Was that the only weapon?'

'I think so,' she sobbed. 'I don't know—'

'We'll search the house,' said Orme.

He left her in the hands of a female officer who asked whether there was somewhere they could take her – to her mother's, perhaps, or a friend?

Claire wasn't sure where she wanted to go. She only knew she couldn't stay in the house. Since Robbie had returned from wherever he got the gun, it had been a prison. No light, no music, no laughter. Just terror. The house would have to be sold. She could never live here. Not now.

'Let's get you and Ocky into dry clothes,' said the female officer. 'Then you can decide where you'd like us to—'

'What about Robbie?'

Orme spoke to her from the bottom of the stairs. 'Don't worry about him,' he said. 'He's our problem now.'

Chapter Twenty

Orme was aware that McLaughlan was exhibiting all the classic symptoms of post-traumatic stress disorder. That explained his behaviour, but it didn't explain how he'd managed to get his hands on a sawn-off shotgun.

He sat with him in the back of an unmarked car, and he told him he was taking him back to the station where he would have to face some questions. His every answer would go some way towards determining his future with the force. Orme therefore had some advice for McLaughlan: 'Be straight with me, and maybe I can help you. Screw me around, and I'll be the first to see you treated like any other villain.'

McLaughlan had seemed dumbstruck by the raid. Maybe, thought Orme, he saw it as a betrayal. He couldn't even begin to imagine what had been going on inside his head. He didn't even ask – the way that McLaughlan was staring out at the suburbs as they headed into town told him he was unlikely to get an answer that made any sense.

Once they were back at the station, Orme put him into the room he regarded as his office. This was unofficial, he told him. He wasn't taking notes, or making judgements: right now, he just wanted to talk to him and find out what was going on. He left Doheny in there with him, then spoke briefly on the phone to a psychologist.

Levinson, the psychologist Orme spoke to, was someone who had long experience of working with men involved in firearms incidents. He was willing to see McLaughlan straight away, but to Orme's surprise, McLaughlan refused to have him involved. Orme, who had already contacted him, was therefore left with the task of telling him he wouldn't be needed.

Not unreasonably, Levinson saw it as a bad sign on the whole. Understandable, thought Orme. Nobody likes to be told their services won't be required, that somebody doesn't appear to have much respect for what you do. He remembered Doheny once telling him that a psychologist had evaluated him along with his team following a particularly traumatic ordeal. Most of the men had come out of it with a score indicating that their emotional stress levels were much on a par with those of a group of toddlers arguing in a sandpit. The psychologist, however, who had tested himself out of interest, had come out with a score that leaped off the scale. Orme smiled at the recollection. But the smile died on his lips when he recollected the state Claire had been in by the time he and his men broke into the house.

In remembering what she'd looked like as she stood at the door to the bathroom, he couldn't help wondering whether he was about to question a man who was yet to learn that his marriage was history.

McLaughlan and Doheny stood up as Orme walked into the office.

Orme gestured for them to sit down, pulled up a chair, and came straight to the point. 'Where did you get the gun, McLaughlan?'

Where did you get the gun? It's a question you've anticipated ever since they got you to the station. The only way you can deal with this is to tell them you can't remember. And maybe, whether you want them to or not, they'll consult a psychologist and ask him whether that's possible. Can a man do something without being aware that he's done it? Could he have got his hands on a weapon without remembering where he got it, or even that he had it?

The answer the psychologist gives will very much depend on how big a dick he is. If he's the kind of guy who sincerely hopes that his patient will share their emotions with the person standing directly to their left, he'll say it's perfectly possible, that one should always give a man the benefit of the doubt. If, on the other hand, he's one of those hard-arsed bastards who won't die happy unless they've done what they can to see every petty villain this side of the river banged up in a high-security unit for the criminally insane, he'll say no.

And he'll be right. Because it's crap. All of it. 'Tell me what happened in your childhood and I will help you to heal yourself.' But nothing short of somebody bringing your brother back to life is ever going to help you, and you're in enough shit without having to watch your Ps and Qs in front of some crank who's got more problems than Freud.

Where did you get the gun, McLaughlan? And you think it's significant that he's calling you by your surname. Normally Orme would call you Robbie. Not today. Because today he had to gather together a team, break into your house and save your wife and son from you, as if anyone who knew you could imagine for a moment that you'd do them any harm.

You were trying to save them. You tell him this, and he looks at you as if you've lost your mind.

Who from?

Swift.

You've seen Swift watching your house?

No, but I've seen his people.

What did they look like?

All different. Never the same man twice.

You seem very sure that these people were watching you, and that Swift is employing them.

Call it a gift.

What if you're wrong? What if there's nobody there?

They were there.

Even as you say it, you sense Doheny tensing up beside you. He thinks you've lost it, and you can't blame him for that. He feels partly responsible. Correction. He feels very responsible, because he was instrumental in persuading you to apply for firearms training in the first place. Your lack of interest had intrigued him. Every man in Flying Squad had applied for firearms training, but not you. You didn't apply, and Doheny couldn't leave it alone. He had to know why.

He asked you what the problem was, and you told him there wasn't a problem – that guns just didn't interest you, that's all.

That's good, said Doheny, and you asked him why it was good. He told you it was hard enough dealing with the psychos on the outside, that the force didn't need any psychos on the inside, and he invited you, personally, to apply.

You still turned him down. He couldn't believe it. It made him all the more determined to have your firearms potential *evaluated. He said you were the kind of man the force was looking for.*

You told him again that you had no interest in guns, but you didn't tell him why. You didn't tell him you were all gunned out – that even as a kid you had handled them, cleaned them, loaded them. You found them in drawers that you'd rummaged through in search of coloured pencils, you pulled them out of cupboards when you looked for clothes or toys, you pushed them off the couch when you wanted to watch Blue Peter. *So guns were of no more interest to you than the knife and fork you ate with. But Doheny wouldn't let it go, and before you knew where you were, you found yourself at Lippett's Hill for training.*

There hadn't been a lot they could teach you about firing a gun. You had the knack, the gift, and you were the envy . . . So you moved on to the next stage and to training designed to prepare you for any and every situation the force could imagine you ever having to deal with.

They trained you well. But no amount of training could have prepared you for the way you're feeling now, or what you have to do when you get out of here.

Chapter Twenty-one

This was Jarvis's least favourite time of day. The sun had moved from the front to the back of the flats, and his living room had been plunged into its usual mid-afternoon depression.

Jarvis's mood followed suit accordingly, and it wasn't lightened any by the view of housing opposite. It was, to say the least, uninspiring – a collection of buildings converted into bedsits, small offices and a dance studio. It was, however, nowhere near as uninspiring as the view George McLaughlan had had on the night he was arrested.

The cells at the station Whalley had taken him to had been built to hold men who had little or no intention of staying where they were put. They were smaller than the average cell and, God knows, thought Jarvis, the average cell in the average British nick was small enough. They were eight feet long by three feet wide. Barely big enough for the bunk that served as a bed.

Jarvis had looked in on George that night and had thought the conditions inhuman, a violation of some international law. Yet it had occurred to him that George might not have noticed. The room where, in childhood, he had shared a bed with his brother had been much the same size, and there, too, the bed had been little more than a bunk. At least he currently had the bed to himself.

Whalley had asked whether Jarvis wanted to question him that night, and to Whalley's surprise, Jarvis had refused, saying, 'I'd rather have a go at him in London.'

Whalley had given Jarvis the kind of look that suggested he knew what was going on: the following day, George was to be taken from Glasgow to London for questioning. Whalley had assumed that Jarvis wanted to wait until there was no one around from Strathclyde to watch as George was beaten into making a confession to the Ladbrokes robbery. 'There's nothing you can do in London that y' cannae do here,' he said, but Jarvis still expressed a preference to wait until he had him on his own territory.

Whalley hadn't pressed him on it. He had assumed that he must have his reasons. And Whalley had been right about that, thought Jarvis, though he'd have been surprised to know what those reasons really were. With Hunter suspended, Jarvis had found himself reporting to a DCI who was a completely unknown quantity to him. He therefore had no idea how his new superior officer was likely to react when he told him he didn't want to be the one to question George.

Not unreasonably, it struck his superior as odd that Jarvis had spent a year hunting George down, had gone to great lengths to capture him, and now appeared reluctant to question him. 'You'd better have a good reason,' he was told, and Jarvis, who felt he had an excellent reason, had a ready answer.

'It's now been established that my former superior officer was tipping George off. If I go in there and question him, and we prosecute, and we don't get a conviction, there's always the chance that someone will point a finger in my direction.'

It sounded as good a reason as any that Jarvis had ever heard, but it wasn't the truth, or anything like the truth.

The plain fact of it was, he felt inadequate. George had laughed at him, and Jarvis was having a problem putting that behind him. You weren't going to crack a villain like George if he had no respect for you. It was hard enough when you'd put the fear of God into them.

Hunter always preferred his villains to be terrified of him, and he wasn't averse to walking into a cell, closing the door behind him and beating them senseless to get the message across that he wasn't about to stand for them wasting his time. Not that he'd have managed it with George but, then, Hunter wouldn't have tried it on with George. Clearly, not only was Hunter aware that George would have killed him, but Hunter liked him, and had struck up some kind of friendship with him. If not friendship, then they certainly had an arrangement and a mutual respect. One thing Jarvis knew for sure was that George had no respect whatsoever for him. He had raised his arms to defend himself, and he'd laughed in his face. How could you question a villain when he couldn't even be arsed to hit you back?

The DCI accepted his reasons for not wanting to be involved any further with this particular case. Another senior detective had therefore been given the job of questioning George. But Jarvis was in court when George stood trial.

Elsa was also in court, immaculate in a linen suit, and a far cry from what she'd looked like the last time he'd seen her. They'd had no contact since George's arrest, and although Jarvis told himself he was well rid of her, he found it painful to be in such close proximity to her, particularly in circumstances such as these. Whether or not she laid the blame for George's capture firmly at his door, he didn't know. Whatever the case, she refused to look at him.

Mostly, she kept her eyes on George, or on the judge, as if she could charm the latter into letting George off lightly, but George hadn't exactly helped himself: he had pleaded not guilty, despite having been positively identified as one of the robbers, and there was no escaping the fact that Crackerjack hadn't been seen by a soul since the day of the robbery.

At one point, Crown Prosecution came right out with it and invited George to admit that owing to his reluctance to get his friend and associate the medical help he needed he had died of gunshot wounds sustained during the robbery. George's only response was to say they could either produce a body or go fuck themselves, so all in all it was going to take more than a few appealing glances from Elsa to persuade the judge to be lenient for her sake.

Even so, the sentence passed on George came as a shock. In that same court a mere five years earlier, robbers more famous than George had received sentences of up to thirty years for the part they played in the Great Train Robbery. A different judge now meted out the sentence of fifteen years. Its severity caused a gasp to pass round the court.

Before Jarvis knew it, the gallery had erupted. Not even he could believe the length of the sentence. He could only imagine that the judge, who had taken a fairly dim view of George's attitude, had made him an example.

Elsa almost collapsed with shock, but George merely stole a look at Iris. She returned his look with a steadfast stare, and neither so much as flinched when the judge said, 'Take him down.'

The noise in the court was phenomenal now, the judge demanding order, and even a press reporter remonstrating that the sentence was excessive.

George might appeal, thought Jarvis, but he wouldn't get very far. The sentence was a sign of the times, a portent of things to come. Serious crime was soaring, and with flogging and hanging gone, the chattering classes were murmuring that the average prison sentence was far from adequate. 'No wonder the streets aren't safe. Society has to be protected from the kind of villain who arms himself with a shotgun.'

Jarvis kept his eyes fixed on George, willing him to turn round, willing him to look shattered by the sentence. He turned, but he didn't look shattered. He met Jarvis's eye, and held his gaze. He carried on holding his gaze even as the men on either side of him led him out of the dock and towards the steps leading down to the cells.

Jarvis sat at the entrance to the steps, a rosewood barrier dividing him from George. He leaned forward, all the better to watch as George began his long descent, and suddenly, George grabbed his arm, held it for a moment.

Instantly, the warders yanked him away, but not before George said something that Jarvis would never forget.

'Keep her warm for me, Mike.'

Jarvis hadn't been able to get over the shock of that comment. For the life of him, he couldn't understand how George had found out, or what he was likely to do about it. All he knew for certain was that George could only have been told after he was arrested, not before, or he'd have done something about it. Maybe someone told him while he was on remand. If so, they clearly hadn't told him it was over. Not that it was likely to make much difference, thought Jarvis. The mere fact that he had ever so much as looked at George's wife would seal his fate. And the fact that George was starting a fifteen-year sentence was of little comfort: it merely meant that George now had fifteen years in which to think up a particularly insidious way of exacting revenge.

In lighter moments, it therefore occurred to Jarvis that anything he wanted to do with his life, he'd better do at some point within the next fifteen years, because once George was released, he would probably leave him in no fit state to do anything more strenuous than blink once for yes and twice for no.

That said, it wasn't funny. Somebody somewhere was on to him. If George knew, then maybe it wouldn't be long before his superior officers also got to know. What then? He could try denying that he and Elsa were ever involved, but he doubted it would do much good. Jarvis was experienced enough to know there was every chance that some bright spark might pull out a photo taken by coppers keeping surveillance on the house, and then they'd list the number of times he'd gone there over the months. They would tell him how long he stayed, what he and Elsa ate, maybe even what stories he read to Robbie before tucking him up for the night. For all Jarvis knew, they might even tell him how often, and for how long, he and Elsa made love in George's bed.

It didn't bear thinking about. And yet he couldn't afford to push it out of his mind: if it came to it, and he got hauled up before a superior officer, he would admit it, but he would tell them it was over and hope for the best.

With luck, thought Jarvis, the next he would see or hear of George would be after his release. In fact, he confidently expected that to be the case, but he hadn't bargained on a visit from Crackerjack's widow.

He had last seen her over a year ago, shortly after the robbery, when he had interviewed her in the hope of finding out if she knew where Crackerjack happened to be. At that time, she had denied that her husband and George were even acquainted, so when Jarvis was told that a Mrs Crowther had turned up at the station demanding to speak to him, his gut feel told him this was going to be interesting.

She wasn't a good-looking woman. Her skin was poor, and nothing, in Jarvis's opinion, looked worse on a woman than skin that was reddened by constant exposure to the kind of wind that could only blow in from a river as vast, as cruel, and as bitterly bloody cold as the Clyde. In addition, she was, in a phrase that Jarvis rarely used at the time, dog-rough.

She had come down from Glasgow by train, carrying her youngest child, a toddler, in her arms, to tell him she was in London because she wasn't getting any joy out of Strathclyde. 'Ah keep telling them I haven't heard from Les since he pissed off tae London tae meet wi' George McLaughlan. Nobody's heard a word from him in a year!'

She's changed her story, thought Jarvis, but before he could ask her why, she added, 'Frankly, Mr Jarvis, ah think he's dead.'

Her youngster, a wean of eighteen months, started to wail. She pulled him up to her lap, and stuck a dummy-shaped toffee in his mouth to shut him up as she said, 'But do you think those *bastards* at Strathclyde will open an investigation intae his disappearance? Will they fuck.'

Jarvis could well understand why Strathclyde Police were reluctant to open an investigation: unless George talked, the likelihood of getting to the bottom of what had happened to Crackerjack was remote.

Suspecting that perhaps she was anxious to remarry, Jarvis said, 'Why is it so important to you to prove the death of your husband?'

Her need had arisen from practical, rather than emotional considerations. 'I've kids tae feed, Mr Jarvis. An' it's a question of insurance.'

Jarvis now understood, but he still didn't see why she'd come to him. 'If you're asking me to put pressure on Strathclyde to look for him, I'm afraid I just don't have that kind of clout.'

'Ah, *fuck* Strathclyde,' she said. 'Ah'm all oot with they yon bastards. Ah want you tae ask George where ye can find the body.'

'What makes you think he'd tell me?'

She had pointed out that it was common courtesy among villains not only to keep their associates' nearest and dearest informed with regard to the true state of play but to ensure that the wives, girlfriends and children of villains were seen right for money wherever possible. George, who hadn't made any attempt to keep his own family fed, was hardly likely to start looking out for her, but if he were at least to divulge that Crackerjack was dead and tell the police where to find his body that would help no end.

It sounded so reasonable that Jarvis found himself agreeing to give it a go. More than that he couldn't promise, although he did concede that, with the court case out of the way, George had nothing to lose by telling the truth.

Satisfied that Jarvis was at least willing to try to do something, she left, and it was only after she'd gone that Jarvis began to regret what he had promised. That 'Keep her warm for me, Mike' still kept him awake at night, and the more he thought about it, the less he wanted to clap eyes on George McLaughlan. The time would come when he would be released, and when it came, Jarvis had every intention of finding him first. Initially he would try to reason with him. If that didn't work, he'd fight him like a man. What he wouldn't do was take out a restraining order. His pride wouldn't let him do that. He was a man. He was a copper. He was also, in all probability, going to be a dead man, and a dead copper, but he wasn't about to go to his grave a coward. He would also tell George the truth – that Elsa had meant something to him, that he'd loved her, that loving her had been the biggest mistake of his life, not because he was about to die on account of it but because she'd betrayed him, and Jarvis doubted he'd ever manage to trust another woman.

He could imagine George's response to that, and he caught a fleeting glimpse of himself in a back-street down by the docks. He would be wearing the stupefied look of the recently brutally murdered, and George would be poking his bloated remains with the toe of a steel-capped boot. *You'll no go fuckin' my wife in future, Mr Jarvis.*

A promise, however, was a promise, and to back out now would be just as much an act of cowardice as the taking out of a restraining order. Consequently, Jarvis resigned himself to the fact that he would shortly find himself in a confined space with a man who very much wanted him dead.

George was serving his sentence at Barlinnie – bleak, depressing, and long regarded as one of the hardest prisons in the country. Jarvis went there within a week of the visit from Crackerjack's wife.

He knew from experience that before they came to accept a lengthy sentence a lot of men went through a kind of grieving process. It was similar to the process people went through when told they were terminally ill. First came denial. Then anger. Then depression. Finally acceptance, though people differed greatly: not everyone went gently into that good night, and not everyone went gently into a long-term prison sentence. Some never came out of denial. Some grew increasingly violent. Some went mad and never truly recovered.

George had skipped the denial, had thought anger too feeble an emotion under the circumstances, so had opted for constant methodical violent rage. The resulting riot had earned him a series of beatings, but it had also earned him a transfer to Barlinnie's Special Unit, and Jarvis wondered how he would fare under such a regime.

The meeting took place in a room strewn with tables and chairs. It stank of disinfectant, and the noise of the prison, though distant, was a constant irritation.

Jarvis hadn't known what to expect in view of 'Keep her warm for me, Mike', but in the event, George made no allusion to it, or to Elsa.

Jarvis hadn't been able to understand it. It was possible, he supposed, that George had already spent long enough in solitary confinement to allow himself to succumb to the desire to try to kill him in front of four prison warders. On the other hand, maybe he was playing with him, trying to lead him to believe that he'd convinced himself his information was incorrect in the hope of catching him unawares when he came out.

Whatever the case, Jarvis hadn't been about to bring it up, and he kept the conversation centred on his reason for being there.

It had been a very one-sided conversation in that Jarvis did most of the talking, but after explaining why Crackerjack's wife had approached him, Jarvis added, 'Do her a favour, George – it's not going to make any difference to your sentence either way, but finding the body will help her feed the kids.'

He had brought a packet of Senior Service with him. He pushed it across the table to George, who opened the packet and took one. It was probably the first decent cigarette he'd had since he'd been arrested, and George smoked it slowly. The smell of it took Jarvis back to the tenements, and to the way in which Iris had held a cigarette to Jimmy's lips.

'Get me some paper,' said George.

Jarvis asked one of the warders to provide them with paper and a pen. The paper had been forthcoming, but a pen had been considered a potential weapon, and George had had to make do with a crayon.

He used it to draw a map of an area flanked by the river Clyde, and described it as being a one-hour bus ride from Glasgow's Central Station. 'I'm doin' this fer Crackerjack's missus, an' that's the only reason I'm doin' it – yer understand?'

Jarvis made it clear that he understood that this wasn't to be considered a victory on the part of the authorities, that George was giving the information out of the goodness of his heart for the benefit of a widow and her children.

That settled, George had drawn a map, and had pushed it across the table to Jarvis, who picked it up and studied it. As he did so, it occurred to him that anyone else would have asked George why he took Crackerjack's body back to Galsgow instead of dumping it locally. Jarvis didn't bother, not only because George would have refused to tell him but because he was pretty certain he could piece the picture together for himself. After Crackerjack had been shot, George got him away from the scene and took him to a place of relative safety. But as it became obvious that Crackerjack was dying, George had been faced with a terrible decision: if he took him to hospital, they'd both get nicked and sent down. If he didn't, Crackerjack would die.

Clearly, George had taken the latter option. Little wonder he didn't want to talk about the whys and wherefores. He had to be living with the fact that Crackerjack might be alive if he'd so much as dumped him on the steps of some local infirmary. All Jarvis said was, 'He was obviously very badly injured. Maybe he wouldn't have made it, no matter what you did.'

He hadn't expected George to make any reply to this, but George, as always, surprised him: 'I tried tae get him tae let me take him tae a hospital. He couldnae face surviving only to end up somewhere like this. Said he'd rather take his fuckin' chances.'

His chances had landed him up on industrial waste-ground some miles from the centre of Glasgow, and in realising how long the remains had been there, Jarvis couldn't help thinking it wasn't going to be a pleasant job to retrieve them.

Chapter Twenty-two

Orme had long been of the opinion that anyone caught with a gun, knife or other lethal weapon should be held indefinitely until such time as a judge or psychiatrist deemed it safe to release them.

In reality, even though he'd put together a team to break into McLaughlan's home, divest him of the gun and bring him in for questioning, Orme couldn't hold him. He would have to release him, if not today, then tomorrow. In the meantime, he would have to decide whether to charge him or give him sick leave.

Despite McLaughlan's insistence that he couldn't remember where he'd got the gun, Orme decided on the latter. The first two options would result in him being thrown out of the force, and Orme wanted, at this stage, to give him the benefit of the doubt. He knew him to be a good officer. This was the first sign of any instability, and let's face it, thought Orme, men had broken down as a result of less traumatic scenarios than the one McLaughlan had gone through only a matter of days ago. What's more, McLaughlan had clearly procured the gun with the intention of protecting his wife and child. At no time had he shown any sign of wanting to hurt them, or himself. He was ill, though he might be denying it right now, and Orme badly wanted to give him some kind of chance.

He told McLaughlan he wasn't the first to have had a bad reaction to having shot someone and he pointed out that he might be in the early stages of a breakdown. He also told him that, as he hadn't been charged, there was nothing he could do to stop him walking out of there any time he liked. Orme, however, was advising him not to go home without first allowing himself to be evaluated by the psychologist. If nothing else, it would look good at the inevitable inquiry – and an inquiry *was* inevitable. Meanwhile, Orme would try to play down what had happened earlier in the day. Filing an accurate report was going to be unavoidable, but the way he described how events had unfolded after Doheny spoke to Claire could make the difference between McLaughlan being kept in the force or thrown out.

He had so far managed to convince everyone who asked that there might have been some misunderstanding with regard to McLaughlan's current emotional state, that perhaps things had sounded worse than they actually were, and that, as a result, Orme had taken the precaution of entering his home without permission, just to ensure that his wife and child were okay, which they were. Ambiguity, thought Orme, long regarded as one of the most powerful tools in a politician's armoury, would serve him well.

Doheny had taken McLaughlan home after telling Orme that he intended to try to get him to meet him later for a drink. Did Orme have any objections?

Orme had had no objection, and after Doheny had gone, he read through further information faxed by Serious

Crimes: Orme had felt it might be useful to know more about Stuart Swift's background, and therefore about his possible state of mind on the day of the robbery. Serious Crimes had therefore provided a report compiled by a welfare officer on the order of the magistrate that Stuart had appeared before as a juvenile.

Orme didn't know how useful it would ultimately prove, but it certainly made interesting reading: Stuart's childhood had been financially and emotionally impoverished. Calvin had been in prison for much of it, and Stuart had lived with his mother in a flat in Soho.

She had been an actress of sorts, who had appeared in a few television commercials but no more than that. Her name had been Barbara Sheldon, and she'd married Calvin when in her early twenties.

The marriage hadn't been happy, and Barbara had disappeared a short while after filing for divorce. The police had their suspicions, but no hard evidence. The file remained open. Within months of Barbara's disappearance, Calvin had found himself on the receiving end of a ten-year sentence for armed robbery. Ray had been left to care for Stuart until his father was released from jail.

It was clearly an unhappy arrangement, with Stuart running away from Ray, and Ray sending out his henchmen to find him and bring him back, and for the first time since the shooting, Orme thought of Stuart as something more than a robber who'd got his due. Small wonder he'd ended up an addict, thought Orme. One way or another, it was a miracle he'd lived as long as he had.

One thing was for sure, thought Orme. Barbara Sheldon, wherever she was, probably wasn't alive.

*   *   *

You walk in to a message on the answering-machine. She's taken Ocky and she's gone to stay with her mother – a complete fucking cliché. You're disappointed, as if she's let you down, as if you'd have preferred it if she'd run to some guy you didn't know was hanging around in the background.

She wants you to know she hasn't left you – it's just that, right now, she can't cope: she needs a slice of sanity, someone to lean on. But you pick up the phone and you dial her mother's number.

And then you replace the receiver and leave her alone. She wanted space. She's got it. Besides, you're just relieved. You know something that neither she, nor Orme, nor Doheny know: the minute you left the station, you were followed. They tailed Doheny's car. They followed you home. They're out there now, and they're watching the house, and unless you shake them off, they'll follow when you meet Doheny later.

Chapter Twenty-three

The river Clyde rose as a mountain stream in the Lowther hills. Much of it flowed through some of the most magnificent countryside Scotland had to offer, but there was nothing magnificent about the industrial wasteground that Jarvis was looking at now.

The land itself was a patchwork of foundations, some of it marking the shape of warehousing facilities built at the turn of the century. At some point in the past five years, Glasgow's planning authority had pulled the warehouses down with the intention of building houses. Maybe those houses would one day be built – Jarvis didn't know. Right now the land stretched out as far as the eye could see, flanking a wide black river, the tide currently low and revealing glutinous mud-flats that looked nothing less than lethal to Jarvis's eye.

He tried to gauge the expanse of land, but failed. It stretched out into the distance, sliced lengthways by a canal that ran parallel to a railway track. The track had been pulled up, or was so overgrown that there was nothing left of it now, just the embankment it ran along and ditches to either side.

The air that came off the river draped itself on his face like an ice-cold cloth. He'd never known anything like it. All around him, dog handlers from Strathclyde huddled deep into overcoats with collars pulled well up around their ears whilst their dogs searched the land that related to the map George had drawn.

Some of the dogs made for the river. Others ran down embankments, skipped along the tow-path of the rubbish-strewn canal or darted under a hump-backed bridge that seemed to Jarvis devoid of all semblance of charm.

One dog in particular caught his attention: he was different from the others, who were all, without exception, German shepherds. This animal was taller, standing a good thirty inches at the shoulder. Most of his height came from legs that were long, his paws as massive as those of an Irish wolfhound. His face was longer, thinner, and his head was very broad. But overall it was his colouring that marked him out as different: the other dogs were black and tan, their short-haired coats gleaming with good grooming. This dog was grey, and his coat was long.

He stood there, lifting his face to the wind, considering his environment and plotting his MO. Then he set off down the railway track that led towards the river. He didn't return for some time, but his handler wasn't unduly concerned.

'He seems a good dog,' said Jarvis.

'He's the best dog in Glasgow. The best,' the handler replied. 'But you wouldn't want tae go pattin' him or anything stupid like that – he'd have your hand off.'

His words sent a shudder through Jarvis. They reminded him of what had happened to Jimmy.

After fifteen minutes the dog returned carrying something. A flexible thing, a breakable thing, it trailed along the ground because it was far too large for the dog to manage it properly. He dropped it at his handler's feet. The man turned to Jarvis. 'Did I not tell you he was a good dog?'

Jarvis, who found himself staring down at a spine stripped of flesh, put his hand out to pat the dog, but remembered what he'd been told and retracted his trembling fingers.

The eyes of the dog were narrow and cold, the purest ice-blue that Jarvis had ever seen. He had no idea what its pedigree was, but he suspected that somewhere down the line someone had mated one of his ancestors with a wolf. What he was looking at now was the result of that mating, several generations on. Tall, rangy and thin, the dog stood over the spine, and dripped saliva on to it as if finding the instinct to eat it almost overpowering.

'Ach,' said the handler, 'you're a good lad, a real good lad. Well done!'

Most dogs, thought Jarvis, would have been ecstatic to have received such praise, but this dog regarded his handler with the kind of cool detachment that Jarvis had come to associate with George. He didn't have to ask in order to know that his handler didn't trust him an inch. I'll bet he never turns his back on it, thought Jarvis. Not for one moment.

It was a strange party that followed the dog back along the track. The other handlers put their dogs on leashes, but this particular dog was left to go on ahead. He paused at intervals to let them all catch up, and at one point, Jarvis said, 'Doesn't it worry you, having a dog like that?'

'I've known him from a pup,' said the handler. 'I know what I'm doing.'

I hope so, for your sake, thought Jarvis.

They walked on, the dog leading them under the bridge and along the embankment. Half a mile on, he suddenly crashed down into one of the ditches, with his handler and Jarvis in pursuit.

Prior to that moment, Jarvis had had no idea that a dog could open its jaws so wide in order to get a purchase on a large and awkward object, for the skull was undoubtedly large and awkward. 'Good lad,' said the handler, nervously. 'Drop it now. Good boy.'

The dog had no intention of relinquishing the skull. He narrowed his ice-blue eyes in threat, and the hair on his neck rose to form a ruff.

'Ach, he'll let it go in a moment. Jis' give him a moment,' said his handler, and, in looking around him, Jarvis found no one willing to argue the toss. If the dog wanted to play with the skull, then that was just fine with them.

Other bones lay scattered around in the grass, the arms, the legs and the ribs – all of them pulled from the clothing worn by the deceased.

'Is this your man?' said the handler, and Jarvis, who knew what Crackerjack had been wearing the day of the Ladbrokes job, took a look at the jacket that was lying close to the dog.

He gave a nod, and the handler said, 'Why do you think George dumped him here rather than in the river?'

Jarvis knew the answer, but kept it to himself: the Clyde, like any river, was predatorial, but whatever it took by way of human life, it generally delivered to the doorstep of the city. If George had dumped Crackerjack in the Clyde, his body would have come to light in a mere matter of hours. The fact that it was punched through with bullets from a Thompson sub-machine-gun would have given the police solid proof that he had been shot by the trigger-happy bookie, and this, plus the bookie's statement naming George as the other robber, would have been enough to persuade the Crown Prosecution Service that there was a good chance of getting a conviction against him.

As it turned out, George's precautions had all been in vain: he wasn't to know that he had been identified as one of the robbers and, ultimately, the fact that Crackerjack had vanished from the face of the earth only served to convince the jury he was dead.

The judge had clearly been angered by George's refusal to reveal where his body was, and Jarvis suspected the judge of holding the view that, with medical help, there was always the possibility that Crackerjack might have lived. If so, it would explain why he had given George such a heavy sentence.

Echoing what Jarvis believed to be the judge's private opinion, the dog handler said, 'Maybe, if he hadn't abandoned him, he'd be alive today.'

'I doubt it,' said Jarvis. 'He has to have been dead before George would dump him anywhere.'

'How can you be so sure?' said the handler.

Jarvis's jealousy of George ran very deep, but it didn't stop him from facing the fact that he wasn't a man without honour. He and Crackerjack had grown up together, had played together as kids, had fought with the same gangs, had done time together. The bonds that were forged between people who had shared the kind of childhood they had shared were developed to a very high degree, and whatever else George might have done he wouldn't have abandoned Crackerjack to die. 'They were friends,' was all he said.

Chapter Twenty-four

Bloomfield's study looked out over playing-fields, acres of green that stretched from the back of the quad to the Berkshire gallops.

The school was currently quiet, these being those rather difficult hours that occurred between prep and supper, when the boys who boarded were left to their own devices and trusted to amuse themselves by reading, painting or whatnot.

Bloomfield, a senior master, held views that differed vastly from those of the somewhat progressive head, and he knew from experience that you never left boys to their own devices, whatever the circumstances, that if you did so, the boys in question would disperse to private parts of the building to abuse, if not themselves, then certainly one another.

Those who could find it within themselves to refrain from entertaining themselves thus could usually be counted upon to amuse themselves by inflicting petty cruelties on younger boys, so when Bloomfield saw Figgis and Devereaux crossing the playing-fields with a younger boy in tow, he was suspicious.

The boy in question was a first-year. Watkins, or Simpkins, or some such. Simpkins, thought Bloomfield. He was almost certain now. The boy was called Simpkins.

Whatever his name, he was being marched towards trees that marked a boundary to the school, and it was his obvious reluctance that alerted Bloomfield to the possibility that he was going against his will. Figgis had him by the arm at one point, but then let him go, only to pluck him along in his wake, or prod him on ahead.

Devereaux, meanwhile, was looking over his shoulder, anxious lest one of the masters should be approaching them from the rear.

He needn't have worried, thought Bloomfield. The only rear he could imagine any of his fellow masters to be approaching belonged to an attractive and utterly inappropriate assistant matron. It happened to be her afternoon off, and three-quarters of the teaching staff were currently engaged in a war of attrition as a result of her inability to decide whom to sleep with next.

He therefore left the oak-panelled study that was his reward for forty years' service, and walked from the back of the quad to the playing-field.

The trio had disappeared by the time he reached the field, but he had every intention of creeping up on them, and he fully expected to catch Figgis and Devereaux in the act of whatever they happened to be doing to Simpkins. However, before he could proceed any further, Simpkins ran from the trees.

Figgis and Devereaux followed, but not at a run. They weren't chasing him, Bloomfield observed. They were merely watching him go.

Simpkins ran straight past him, and Bloomfield called

his name, but Simpkins ignored him, and Bloomfield turned to watch as he ran to the quad.

He disappeared through an archway that linked the quad to the fields, at which point Bloomfield turned his attention back to the older boys.

Figgis had been so amused by the sight of Simpkins's panic-stricken departure that he hadn't noticed Bloomfield bearing down on them. It took a dig in the ribs from Devereaux to warn him that this could mean trouble, and Figgis duly wiped the smirk from his face.

When still several yards from the boys, Bloomfield called out to them: 'What were you doing to Simpkins?'

Figgis, who was in the habit of affecting congenital stupidity, immediately adopted the attitude of one who has been deeply and unfairly wounded to the quick. 'Me, sir? Nothing, sir.'

'Then why was he running away?'

'Don't know, sir.'

'You took him into the trees.'

'I didn't—'

'I saw you, Figgis. Don't argue.'

'I wasn't arguing, sir.'

'And don't contradict me.'

'I wasn't—'

'You, Devereaux, what were you doing in the trees – and what in God's name have you got in your eyes?'

Devereaux, of French and North African extraction, had skin the colour of Bloomfield's walking boots. His dark brown eyes, however, were currently a luminescent green, Devereaux having got his hands on a pair of theatrical contact lenses. 'Me, sir? Nothing, sir. They've always been this colour.'

227

'You look bloody ridiculous. What do you look?'

'Bloody ridiculous, sir.'

'Where did you get them?'

'I borrowed them, sir.'

'Who from?'

'Don't remember, sir.'

'Take them out this instant.'

'Can't, sir. They're stuck to my eyes.'

'My study, five a.m. tomorrow – both of you – and bring cross-country kit.'

They groaned, yet still stood there, as if waiting for further punishment, and suddenly Bloomfield felt completely drained of energy. 'Oh, *go away*,' he said, and they edged past him warily, Devereaux poking around in his eyes to rid himself of the contacts before he was seen by the head.

Bloomfield stood with his back to the trees, watching the two boys go. When they were half-way to the quad, he started to follow. And then he changed his mind. He wasn't sure why. It had been his intention to retrace his steps, to return to the calm of his study and smoke a pipe before supper. But Simpkins had seemed frightened, and Bloomfield couldn't quite believe that it was Devereaux's alien eyes that had put the fear of God into him.

What had happened once they entered the trees?

Had they threatened him? Hit him? Hurt him?

He reasoned that they couldn't have had *time* to do anything too awful. They hadn't been in the trees for more than a moment before Simpkins ran out.

But he hadn't just run, thought Bloomfield. He had fled, not even pausing to answer when Bloomfield had shouted his name.

He turned to face the trees, then entered, following a path carved out by endless generations of illicit smokers.

In all, it was a pleasant enough environment, even at this time of year, with half the trees devoid of leaf, and the ground a rainsoaked mulch that soiled his shoes.

He felt the moisture creeping through the leather, looked down, and allowed his eye to follow the path to a pine. It seemed out of place among the smaller, younger oaks, a monolith that reached up into the sky. It was green, and very full, almost the perfect Christmas tree, its shape pleasingly symmetrical; and sitting on a branch that stuck out level with his chest, there rested a single decoration.

At first, Bloomfield wasn't quite sure what the decoration was, other than that it was round, purple and bloated. He therefore approached it with a view to taking a closer look, and as he did so, he became aware that certain physical changes were occurring in his body. He had no control over them, and could no more have slowed the beating of his heart than prevent himself breathing in short, sharp gasps.

As he neared it, he wondered where it had come from, and how it had come to be lodged in the branches of a tree. And then he realised that some boy – Figgis, perhaps, or Devereaux – must have found it and propped it in the tree for full effect.

Whoever that boy was, perhaps it had also been he who had drawn a pair of spectacles round the eye sockets, and an Adolf Hitler moustache beneath what was left of the nose.

Someone had thoughtfully, *carefully*, placed an old school cap on the skull, the peak pulled over the forehead.

And around what was left of the neck, securing the head to a branch, was an old school tie.

For one horrible moment, Bloomfield considered the possibility that the school might be missing a pupil, that for the past week or so someone had been answering to the name of that missing pupil during morning registration.

And then he composed himself. The head was that of a man. From what could be seen of his hair, it appeared to be grey, as were the whiskers on the jowl.

He knew he shouldn't touch it, and yet, he felt compelled to reach out, and pluck from its lips, the cigarette that was jammed between the teeth.

The lips made no protest as Bloomfield let the cigarette fall to the ground. He didn't know what had made him remove it, he only knew it would be considered wrong if he were to succumb to the further temptation to knock the head off the branch, to bury it, to pretend that it had never been there at all.

He turned and left the belt of trees, forcing himself to walk slowly, to breathe evenly, and gather his thoughts before he reached his study and called the police.

Chapter Twenty-five

Doheny had purposely chosen a pub patronised by the police. There were civilians in there, but most of the people crowding round the bar were off-duty coppers, some with their wives or girlfriends, most with people they worked with every day; and if most of them banged their heads on lintels erected at a time when the average height for a copper was five foot nothing, that was okay.

It was warm in there, and comfortable. It was also safe. Every time the door opened, sixty pairs of eyes weighed up who was walking in. If the visitor wasn't a copper, the eyes stayed focused until the outsider had finished his drink and fucked off.

McLaughlan had got there early and Doheny saw him the instant he walked in. He stood at the bar with an untouched pint of bitter in front of him, and when he saw Doheny, he ordered one for him.

Doheny shook his way out of a leather Timberland jacket, almost identical to the one Fischer had been wearing on the day of the robbery, and hung it on the back of a chair in the knowledge that this was probably the only pub in north London where you could do that without serious risk of having it ripped off. Normally, he was completely relaxed with McLaughlan. Right now, the guy even *looked* like a stranger.

Doheny had sat in on the session with Orme, and later there had been meetings with other, more senior officers. In the weeks and months to come, there would be further meetings, and when they occurred, McLaughlan would have a lawyer and other representatives present. That's if he had any sense. After today, Doheny wasn't sure that McLaughlan was aware of just how much trouble he was in.

Later, he intended to try to talk to him about the value of a report from a police psychologist. As Orme had tried to impress on him earlier, a good report could prevent him from being thrown out of the force, though nothing on God's earth was going persuade anyone to let him anywhere near a squad in which the men handled firearms. From now on, Flying Squad, Serious Crimes, Murder Squad, Drug Squad, and squads detailed to protect royalty and VIPS were out. McLaughlan would end up sitting behind a desk, filing reports, dealing with traffic.

It wasn't a future Doheny could have looked forward to with any degree of enthusiasm. His bet was that McLaughlan would quit. Even so, he intended to persuade him to heed Orme's advice: if he did so, he might just leave with his pension intact.

It felt bizarre to be in McLaughlan's company socially after everything that had happened earlier on. Doheny hardly knew what to say to him, and McLaughlan appeared not to be interested in making the kind of small-talk that Doheny was relying on to ease them on to more important topics. What he did say was so unexpected, Doheny wasn't sure how to react.

'On the way here, I was tailed.'

'Robbie,' said Doheny, 'relax—'

But McLaughlan said it again, raising his voice as he tried to impress it on Doheny: 'I'm telling you I was tailed.'

Doheny picked up McLaughlan's pint as well as his own, put them on the table with the chair that held his coat and said, 'Sit down.'

McLaughlan sat obediently, but he wouldn't look at Doheny, who found himself with a packet of crisps he hadn't asked for – a gift from a girl at the bar who, for some months, had been trying to win her way into his trousers by remembering what he drank, and that he liked a particular brand of crisps with the old-fashioned twist of salt in dark blue paper.

Doheny needed a minute to think before he said anything, so he opened the crisps and played for time by dipping a gunman's small neat hand inside for the twist of salt. 'If you'd take Orme's advice and see the psychologist, you'd find out how common it is for men in your situation to think they're being followed.'

'What do I have to do to make you believe me?'

'It's a syndrome,' said Doheny.

'They're watching the house.'

Oh, fuck, thought Doheny.

'I was tailed.'

Doheny had no intention of brushing McLaughlan's fears aside, but neither did he want to pander to them. 'Robbie—'

'A bike – not big, a trials bike maybe – I couldn't shake it.'

His voice was manic now, manic and rising in volume. People were looking their way, and Doheny didn't want it getting around that McLaughlan had problems. He suddenly stood up, grabbing McLaughlan's arm and pulling him to his feet. 'Let's get some air,' he said.

He got him outside where he emptied the crisps on the ground and handed the bag to him, saying, 'Breathe into this.'

McLaughlan, who knew this was the standard method of stopping someone hyperventilating, tried, but it took him a good few seconds to get it together. 'Take it easy,' Doheny told him, and they leaned with their backs to the wall of the pub in much the way that they'd leaned with their backs to the alley only seconds before Orme had given the order to attack.

McLaughlan breathed into the bag, then sucked the carbon dioxide out, and as the moments passed, he felt his heart-rate starting to slow, and his thoughts beginning to clear.

He took the bag from his mouth and bent forward, his hands to his knees. Doheny watched him. 'Okay?'

McLaughlan wanted to speak, to impress it on Doheny that he hadn't been imagining all this. But he said nothing, afraid that the voice that came out of him would be the same manic voice Doheny had heard in the pub, that Claire had heard when he ran from the house to beg her not to leave. How could he make them believe him when he sounded as though he was going out of his mind?

Doheny was asking him questions now, but the skin of

the bubble had thickened. It deadened the sound of his voice, reducing it to a distant monotone.

Then something pierced the skin of the bubble with all the ease of a bullet. A trials bike, the rider in black, no logo on the clothing.

Doheny said something but the bubble bounced his words back into the air and McLaughlan lost them. He had blown into the bag for one last time, but when he saw the bike, he hadn't breathed out of it. Instead, he had held the neck of the bag, and had trapped the air inside. The colour of the bag, the fact that it was lined with foil – these things reminded him of the silver, globe-shaped balloon.

He wanted to shout a warning but found himself struck dumb by what he knew to be coming. He slammed his fist against the bag and the trapped air exploded with a sound like the pop of a bullet.

Doheny fell to the ground, his skull torn apart by the impact. And then the bike was gone, and McLaughlan was alone.

Doheny, who was kneeling up, his hands to his face, was dying. The crown of his skull had been blown away, and no amount of help from whatever source was going to save him. The lolling of the head, the toneless cries – these were the protestations of a man who was already dead.

The sound of gunshot had brought people running out on to the street, some from a nearby restaurant but most from the pub where Doheny had met with McLaughlan. They stood around Doheny, most too shocked to do anything, others trying to help him as best they could.

But in the moments that followed, Doheny fell face forward, as if he were praying to Allah. Then he was silent.

Chapter Twenty-six

Orme was standing outside the gates of the Swifts' prestigious country home in Berkshire. He, like the team of armed police he'd brought with him, was dressed as if expecting to be caught up in a gun battle.

Once the surveillance camera had been immobilised, he gave the order for some of his men to scale the massive wrought-iron gates. Others scaled the razorwire-topped wall and jumped down into the garden. Calvin, thought Orme, wouldn't be impressed if he saw his Dobermans curling their lips then skulking away from the sonic device the police were using against them, like some high-tech cattle prod.

They barked, but although there were lights on in the house nobody investigated, and Orme considered his options: he could batter down the elegant Georgian front door or he could knock on it. Circumstances dictated that he should knock, but Doheny's murder had enraged and saddened him to such an extent that he gave the order for hydraulic rams to be used.

He found the door to be genuine. It took three cracks from the ram to break it from hinges that had held it firm for over a hundred and fifty years. Men were entering the house from other vantage-points – two back doors and a window – but the team got into the house in complete unison.

The elegant hallway was suddenly lit as if by neon strips, Sherryl stood on a landing, blinking into the light. She'd been sleeping, and it showed, but she shook off her confusion and collected herself in a way that Orme was sure would have made Ray proud. 'What the fuck do *you* want?'

Orme wanted plenty: he wanted to take the Swifts to Tower Bridge and keep them there for as long as the law would allow. While he had them in custody, he intended to let them know that if he heard so much as a whisper, now or ever, that they were in any way responsible for Doheny's death, he would hound them from here to the grave until he brought them to justice. He'd give them no peace. He'd broker no deals. He'd see them killed, if that was what it took. 'Where are they?' he said.

Sherryl put on a dressing-gown. 'Where are who?'

Orme was up the stairs and on the landing in three short strides. It acted as a signal to his men who dispersed through the house to look for Calvin, Ray, or anyone else they could lay their hands on. And as they moved through the rooms, they did so with the degree of caution men tend to exhibit when expecting to be shot at.

'I want them,' said Orme. '*And I want them now.*'

As if completely unperturbed that the house had been broken into by armed police, Sherryl replied, 'Well, you'll just have to want,' and, her voice sounding smug, she added, 'They're not here.'

Orme could happily have reopened the split lip for

her, but refrained. He forced himself to stay under control.

'They've taken a little holiday,' she said. 'Spain. They're partial to Spain. You ever been to Spain? Weather's *lovely* this time of year.'

Orme, who found her insolence infuriating, said, 'When did they leave?'

'Night before last.' Her voice hardening now, she went on, 'And if you don't believe me, check with Heathrow!'

He pushed her away, and ran past her to search the upper rooms with a handful of his men. He wouldn't have to check with Heathrow or anybody else to know what he would find: whenever a serious crime was committed and all fingers were pointing in the direction of the Swifts, documentation invariably proved they were on the continent at the time the crime took place. It was an easy and effective alibi, provided you could afford to pay a couple of people who looked similar to you to fly out on your passport. Orme didn't doubt the Swifts were still in England. But he also didn't doubt that he wasn't about to find them at home. He hadn't really expected to, but he'd had to try on the off-chance.

He and his men searched every room in the house and more besides, and if they found it necessary to turn over a few items of antique furniture, chipping and scratching them in the process, then Orme was sure that Calvin would understand in the circumstances.

Sherryl stood in the doorway watching. 'Bastards,' she said, and Orme advised her to watch her lip. He hadn't meant it as a literal threat, but she took it as one, lifting a hand to her mouth and feeling for the scab that had formed as a result of her launching into him last time he was there.

She flounced out of the room, and as Orme watched her go one of his men said, 'What now?'

Bloody good question, thought Orme.

He had been at home and off-duty when he heard the news about Doheny's murder. He had gone straight to the scene, and from there he had gone to Doheny's home where he broke the news to his wife.

Eventually he had left Doheny's wife and children in the hands of family and friends, and had gone to the station to get a team together to search the Swifts' property. But this had, as much as anything, been a knee-jerk reaction to the murder. He had wanted to do something positive, something proactive, something that would send the Swifts into a fury, though if he'd found them at home he didn't doubt that they would have been all wide-eyed innocence: *A murder, Leonardo? One of your own? Goodness me – I don't know what the world's coming to. I've a good mind to drop a line to my MP.*

There was another reason why he had acted so quickly: in her shock and disbelief, Doheny's wife had asked him two, very simple questions: The first was, *Who?*. The second was, *Why?*. And Orme couldn't give her an answer. He had assumed, automatically, that the Swifts were behind Doheny's death, because this was what he wanted to believe. Or, rather, he didn't want to believe the alternative, which was that Doheny had been shot by McLaughlan. Nevertheless, he had to consider the possibility: there was no doubt that they were together moments before the shooting; a number of off-duty coppers had reported seeing them in the pub. Those same off-duty coppers had also reported seeing Doheny drag McLaughlan outside, so it looked as though some problem had arisen between them. But whether that problem had resulted in McLaughlan shooting Doheny, who could say? It was something Orme didn't even want to contemplate. It was possible that McLaughlan had been right when he had said he suspected he was being watched, and it was possible that Doheny had been shot in a case of mistaken identity. But if McLaughlan was in the clear, why had he done a runner?

Whoever the killer was, he was a confident, accurate shot. He had only fired once, because that was all it had taken. An amateur would have put bullets all over the place, but the killer had planted a single bullet in the back of Doheny's skull. This, more than anything else, indicated that he was a professional. But, then, hitmen were generally trained in the use of firearms, thought Orme.

He didn't want to believe that McLaughlan had shot Doheny, and yet he had to face the fact that McLaughlan was also a professional hitman – it was just that he had been trained and employed by the police. And something else, thought Orme: Doheny was five foot seven, which was small by the Met's standards. McLaughlan, on the other hand, was right at the other end of the scale at six foot five. It just wasn't that easy to make a mistake when your target was almost a foot taller than the man beside him.

It didn't look good.

It seemed to Orme a very long time ago that he and his men had broken into McLaughlan's house to divest him of the gun. In fact, it had happened less than twelve hours ago, and after McLaughlan was taken back to the station, Claire had opted to stay with her mother in Radnage.

As soon as she had been driven there, McLaughlan's house had been searched. No other weapons had been found, but McLaughlan had managed to get his hands on a sawn-off when he wanted one, which meant he must have a contact – someone who could supply him with a weapon. Maybe, after leaving the station, he had returned to his contact to buy another gun?

Orme had another problem to negotiate: his own senior officers would want to know what had possessed him to allow McLaughlan to leave the station within hours of being taken in by an entire squad of armed men.

Orme intended to argue that short of charging him with illegal possession of a firearm, which would have spelled the end of his career, he couldn't keep him. And it was all well and good determining, in hindsight, what he should have done: the thing was, he had evaluated the situation at the time, and he had come to the conclusion that McLaughlan wasn't a danger to himself or anyone else.

Orme hoped that, ultimately, his senior officers would understand his desire to protect 'one of their own', particularly after he told them that, in his opinion, McLaughlan's fear that the dead man's family might hire a hitman to kill him wasn't entirely unreasonable: the Swifts were a notoriously vengeful family – you only had to look at what Calvin was rumoured to have done to a former girlfriend to know that. And where was Calvin's wife? Missing for almost a decade.

It looked very much as though someone from within the force had revealed that Ash had grassed Stuart, so who could put their hand on their heart and swear that McLaughlan, or his family, wouldn't be next? And it wasn't as though McLaughlan had been threatening anyone. He'd got his hands on a gun because he wanted to protect his family. It wasn't unreasonable, thought Orme.

But it *was* a crime, and it *was* enough to get him thrown out of the force. And what if I was wrong? thought Orme. What if McLaughlan has lost it, big time, and he's out there waving an AK-47 in somebody's face?

First thing tomorrow, he intended to go to the prison where Leach was on remand and have another crack at him, see if he could shed any light on where the Swifts might be. Unlikely – but you never knew.

In the meantime, he had already alerted Thames Valley that the wife of one of his men was currently at an address in Radnage, that there might be a serious situation in development, and that it might be wise to keep a patrol outside the address. It might also be advisable to have an ARV in the area.

Once he'd dealt with Leach, he would call on Claire. He wanted to be the one to tell her about Doheny, and he wanted to make sure that all the right precautions were being taken for her safety. Right now, however, it was late. Orme felt there was nothing more he could do, and he needed to get some sleep. McLaughlan, wherever he was, was in for a cold night sleeping rough unless he had friends he could turn to. He wondered where he was. He wondered what he'd done. Please, God, thought Orme. Let it be Swift. Don't let it be McLaughlan.

Chapter Twenty-seven

Orme will be looking for you. He knows you were with Doheny. He'll want to know why you disappeared when the place started crawling with police and paramedics. Maybe you had another gun? Maybe you shot Doheny?

For the first time in your life you realise what it's like to have to run and hide, and it brings your father to mind. You find yourself thinking that maybe he would help if he knew your situation.

The last time you saw him, he'd just been released from prison. You'd gone to the Gorbals to find him, and you'd gone expecting to feel nothing for the place. But that was when you learned that no one is given the option of deciding where they belong. Places claim people. It isn't the other way round. And places like the Gorbals run through the veins like a hereditary disease. You were born there. You spent the first few years of your life crawling around some courtyard like your brother and father before you. So your surroundings spoke to you in a way that threatened never to let you leave. You breathed the air and it tasted of the river, of rusting steel, of familiar people, so for the first time in your life, you understood what had brought him back when he was released.

The tenements were gone, and in their place were tower blocks, twenty storeys high. You had an address for him and it led you to one of the blocks. It was accessed by a steel-framed door, the meshed-glass panels broken. You didn't have to look at the lift to know it wouldn't work, so you took the stairs to the twentieth floor, bare concrete underfoot and the smell of urine getting you deep in the lungs.

You hammered on the door to one of the flats, and he opened it, a flicker of surprise expanding, then closing the pupils of his eyes. It was as if they were shutting you down, or shutting you out. He started to close the door on you and you jammed your foot in the doorway, your head so close to his face you could smell his sweat. He gave it up. He went back into the flat, leaving you to follow, and you walked in behind him.

You'd never been there before. You didn't know the room. But you knew every item of furniture in it, and it was somehow disturbing to see such familiar things in unfamiliar surroundings. Over the years, people had rested hot mugs on every wooden surface, the tables, the arms of the chairs, a decoration of pale beige rings against a background of cheap veneers.

There were photographs of Jimmy along one wall, and some of Iris and Elsa, but none of you. There was just one snapshot of Tam, and when you looked at that photo, it took you a good few minutes to realise who it was. You'd wanted to say that this wasn't what he'd looked like, that this wasn't how you remembered him, and then you realised that, over the years, your memory had lied. It had built up a picture of Tam that wasn't true. He'd looked like Iris, plain and strong, and nobody would have taken you for brothers.

George stood at the window, as far from you as the room

would allow him to get. He was leaning against the sill, his back to a view of tower blocks that stretched away as far as the eye could see. He asked you what the occasion was, and you told him you were there to deliver a message.

'Let's have it, then,' he said, so you delivered it. You walked up to him. You stood about two feet away, and you made your feelings known with a series of blows to the gut. 'You're the worst fucking father a kid could ever have had. We used to lie awake at night just praying the coppers would come to the door and tell us you were dead – and if you so much as lay a finger on Jarvis, or my mother—'

That power behind those punches would have brought a lesser man down. Your father doubled in shock, but he didn't go down, and when he laid into you, it gave you some insight into what it must have been like to be hit by Jimmy – like jumping from the roof of a very high building. Absolute impact. All internal organs turned to liquid.

It was Iris who saved you, Iris who walked in to find you lying on the floor, your father hauling you back to your feet then knocking you down again. She went for him, her fists like iron balls. They bounced against his back and face with all the impact of marbles. But he stopped.

You wanted to walk out of there with some semblance of dignity, but you couldn't get up, and you lay there, fighting for breath, blood all over your hands, your face, the floor. He shoved a boot in your ribs and it was vicious, the kind of rib-cracking kick that can puncture a lung. 'Get up,' he said, and you couldn't get up. You vomited blood, but you couldn't get up, and the last thing you can do is go to him now.

So you walk the streets and you look for some doorway to hide in for the night. Orme might find you before morning, and *if he doesn't, Swift or one of his men might do the honours. The bullet that killed Doheny was meant for you. This time, they got it wrong. Next time, they'll get it right.*

Chapter Twenty-eight

The morning after Doheny's death, Orme paid Leach a visit. He came to the conclusion that Leach had lost a bit of weight since he had last seen him, but that was par for the course: those on remand were known to shed more weight than the average prisoner. People who had been tried and convicted tended to settle down after a while. They knew their fate, and were serving their sentence. People in Leach's position, however, tended to worry a lot.

Orme had gone there with the intention of doing little to lessen Leach's worries. 'One of my men was shot last night.'

For a moment, Leach looked terrified, as if afraid that Orme was about to hold him personally responsible. He said something that might have made Orme laugh had the victim not been Doheny: 'I was in my cell all night.'

'Vinny,' said Orme, and his tone sent a chill through Leach, 'when I first questioned you, you told me you'd been employed to do some maintenance work for Calvin.'

'What about it?' said Leach.

'What was the address of the property?'

J. WALLIS MARTIN

Leach had a knack of allowing fear to invest his features with the characteristics of a terrified dog. His lip half curled, and his voice came out in a whimper. 'I can't remember.'

Orme replied, 'The man who was shot – Doheny – he was one of our best officers, but more than that, he was somebody's husband and somebody's dad, so if I discover the Swifts were behind his murder, I'll make sure that when your case comes to trial, the jury knows you tried to conceal their whereabouts.'

'I don't know where they are.'

'You know the address of that property.'

'Please, Mr Orme, you know I can't say where it is. I've got kids as well.'

'You've also got twenty-four hours,' said Orme. 'If I don't hear from you in that time, I promise you, Vinny, I'll find a way of making sure your name gets mentioned in connection with Doheny's murder.'

Orme left him with that thought, and as he drove from the prison, he realised that he had yet to have a session with Leach that didn't either begin or end with Leach bursting into tears. It wasn't the kind of behaviour most people would associate with the average armed robber, but it was very common behaviour for captured armed robbers to exhibit.

There had to be less stressful professions, thought Orme.

He returned to the station where a report from Forensic was sitting on his desk. It informed him that Doheny had been killed by a 9mm bullet, and that the shot had been fired from a distance of approximately eight feet. It also informed him that various weapons could be used to fire a 9mm bullet: a Smith and Wesson Model 10, a Browning, and a Heckler and Koch MP5 to name but a few. But Forensic were sticking their neck out and stating that, in this case, the weapon used was most likely a Glock 17.

He didn't welcome the news, not least because it was well known that the Glock was McLaughlan's weapon of choice: like most officers trained in the use of firearms, he had, in the past, comprised part of the crew that manned an Armed Response Vehicle, and the handguns carried in ARVs were usually Smith and Wesson Model 10s.

They were six-shot, .38 calibre revolvers which, in the hands of an average shot, were accurate up to a distance of 25 yards. In the hands of a crack shot like McLaughlan, they were accurate to an even greater distance, and yet McLaughlan had never been able to get on with them. No particular reason. As guns went, they were among the best in the world. But McLaughlan had requested special permission to use the Glock, a self-loading automatic with a seventeen-round magazine.

Each to their own, thought Orme, who preferred the Model 10. But then, although trained in the use of fire-arms, he wasn't a marksman, a *hitman*.

Over recent years, the Glock 17 had become standard issue. But they were only issued when necessary, and only then on the order of a commanding officer. And the men to whom they had been issued returned them to the officer responsible for ensuring that each and every one was accounted for and returned to the firearms safe. It was therefore unlikely that McLaughlan would have managed to circumnavigate the usual security pre-cautions: men were checked in and out of the station through metal detectors of a kind used in airports. A gun would have set the alarms off. If he'd tried to steal a gun, he would have been caught, thought Orme.

And then he told himself that he wouldn't necessarily have been caught. As a senior police officer, he of all people was aware that when someone intended to commit a criminal act, they could sometimes be extremely creative with regard to how they went about it. If McLaughlan had wanted to steal a Glock from the force, he would have achieved it somehow.

But it wouldn't have been worth the bother, thought Orme, let alone the risk, not when you considered that McLaughlan would know well enough who was currently dealing in illegal weapons. The market was crawling with Glock 17s, and whilst they didn't come cheap, making an illegal purchase was a lot less risky than trying to get a gun past police security.

He tried to stop himself from thinking along these lines, but the fact of it was he couldn't be sure that a hitman had shot Doheny, and there was something else: no matter which way he looked at it, Orme couldn't see how any professional hitman could possibly have mistaken Doheny for McLaughlan. They were different physical types. And there was no escaping the fact that McLaughlan had left the scene after the shooting.

The question was, thought Orme, where had he gone? Not home. That much was obvious. The first thing Orme had done was put his house under surveillance in case he turned up. The fact that he hadn't implied that he had assumed it was being watched – if not by one of Swift's men, then certainly by police.

There was no point wasting resources covering a house

when its owner had more sense than to show up, so he lifted the surveillance, and told his men to concentrate their energies on assisting in the search for McLaughlan. He was six-five. Wherever he was, it wasn't in someone's conservatory, curled up under a plant-pot. The guy was huge. He was noticeable. He was *findable*, thought Orme.

When Orme phoned Claire to tell her he was on his way to see her, she said, 'There's been a police car outside the house since last night.'

'Just a precaution,' said Orme.

'Against what?'

'I'll explain when I see you.'

He left the station and headed out of London. He had an address for Claire, but no preconceptions with regard to the kind of house he would find when he got to her. With one of his men dead and another missing, it was something he hadn't given any thought to.

If asked, he would have said he imagined Claire's mother to live in a semi in some suburb, so it came as a surprise when he pulled up in front of a former vicarage. He'd had Claire down as a working-class girl married to a copper, but the house indicated otherwise. It had to be worth a few bob, thought Orme. Anything detached that stood in its own grounds and was a mere eighty minutes from central London had to be worth a fortune.

He pulled up behind a patrol car, showed his ID to the men sitting inside it, and spoke with them briefly. They'd replaced an earlier shift who'd been on since the night before. So far as they knew, there hadn't been a car or an individual seen along the quiet road that led to the former vicarage in hours. They looked bored, thought Orme, as though nothing had ever been known to disturb the almost genteel tranquillity of upper-middle-class households buried in the country.

He walked down the drive, making for a property that had been built to take servants. He doubted there were servants now. He doubted there was the money. It was large, charming, but shabby, its shabbiness concealed by ivy that covered not only the walls but most of the roof.

The garden, he observed, was typically English. It had its bright spots, where sun-loving plants would blossom come the summer. But mostly it was dark, a portion of it walled, the wall itself almost totally hidden by trees.

Now that he'd seen it, he wished he'd asked for more than one patrol. It was difficult to cover a house of this type, and there was no way a couple of uniformed men could hope to prevent anyone entering it without being seen. The sooner he got Claire away from here, the better.

An older woman, who bore an unmistakable resemblance to Claire, appeared at the door. Orme introduced himself, and was invited into a sitting room.

Like the garden, it also had its bright spots. For the most part, however, the furnishings were dark and heavy, and it seemed a fitting place to tell Claire that the night before, on a London street so far removed from their current surroundings as to appear to belong to a different time, a different world, Doheny had been shot dead.

He doubted she could have taken the news more badly if it had been her husband, rather than his partner. But then, thought Orme, she'd known Doheny well. Over the past few years, the Dohenys and the McLaughlans had socialised, had even taken a holiday together. And then came the questions – questions that Doheny's wife had asked.

Where was he?

What was he doing there?

Have you any idea who shot him?

Orme replied that Doheny had arranged to meet Robbie for a drink after he was released, pending a decision with regard to whether he would face charges over the gun. 'He wanted to try to talk some sense into him,' said Orme. 'Robbie had refused to allow a psychologist to evaluate him, and that wasn't going to look good in the inquiry into his behaviour. Doheny hoped to persuade him to be evaluated so we could put his behaviour down to the shock of shooting Swift.'

'But you said they were outside.'

'Witnesses say Doheny suddenly led Robbie outside. We don't know why. All we know is, Robbie looked agitated, and Doheny appeared to be trying to help him in some way.'

'And when he got outside, he was shot?'

She couldn't visualise the sequence of events. Orme could hardly blame her. He'd had difficulty seeing them for himself. 'They walked out of the pub. A couple of minutes elapsed. People inside the pub heard a shot. They ran outside. Doheny was clearly very badly injured. Robbie was just standing there.'

Orme didn't add that not one among the many off-duty coppers present had thought to search McLaughlan for a gun. And why should they? He was known to them. He was a copper. It simply hadn't occurred to anyone to search him, though some had searched the road in case the killer had thrown down his weapon before leaving the scene.

If Claire had picked up on a sub-text to the words 'just standing there' she didn't say so. She slumped on to a horsehair sofa, its walnut back dark with age, the grain of the wood very fine. The wall opposite her was almost entirely taken up by the fading painting of a chestnut gelding pulling hay from a rack suffused by sunlight. She kept her eyes on it as she said, 'The bullet was meant for Robbie.'

Orme made no comment. Maybe it was. Maybe it wasn't. Maybe the bullet came from McLaughlan's gun?

Claire added, 'Is that why there's a patrol outside the house – because of Swift?'

Orme wanted to reply, 'Possibly', but refrained.

'Robbie was right, wasn't he? We *were* being watched.'

Again, Orme made no comment. Maybe they were being watched. Maybe not. If McLaughlan shot Doheny, Claire was in no danger from Swift, but she might well be in a different kind of danger.

'What must he think of me?' said Claire. 'How can he ever forgive me for calling Doheny, telling him he had a gun, when all he was trying to do was protect us from Swift?'

Orme wasn't keen to allow her to fix on the idea that the danger was from Swift. To do so might make it all the more difficult for her to come to terms with the facts if it transpired that her husband had killed Doheny. 'Claire,' he said, 'I want you to come back to London with me – you and Ocky.'

She looked up. 'Why?'

'It's not easy to protect someone in a domestic situation,

particularly one where the house and garden are as big, as complex, as this. You need to go to a safe-house.'

'I'd rather stay here. Can't you put men inside the house?'

'It would make life easier if you'd go to a house that's less difficult to cover.'

She wasn't listening. Something had just occurred to her, something she felt she should have asked the minute Orme broke the news about Doheny. 'Where's Robbie?'

Orme was reluctant to admit he didn't know, and if he were further to admit that all units were on the look-out for him, Claire would start to piece together the situation for herself. McLaughlan might be in the clear, in which case, he decided, it would be cruel to distress her unnecessarily. He therefore answered her question with a question: 'Have you heard from him?'

'No, but I left a message on the answerphone to tell him where I was.'

Even if she hadn't done that, thought Orme, McLaughlan would ultimately have guessed where she was. It made him all the more determined to get her away from there and into a safe-house. He said, 'Well, like I say, I want you to come back to London with me – *now* – and bring Ocky.'

'I'd rather stay here.'

In the knowledge that he couldn't actually force her into a safe-house, Orme replied, 'I'd rather you didn't.'

'Why?'

He phrased his reply very carefully in an effort to avoid implying there might be a problem with McLaughlan. 'If Doheny was shot by a hitman, there's no guarantee that same hitman won't come looking for you.'

His effort was in vain. Instantly she picked him up on the slip. 'You said *if* Doheny was shot by a hitman. What did you mean by *if*?'

For a moment, they looked at one another, Orme considering how best to invalidate that slip of the tongue and finally realising he couldn't. He had no choice now but to come clean with her:

'There's a possibility Robbie might have shot Doheny. Right now, we can't be sure he didn't. He left the scene. We don't know where he is.'

Orme's words stopped her as effectively as any bullet. For a minute, Claire looked stunned. He half expected to have to rush forward and catch her as she fell, but all she said, when she found her voice, was, 'Get out.'

'Claire,' said Orme.

'Get out!'

The sound of shouting brought her mother to the doorway. She stood there, a soft yellow duster in work-roughened hands, and she looked in rather nervously, as if the house were no longer her own but the home of someone who had merely employed her to dust, and iron, and wash: 'Is everything all right?'

Claire was crying now. 'How can you even *think* he'd shoot Doheny?'

Her mother darted towards her as Ocky ran into the room. He took one look at Claire, and promptly burst into tears.

Enough! thought Orme, who barked a command at Claire's mother: 'Look after Ocky. I'll deal with Claire.'

'Well, I'm really not sure—'

'Just do it,' said Orme, and after she ushered Ocky out of the room, he closed the door, then turned his attention to Claire. She kept her back to him, incensed by his suggestion, and Orme was tempted to remind her that not so long ago, he'd had to rescue her from a situation in which her husband was holding her at gunpoint in the bathroom of their home.

Orme didn't care one way or another whether she looked at him or not. She could hear him well enough, and that was what mattered. 'Now, you just listen to me . . .'

Ocky ran into the garden, calling for his mummy. It was a much bigger garden than the one at their new house. No giant puddle to splash in, but it went right round the side of the house and disappeared into trees.

He ran right down to the bottom, his chin puckered with the effort of biting back the tears. Granny had told him to be a big boy and play outside while she listened at the door to what the man was saying to Mummy. He was trying to be big. But seeing Mummy cry made him cry too.

There were trees at the bottom of the garden, and beyond them, Ocky could see a wall. He could also see something else, something that made him afraid . . .

A figure that wasn't a figure, but seemed to be more of a shadow, stood with its back to the wall that was hidden by trees.

'Hello, Ocky,' the shadow said. 'I've got something for you.'

And then it held out a present.

A silver, globe-shaped balloon.

Chapter Twenty-nine

Jarvis noted that the discovery of a human head in the grounds of one of England's better-known public schools made front-page news, whereas the murder of an off-duty police officer had warranted no more than a column on the second page.

He wasn't amused.

Like many of his contemporaries, Jarvis could remember precisely where he had been and what he had been doing when, in 1966, three police officers were shot and killed in Shepherd's Bush. Prior to their murder, it hadn't been thought necessary to train police officers to use guns, and the squad that had ultimately become known as Force Firearms had come about as a direct result of their deaths.

In Jarvis's view, Doheny's murder was more shocking than the fact of Ash's miserable face peering out from beneath some schoolboy's cap. Trouble was, it was nowhere near as interesting to the majority of people. What sold newspapers was sensational front-page news, and Ash's severed head had grabbed the imagination of a nation bored by politics, tax proposals, and England's rather dismal performance against Sri Lanka.

The better class of newspaper had devoted much of its coverage to observations made by the police, namely that Forensic had so far failed to discover how the head had come to be where it was found. Certain of the pupils attending the school were the sons of prominent figures. Kidnap was considered an extremely remote possibility – this was England, not Italy – but it was, none the less, a possibility, and security at the school was therefore high.

Security cameras covered every square foot, from the corridors to the dormitories. Even the showers and lavatories were covered, as were the staff quarters, the quad and the playing-fields, and as the tapes were kept for three months before being re-used, it had been possible for police to say with some degree of certainty that nobody had entered the school property with a head tucked under their arm. To quote a senior officer: 'It was as if the head had been dropped from the heavens and landed in the trees.'

Except, of course, that it hadn't landed in the trees at all. Two boys had found it lying at the foot of an imported Canadian pine, and over a period of days, they had shown it to every boy in the school who was willing to pay five pounds for the privilege.

Notwithstanding the level of security at the school, the tabloids had somehow managed to get their hands on the boys in question. One of them, Devereaux, had attempted to convince the journalist interviewing him that the luminescent green of his eyes had resulted from radiotherapy, and had then accused Figgis of sticking the head in the branches of the pine.

Figgis had retaliated by letting it be known that it was Devereaux who had adorned the head with an Adolf Hitler moustache, but neither boy would admit to who had stuck a cigarette between its lips.

The head had been removed from the school, as had Figgis and Devereaux, the former awaiting formal identification, the latter awaiting a decision relating to their future at the school.

Jarvis was less interested in how the head had come to be where it was found than in what the boys who had found it had done to it, because for him, there was suddenly an abstract but potential link between what had happened to Ash and the disappearance of Tam McLaughlan.

It was almost thirty years since Tam had vanished, and over those years, the question of what might have happened to him had sometimes positively plagued Jarvis. He had considered every possibility from every conceivable angle, but the one possibility staring him in the face had somehow managed to elude him.

Until now.

Neither Figgis nor Devereaux was evil. What they had done was something thousands of other young adolescent males would have done in their position: they had – initially at any rate – kept the macabre discovery to themselves. They had returned to it, time and again, to see how it was coming along, and to find out whether the birds had yet managed to get at the tongue as well as the eyes.

Ultimately, however, they hadn't been able to resist the temptation to show it off, and they had revealed their find to others. They had, however, made it clear that the head was theirs. After all, they had found it. They were therefore entitled to call the shots with regard to who saw it, and when, and for how much.

The fact that almost every boy in the school had paid to see it told Jarvis something he should have realised long ago. Most boys were more fascinated than horrified by such things.

He thought back to the industrial wasteground where Crackerjack's body was found and something suddenly occurred to him: what if Tam and Robbie had known where their father had dumped it? What if they went up to Glasgow not to find George but to find out what the body looked like after lying in a ditch for a couple of weeks? And what if that's where Tam had come to harm?

It still didn't explain why Robbie wouldn't tell them what had happened, but Robbie had been a complex kid, a sensitive and secretive child. There was no telling what went on in the mind of a kid like that.

There had been occasions when Jarvis had come close to suggesting he should see a child psychologist, but times were different then. The mere suggestion that someone might be in need of a psychologist, or other professional who specialised in helping people deal with mental illness or emotional trauma was enough to get them labelled for life, along with their family, as unstable. Consequently Elsa wouldn't hear of it, and it had been left to Jarvis to try to sort him out.

He'd failed. He'd known that. There had been minor triumphs, but mostly he had failed to get to the root of Robbie's problem. And whatever that problem was, it was something serious, he knew that much.

There had been many occasions when Elsa had turned to Jarvis for help when it got too much. Even though they were through, she had phoned him at home some weeks after Crackerjack's body was found, and she had sobbed down the phone, 'Mike, I need your help with Robbie. Please, Mike, don't hang up.'

This is it, thought Jarvis. He can't cope with it any more. He's going to tell us what happened. 'What's wrong?'

He had expected her to give one of a dozen potential answers, but none came anywhere close to Elsa's: 'I can't get him out of the cellar.'

Jarvis had been about to ask her what he was doing in the cellar in the first place, and what she meant by being unable to get Robbie out of it, but the line went dead, and because he couldn't be sure what was going on, he decided to go to the house and try to find out. His common sense had screamed at him not to, had told him to phone her back and tell her there were societies and support groups that made it their business to help the wives and children of prisoners – but she'd sounded so desperate he hadn't been able to bring himself to do it. *You're a fool*, his common sense told him. *Phone her back and tell her it isn't your problem.*

The minute he got to the house, she opened the door – no more waiting around on the step while she fumbled with the bolts. With George in prison, there was no longer any need to make sure he couldn't just stick his key in the lock and walk in on them. He gave her a nod of acknowledgement, and she led him into one of the downstairs rooms. 'Talk to him, Mike, he'll listen to you. Tell him to come out the cellar.'

The house had seemed to smell – which it never had

before. She couldn't have cleaned the place in weeks, thought Jarvis – and then he noticed something else: quite a few items of furniture appeared to be missing. An armchair. A table. A lamp. Just bits and pieces, really, but enough for him to notice. 'Half your furniture's gone – what's going on?'

She waved her hand as if to say it was the least of her worries. 'Talk to him,' she pleaded. 'See if you can get him to come out.'

Jarvis left the question of the furniture for the moment, walked out into the hall and tried the door to the cellar. It had been bolted from within, and he shouted as he knocked: 'Robbie, how about opening up?'

There was the sound of scuffling, as if a mouse had scrambled under the skirting. But the door stayed closed, and Jarvis said, 'If you don't open up, I'll—'

I'll what? he thought. He could hardly threaten to smash down the door. Even if he tried, he doubted he'd be able to do it. George had built it in such a way as to ensure that, should the need arise, it would buy him time. It would take a hydraulic ram to make any impression on it, and Jarvis didn't even have a hammer to hand.

'Robbie,' he said, 'either you open up or I'm off. Sorry, but that's the way it is.'

This time, there was no sound at all, and Jarvis said, 'Suit yourself.'

He made as if to go, and Elsa cried out, 'Mike, please!'

'Not my problem,' said Jarvis.

The bolts were drawn.

Just for a moment, it occurred to him that if he had any sense he'd carry on walking, but he turned to find Robbie standing at the entrance to the cellar.

In all the time he'd known him, Jarvis had never seen him in such a state. He was dirty, and the dirt was of a kind that accumulates over a period of days or weeks. 'It's not my fault,' said Elsa, as if anticipating a comment. 'He won't let me near him.' She darted towards Robbie, adding, 'You stink.' She turned to Jarvis. 'He stinks, doesn't he, Mike? Tell him he stinks.'

In view of the fact that Robbie had done as he was told, Jarvis felt he couldn't just leave. He walked up to him, bent down, leaned his hands on his knees and made a conscious effort to soften his voice. 'What were you doing in there?'

For the second time that afternoon, Jarvis got an answer he didn't expect.

'Hiding from Jimmy.'

The words had come out in a rush, and with them a torrent of tears. They triggered Elsa off and Jarvis had done the only thing he could think of at the time: he'd parked them both in the living room and he'd gone into the kitchen to put the kettle on. If nothing else, he needed time to think.

He'd found a tin of loose tea – Typhoo, funny how that kind of detail stayed in your mind down the years – but the sugar bowl was empty, and on looking in the cupboard for a bag to refill it, he'd found the cupboard bare of everything bar a packet of rice and half a loaf of bread.

He opened the fridge. No milk, no butter, none of the basics, just a piece of corned beef wrapped in greaseproof paper.

He closed the fridge and walked back into the room, finding Robbie sitting on the carpet and Elsa on the couch.

Neither so much as looked up when he told them he was nipping across the road for a few bits and pieces.

He returned five minutes later with enough to last them a couple of days at any rate, and then he made up his mind that he'd done his bit, that he could leave with an easy conscience, yet that comment of Robbie's still hung on the air:

Hiding from Jimmy.

He sat on the carpet next to him and said, 'Why were you hiding from Jimmy?'

'He's after me,' said Robbie, and Jarvis understood. A much-loved elderly relative could turn, upon death, into a ghoul in a child's imagination. How much worse must it be for a child when the deceased had been feared when alive?

Without even looking at Elsa he said, 'Got any photos of Jimmy?'

'What kind of photos?'

Jarvis had been obliged to spell it out. 'Photos taken before he lost his hands.'

She'd gone to a drawer and had pulled out a polythene bag full of photographs, some of them bent, none of them protected in any way.

Jarvis had gone through them, and it hadn't been a pleasant experience to be faced by an even younger, stronger, better-looking George. There'd been George with Elsa before they were married. George with Tam and Robbie when they were born. George on a boat. George in a car. George in the Highlands of Scotland with Elsa in a blue print frock. He only wished there was also a picture of George in a cell in Barlinnie. *Not so handsome now, George. Not so cocky, either.*

He'd found what he was looking for, and he said to Robbie, 'Come here.'

Robbie had got up, had gone over to him, had sat on his knee on the couch. And Jarvis had shown him a photograph of himself with his uncle Jimmy.

Robbie had been a toddler, just old enough to sit on Jimmy's shoulders and not lose his balance. But Jimmy hadn't taken any chances. He'd held him there, his hands like massive cradles.

'Sometimes,' said Jarvis, 'things happen to people – things they can't cope with. It changes them. It makes them hard to live with.' He handed the photo to Robbie. 'You've always been told never to mess with drugs.'

Robbie kept his eyes on the photograph, but nodded.

'That's because this family knows better than most the kind of misery it can lead to. Your uncle Jimmy, he got involved with some very bad people, Robbie.'

'I know. My dad said.'

'He did something stupid. He stole from them.' Jarvis was telling him things he already knew, but he felt it wouldn't do any harm to spell out the facts. 'He thought he could get away with it because of who he was.'

'Because he was a famous boxer?'

'Something like that,' said Jarvis. He hadn't been going to say what the dealers had done to Jimmy when they got hold of him. Robbie knew well enough what they'd done. There was no need to go into it. He would have left it at that, but it was almost as if Robbie had felt the need to talk it through and lay it to rest in his mind.

'They cut off his hands with a chainsaw,' said Robbie, and Jarvis saw Elsa shudder. Robbie looked up from the photo. 'He couldn't box no more.'

'Robbie—' said Jarvis.

He sounded hysterical now. 'That's why he went mad. He couldn't box no more.'

Jarvis took the photo and looked at it himself. Jimmy and George had shared certain traits. Neither had ever had any respect for authority, but perhaps that was only to be expected of the sons of a man who had died in a labour camp – he didn't know. He only knew that each had regarded himself as above or beyond the law, that each had been so extraordinarily strong he had seemed almost to think himself invulnerable, immortal.

Neither had proved invulnerable, and Jimmy had been murdered, possibly by the people who had cut off his hands. The message had gone out to every minor drug-dealer in the country: mess with who you like, but not with the Lebanese.

Jimmy had been found wandering round the docks with tourniquets round his arms. They hadn't wanted to kill him. They'd wanted to make a point.

'He loved you,' said Jarvis, and gave him the photo. 'Keep it. Every time you think he's come back from the dead, take a look at it, and ask yourself whether, if you had a nephew you loved, you'd want him to go through what you're going through.'

It was logical. It made sense. Jarvis hoped it would work.

He stood up to go, and Elsa stood up with him. And then, just as he was leaving, she said, 'Mike, can you take the ship?'

For a minute, Jarvis had had absolutely no idea what she was talking about. It had seemed a very long time since he had turned up at the house with matches and glue, but since the day that Tam had performed his minor miracle of repair on the shattered hull, the ship had been gathering dust on a table in one of the rooms.

He had asked why she wanted him to take it, and she told him they were moving and couldn't look after it properly.

Jarvis had told himself that it was no concern of his if Elsa was moving, but curiosity got the better of him, and he asked where she was going.

She replied that they were being evicted for non-payment of rent. Social services had stepped in to put a roof over their heads, but the best they could do in the short term was put them in bed-and-breakfast. She'd mentioned the name of the place, and Jarvis had recognised it as one of a number of establishments that came to police attention from time to time. It was too far from any of the London colleges to attract students, and the owner lined his pockets by filling it with a mixture of problem families, drug-users and alcoholics.

He now understood why the place seemed stripped of furniture. Times had been hard, and Elsa had sold off what she could. Besides, when social services put you into temporary accommodation, it was rarely possible to take anything other than a few personal items with you: there wouldn't be room in a bedsit for the occupant's household furniture.

Normally, he would have taken the ship without a moment's hesitation, but he considered his relationship with Elsa to be over, and he didn't want to have anything in his possession that would give her an excuse to get in touch with him down the road. Having said that, he knew that if he refused the ship might get broken or

stolen, and you couldn't put a value on something like
that. Tam had made it, and if, as he suspected, Tam was
dead, the ship would turn out to be just about the only
thing Elsa would ever have to remember him by – that
and a few old photos. Whatever she might have done, he
didn't want to see her deprived of it, and he said, 'I'll go
get a box.'

He had returned to the shop for an empty cardboard
box. He took it back to the house, placed the ship inside
it, and packed it with balls of newspaper.

As he did so, Elsa wandered upstairs. She seemed
suddenly dazed, as if she wasn't sure where she was
any more, and after he'd packed newspaper around the
ship and taped the lid, Jarvis went to find her.

All three beds were gone from the bedrooms, along
with a wardrobe, the basketweave ottoman, and a radio-
gram that for reasons lost on Jarvis had always resided
in a back room, out of sight. 'What's all this?' he asked
her.

'We have to be out by tomorrow.'

They would be spending their last night sleeping on
the floor, thought Jarvis. In all, George had more home
comforts in Barlinnie than his wife and child had here.

He had gone back down and Elsa had followed him,
standing in the kitchen and looking at the food he'd
bought earlier. 'It isn't much,' said Jarvis, 'but it'll see you
through tonight and over breakfast.' He hadn't added,
'And then you're on your own,' but the words hung in
the air and she caught them deftly.

'I didn't ask for it to be like this, you know, it's not
my fault.'

There had once been a time when Jarvis had believed

THE LONG CLOSE CALL

she'd done a fantastic job of bringing up her boys, considering her circumstances. But that was before he had
grown to know her better. She had made her bed and
she had lain on it. But she had continued to lie on it even
after her boys had suffered as a result, and suddenly he
lost patience with her. 'Yes,' he said, 'it is.'

She had looked at him like a small, hurt child, so he'd
treated her like one. 'Elsa,' he said, 'what have you done
with your Giro?'

'It doesn't go very far.'

'What's Robbie supposed to eat?'

'I can't work miracles, Mike.'

And suddenly he had found the whole experience of
being alone with her exasperating, as much as anything.
She reached out for him, as he had guessed she might, and
he responded by telling her that the image of what had
greeted him when Whalley's men had battered down the
door was one that would stay with him the rest of his life.
He had expected his outburst to produce a sullen apology,
but Elsa hadn't apologised on the night that George was
arrested, and she wasn't about to apologise to him now.
'George is my husband,' she said, and Jarvis pushed past
her, went into the back room and picked up the ship.

He carried it into the hall, wanting, now, to leave as
quickly as possible, to avoid the pull he felt towards
her, and avoid also the question in Robbie's eyes. *Are
you coming back?* But he wasn't about to leave without
saying, 'George knew about us.'

She didn't deny it.

'Who told him?'

She couldn't look at him.

'Thought so,' said Jarvis. 'What made you tell him?'

'I was frightened he might find out.'

'You were frightened so you thought the best way to deal with it would be to tell him about us? I don't quite see the logic.'

'I told him I'd gone after you because you were the one looking for him. I promised to tip him off about whatever you were doing.'

'And did you?' said Jarvis.

'*No!*'

'How does it make you feel to realise he was happy to let you screw another man if that was what it took to help him stay free?'

No reply.

'I don't think I even know what to say to you.'

Still no reply.

'Elsa – look at yourself.'

She hadn't made any reply to that, either, and suddenly, Jarvis was on to her like a pit-bull. 'Look at the state of you! Look at the state of the house, of Robbie – what do think his future's going to be?'

With Robbie at her heels, she had followed him out of the house as Jarvis had carried the box to the car. He got it on to the back seat with no help from Elsa or Robbie. They just watched him, Elsa quietly furious, Robbie seeming resentful. So Jarvis had got in the car, had started it, had put it into gear—

—and had put it back into neutral.

He had sat there, the engine ticking over. And he wanted more than anything to drive away. But he couldn't do it.

He should have just driven away. He knew that now. But it's always easy to know these things in hindsight, thought Jarvis. At the time, he had no way of knowing that he was just about to blow the only chance of real happiness that he would ever have, that if he'd driven away, he might have met a woman who would provide him with the children he longed for, the peace he deserved, the home he felt he had never truly had. As it was, he reached back and opened the rear door nearest the pavement. He called out to Robbie, 'Get in.'

Robbie climbed in, just small enough to squeeze up next to the box, but Elsa didn't follow, and Jarvis looked at her as if daring her to turn the offer down. 'What about you?'

She wouldn't even look at him, but she hadn't stopped Robbie, and he knew she wasn't about to refuse the only offer of help that was likely to come her way. 'I won't offer twice.'

She'd climbed in beside him. What choice did she have? And Jarvis had taken them back to the flat he had been living in at the time. He had told himself he was doing it for Robbie, but that was a lie, as was the declaration that he was doing it because he hadn't been able to find it within himself to leave them both to spend the night in a house where there was no heating, no furniture, and very little food.

He told himself he was big enough to forgive her, that with George out of the way his relationship with Elsa would have the chance it had never had with George always there in the background. But once she was under his roof, he had laid down terms: he would pay for them to stay somewhere decent for a couple of months whilst he put in for a transfer. Sussex, Cardiff, Yorkshire – somewhere where there wasn't the slightest chance of anyone knowing she was the wife of a convicted armed robber. They would live together as man and wife. She would call herself Mrs Jarvis. In the meantime, she would file for divorce, and when it came through, they would marry. If George was agreeable, he would formally adopt Robbie. In the meantime, George's name wasn't to be mentioned in front of him. The terms were non-negotiable. She could take it or she could leave it. But it wasn't up for discussion.

'It's up to you,' said Jarvis. 'So what's it to be?'

She had nodded her acceptance like a little girl. A very fast nod, a nervous, bobbing motion, as if she had thought herself lucky to get off quite so lightly. 'Say it,' said Jarvis, and Elsa had nodded again, her lips tight shut, her eyes very wide. '*Say it*,' said Jarvis. '*Say* that you agree.'

'I agree,' she mumbled, and although it wasn't the most enthusiastic declaration of intent that Jarvis had ever heard, he had believed her to be sincere.

It was just that, at the back of his mind, he kept hearing George McLaughlan, his fingers gripping his arm as he said: 'Keep her warm for me, Mike.'

Chapter Thirty

The canvas bag that held the document case was growing frayed around the edges. Margaret Hastie had been intending to replace it for some time. As the wife of a barrister, it would be incumbent on her to pay more attention to the way she spoke, conducted herself, and dressed – and a woman could not be considered well dressed if her accessories were falling apart.

Right now, however, it wasn't just the canvas bag that was falling apart at the seams. She had missed a luncheon appointment with Edward, and Edward would want to know why.

He would also want to know why she had kept him waiting for the documents he had asked for, and, if asked, she would tell him that she had needed the afternoon to gather her thoughts after taking her engagement ring to a jeweller for an insurance valuation.

The jeweller had examined the stone, which was set in eighteen-carat white gold, and had handed back the ring with a rueful smile. 'It isn't worth insuring.'

Margaret Hastie had felt the floor of the shop give a distinct lurch as the jeweller went on to explain that the stone was a cubic zirconia. 'Very pretty,' he said. 'Very realistic – but hardly worth a thing, I do assure you—'

She had left the shop convinced that the jeweller had been mistaken. And then she had grown angry, but not with Edward: the jeweller had been about to offer her money for the ring. Having told her it was barely worth anything, he had been about to try to persuade her to part with it for scrap. After all, he had mentioned that the scrap value of the white-gold setting was roughly eighty pounds, and that if she wished him to do so, he would happily write a certificate to that effect, though he was still of the opinion that, such was its lack of value, it was hardly worth the bother.

Too shocked to speak, she had simply walked out of the shop, taking the ring with her, and jamming it back on her finger as if she had come close to having it stolen. And after leaving the shop, she had made for the restaurant Edward had suggested, but had got off the tube a stop early, and had slipped into Regent's Park.

She had sat on a bench, turning the ring on her finger, her anger rising and falling, then finally dissipating altogether.

Someone – a woman – had stopped to ask if she was all right, had offered her a tissue, and had hovered over her as she mopped her face, her chin, and dabbed at her blouse. 'I'm fine,' she said. 'I'm fine.' And the woman had gone away.

But Margaret hadn't gone away. She had sat in Regent's Park until the two hours that flexi-time allowed her to take at lunch had long passed by. It was late afternoon. Soon, the rest of the staff would be willing the hands of the clock to reach 4.30 p.m., it being a tradition that the weekend started early in her department. They would wonder where she had got to. Or, rather, they would wonder why she hadn't returned to the office that afternoon.

The grass in Regent's Park was a dull olive green, the cloud overhead having stripped it of the luminescent qualities it sometimes had in summer. A bush that held crimson blossom in early spring was now a thicket of bare twigs. It blocked her view of a path from which a man in his early thirties emerged with a colleague. They were dressed in suits, which was why, at first, she thought they might be bankers. But neither man was a banker.

The older of the two approached her first. 'Margaret?' he said, and it didn't even occur to her to wonder how he knew her name. He held his hand out – not as if asking her to take it but as if asking for her bag, and she gave it to him, standing up as he opened it and pulled out the document case.

'How did you find out?' she said.

'You've been watched for some time,' he told her, and she just gave a nod of acceptance, then said, 'I didn't know until I had the ring valued.'

He didn't know what she meant.

'It doesn't matter,' she said, and she followed them out of the park and into a car that was waiting. Dark and sleek, it was the kind of car she had previously associated with James Bond movies. So this is where our taxes go, she thought, and she said, 'I'll tell you everything. I've nothing to gain from protecting him.'

The younger of the two men – the one who had

apologised as he cuffed one of her wrists to his – smiled
and patted her hand, his palms cool, his skin very soft to
the touch. 'We're so glad you see it that way. It's going
to save us all a lot of trouble.'

Chapter Thirty-one

McLaughlan had spent the night in the garden of a house that appeared to be empty. The lights were on a timer. He knew, because he'd watched the house for a while before entering the garden and washing Doheny's blood from his face, hands and clothes in an ornamental pond.

The scent of blood had brought two Koi gliding towards him with macabre interest. He wafted the water, and they slid away, their mouths taking gulps of death as they made for the safety of a miniature Japanese bridge.

He had slept in the garden, up by the wall that divided it from the road. He knew this to be safer than spending the night in a doorway. Unless the owners of the house, or a neighbour, spotted him, he would go unnoticed. And when morning came, he got up before it was completely light and wandered down the main street of a suburb where he bought the morning paper. The street vendor who sold it to him looked him over as if he recognised him, and for the first time in his life, McLaughlan realised what it must feel like to be in his father's shoes, to be watching over his shoulder, or reading threats that didn't exist into even the most

281

casual glance from a stranger. At six foot five he knew himself to be conspicuous. Any passing patrol might pick him up. There was nothing he could do but risk it: he couldn't spend the rest of his life in somebody's garden.

He took the paper to a park and sat down with it to read it. The first thing he saw was the headline relating to the discovery of a severed head. Forensic had confirmed it was that of Gerald Ash, and under any other circumstances, McLaughlan would have been fascinated. Right now, he couldn't even bring himself to read the article in depth. His eyes skimmed over the basic details, then searched the page for news of Doheny's murder: 'Police are looking for a man who fits the following description . . . He was seen drinking with the dead man only minutes before the shooting, but left the scene when paramedics arrived.'

That's all I need, thought McLaughlan. Much as he had feared, he was suspected of having shot Doheny, and who could blame anyone for that when he'd been taken down by his own team and divested of a shotgun only hours earlier? It was enough to persuade him that his instincts of the night before had been sound. He couldn't turn to Orme. He wouldn't be believed.

He spent the day walking through suburbs he knew to be quiet, suburbs where passing patrols were fewer than in some of the more troubled areas of London. And in late afternoon he walked into a café and drank coffee that sent his heartbeat through the roof. It was warm in there – warm in the way it had been warm in the buffet at Glasgow Central. Now, as then, he had little money on him, and no warm clothing, and the cold that had been forecast in the early-morning paper was settling on the darkening London streets.

He sat at a window, looking out, lowering his eyes when a patrol cruised by. It didn't stop but carried on, and he might have relaxed if not for the fact that he then saw something that made his stomach turn: a kid with a silver balloon had passed the café. He was older than the little boy who'd got caught up in the robbery. This was a child of nine or ten, but the balloon was identical.

Such popular things, those balloons, thought McLaughlan. He'd never noticed before just how common they were.

He finished the coffee, and left the café, the cold biting through his clothing the minute he stepped out.

Last night had been cold. Tonight, the temperatures would drop to a life-threatening degree, and he couldn't face another night in a garden. Nor could he risk the usual haunts of the homeless: the hostels, the shelters, the places that would be searched by the police. He had to find somewhere to go, or somebody who might help him, and he thought of contacting Claire, but decided against it. Not only would he risk the call being traced, but Claire had had a series of bad shocks over the past couple of days: whatever he told her, she wouldn't know what to believe.

He turned away from the direction that had been taken by the child with the balloon. He couldn't stand to see it, bobbing, as it was, above the heads of the people on the street.

Chapter Thirty-two

Frost was beginning to form on vehicles parked below the flat. The sky was a cool dark blue – no cloud to trap warm air between the pavement and the stars. Tonight would be bitter, thought Jarvis.

He pulled the curtains and turned up the central heating, then settled down to watch the last of the afternoon's racing from Aintree. The horses seemed to shrivel the minute the striped woollen blankets were whipped away from their saddles, and the jockeys shortened the reins as if attempting to get a purchase on ribbons of ice.

He liked to watch the horses, though he rarely put money on any. And a good job too, thought Jarvis, for whatever he backed invariably limped in last. He was notorious for putting the kiss of death on the odds-on favourite. So much so that Hunter, a gambling man if ever there was one, had once addressed the team with: 'If ever we find Jarvis lying face down in a ditch, don't look to any of the local villains, just phone round every trainer in Lambourn and you'll soon find out who shot him.'

Hunter, thought Jarvis. You had to laugh. He'd exhibited a certain panache in court, the kind of cavalier attitude that prompted the press to suggest that perhaps he was mad. He had come out of prison to write a book about some of the more notorious villains he'd had dealings with in the past. It had done very well. Jarvis had a copy, a first edition that Hunter had inscribed: 'To an old fool, from an old villain'.

In it, George had been portrayed as one of the men who had stood on the platform at Glasgow's Central Station when it was rumoured that the Krays were on their way.

According to legend, the Krays had intended to stake their claim north of the border, but they hadn't anticipated a welcoming party comprised of men like George. They had taken one look at that welcoming party, and hadn't even bothered to disembark. Ultimately, the train had chugged them back to London, where they remained.

Very wise, thought Jarvis. You wouldn't want to get off a train and come up against the likes of George McLaughlan. And Glasgow was full of men like him: big, powerful, brutal men who, in earlier times, had scrambled over Hadrian's wall to give the Romans a hiding.

The race was in progress, one in which a chestnut colt that Jarvis had quite fancied took a left turn when the rest of the field turned right. Having failed in his bid to become the next equine Vasco de Gama, the colt then divested himself of his jockey, sauntered to a halt, and began to crop the grass. It was par for the course, thought Jarvis, who was so amused by his own pun that it took a moment or two for him to realise someone was at the door.

He rarely got visitors at this time, and his initial

reaction was to be wary. He knew all the tricks villains could pull to gain access to the home of an elderly person.

He checked the spy-hole but his visitor was standing with his back to it. Jarvis tested the chain to make sure it was secure, and his visitor turned round as the door was opened.

'Mike,' said McLaughlan, and Jarvis's first reaction was to think there must be something wrong with Elsa. What would bring him here after so many years if not Elsa? Maybe she's ill?

'I need to come in – just for a while. I need to talk to you—'

Jarvis opened the door and McLaughlan walked into a flat that he had last seen years ago. Slightly different décor, perhaps, but essentially the same, cheap, cheerful, comfortable place he remembered. And on that occasion, Jarvis had asked him, politely, to leave him alone in future. 'No offence,' he'd said. 'It's just I need to make a complete break with the past – and that includes you.'

And here I am, thought McLaughlan, a physical reminder of the past he would rather forget.

He sat down as Jarvis switched off the television and just stood there. He didn't know what to say to Robbie. What did you say to people who turned up on the doorstep after so many years, particularly when, the last time you saw them, you had asked them not to come back?

In different circumstances, he might, perhaps, have been able to kick off by telling Robbie he was looking well, before moving on to ask why he was there. But he found himself unable to use that particular opener because Robbie looked anything but well. He appeared not to have shaved for a couple of days, and his clothes showed every sign of his having slept in them. He smelt of the streets, of traffic and cafés, of air that was thick with pollution. And now that Jarvis had let him in, he didn't seem inclined to talk. He just sat there, looking rough.

'Drink?' offered Jarvis.

'Tea,' said McLaughlan. 'I'd really like some tea.'

Jarvis went into the kitchen, expecting him to follow, but he didn't. He took a look at him once or twice while he waited for the kettle, but Robbie just sat there as if, now that he'd found somewhere comfortable, nothing was going to shift him.

'Fancy a bite to eat?' said Jarvis, and McLaughlan gave a nod. 'Anything in particular? Fry-up? Soup?'

McLaughlan shook his head.

Fry-up, Jarvis decided. Robbie had always been partial to a fry-up.

Nothing much changes, thought Jarvis, as he pulled the bacon and eggs from a fridge that was always full to bursting with food. He seemed to have spent a great deal of time feeding Robbie. It seemed almost natural to be cooking for him within minutes of his turning up out of the blue. Robbie and food – the association was one that Jarvis had made from the first.

He would expect him to ask after Elsa, Jarvis decided. He didn't want to but felt it might look strange if he didn't, so once he'd got the bacon on, he poked his head round the door and said, 'How's Elsa?'

He was still sitting there, staring at a blank screen. 'I wouldn't know.'

Jarvis wondered what he had meant by that. Maybe

there'd been some argument between them. At least it indicated that Elsa was still alive. She'd be old, of course, thought Jarvis. I wouldn't know her now.

And yet, that wasn't true. He'd know Elsa anywhere, however old she was. You couldn't love someone as he had loved her and not know them instantly if you happened to meet them years down the road.

He didn't want to meet her, that was the thing. He hadn't even wanted to ask after her. Well, he had asked, and Robbie's 'I wouldn't know' had put an end to the need for further enquiry or discussion. Jarvis felt that it let him off the hook. He could cope with Robbie being there provided he wasn't going to start talking about the past. If all he wanted was a meal, maybe a few quid, he could help him out. If he wanted something more, like an explanation of why Jarvis had walked out on him and Elsa for no apparent reason, then he couldn't oblige.

But the mere fact of Robbie's being there was enough to dredge up memories that were painful, Jarvis decided. And then he decided he wasn't being fair: for years, he'd dwelt on the past. It wasn't a recent thing. Every time he attended a funeral, read of a robbery or saw a police car, he found himself thinking of the period when Elsa was in his life.

He had, of course, expected Elsa to keep her side of the bargain, just as he had expected George's incarceration to result in a marked improvement in their relationship. And, in some respects, his expectations had been met: Elsa had changed her name to Jarvis after the move, and she had also refrained from mentioning George. But she sometimes lapsed into silences that could go on for hours on end.

'What are you thinking, Elsa?'

'I wasn't thinking anything in particular.'

It was at times like these that he sensed George's presence as strongly as if he had burst his way into the room. But worse still were the times when he made love to Elsa only to find that, once again, she was somewhere other than with him. At times like these, her responses were mechanical, the sex nothing more than routine, a series of physical acts to be performed as if for his satisfaction alone, something she knew she must do to keep him quiet, keep him happy.

'You do love me, Elsa?'

'Why do you ask?'

And then there were the unexplained absences from home, the weekends spent in Glasgow on the pretext that Iris wasn't as well as she might be. 'I'm just off to stay with Iris a couple of days. She could do with a hand.'

Sometimes Robbie would stay behind. Sometimes she took him with her. And on the occasions when Elsa took him with her, Robbie returned exhibiting all the symptoms of a youngster mortified with guilt.

'Is there anything I can get you?'

'I bought you some of those mints you like.'

So Jarvis had never asked him to confirm what he suspected to be the case: that Elsa had gone to Glasgow for the sole purpose of visiting George, not Iris. Where she took receipt of the visiting orders, he didn't know. Perhaps they were posted to the same address that George's letters were sent to? He had never found a letter from George to Elsa. He had no proof that any were written or sent. But sometimes you don't need proof, thought Jarvis. Sometimes you just *know*.

He had hoped that, in time, Elsa's love for George would slowly die. Fifteen years was a long time to love someone who wasn't there, and Jarvis had made life good for her. For the first time ever she had a decent home, and a man who put a decent wage on the table. Surely that counted for something? Surely that counted for more than her lust for a villain like George?

'I need to know you're committed to me, Elsa. I need to know that you didn't move in with me purely because you had nowhere else to go.'

'What do I need to do to prove it?'

'File for divorce from George.'

'I couldn't, Mike – not while he's inside.'

'You promised.'

'I hadn't thought it through when I made that promise. I promise you now, I'll do it when he's out.'

He had wanted, so badly, to believe her. And when you want something badly enough, you'll make yourself believe it. So Jarvis had persuaded himself that her reluctance was born of a misguided sense of compassion, until, one day, he had rooted around in a biscuit tin. He could see it now – a big red tin that had once been packed with shortbread. The shortbread had long ago been eaten, and now it housed an assortment of birth, marriage and death certificates, along with a certificate stating that Tam had made his first communion at St Mungo's. Beneath the certificates were buttons, safety-pins, and a roll of Sellotape – and that was what he'd been looking for: the Sellotape.

How many times, over the years, had he opened that tin? He had no idea. He only knew that, as he pulled out the certificates, he had suddenly realised that something of paramount importance was missing.

Twelve years that tin had sat on a shelf in the kitchen. If only he'd realised what was missing earlier. But he hadn't. So for twelve years he'd fooled himself that the Brighton flat with its roof garden and its five-minute walk to the sea had filled Elsa's life, as it slowly grew to fill his.

During those years, Robbie had grown up. He was twenty-two, and still living at home. Jarvis had expected him to leave. But, as it happened, Jarvis had left before him. *Who would have thought that I'd be the one to go? Who would have thought that the day would come when I would leave without a word of explanation?*

He had always thought it a kid's trick, walking out. He'd believed that men who were mature, who prided themselves on being able to communicate their feelings, on being able to keep a relationship together, didn't walk out without a word of explanation. They didn't just stick their coat on, take a last look round, then walk out on their family, their job.

He understood it now, the way some men could simply disappear. *I'm just off down to the shop for a packet of fags.* And that would be that.

He'd come back to London, to familiar streets, familiar villains, and the only place where he'd ever felt at home.

Robbie had tracked him down in the end, though it took him a good few months. 'Why did you walk out on us?'

'No hard feelings, Robbie. It's nothing you've done – it's just that I want to make a complete break with the past.'

'She's going out of her mind to know where you are.'

'No, she's not – and she'll be all right. George will be out in no time.'

'She'll never go back to him.'

'Oh, won't she? You just watch.'

He'd been right, of course. Going back to George had been precisely what Elsa had done, precisely what she'd always intended to do. And after George was released from Barlinnie, they'd gone to live with Iris. The tenement where she'd raised her boys had been blown down, first by the hurricane and later by Glasgow's town planners. A tower block had been built where it once stood.

Jarvis had sometimes imagined Elsa staring out from that block. The scene that spread out before her must have looked more like a moonscape than a landscape, he decided. No grass. Just pits and ruts, and tower blocks rising out of them like ancient monoliths. He wondered whether, in looking out on them, she ever thought back to that garden flat in Brighton. If so, did she have regrets? And if so, did they relate to what she had lost, or to the fact that for twelve long years she'd lied to him, lied to herself?

The former, probably, thought Jarvis.

Over the years that followed, he had managed to get his life into some kind of order. He'd taken early retirement, and then a job as security guard at a casino in the West End. He'd done all right. And he'd even considered settling down now and then. But, after Elsa, he'd somehow never managed to meet anyone he'd felt he could commit to. And this, thought Jarvis, looking around his flat, is the result: no photos of grandchildren, of past family holidays, of family celebrations. You were a bloody fool, he thought. And this is your comeuppance.

He carried the fry-up through to Robbie, who balanced it on his knee and ate it as if he hadn't eaten in weeks. Strange, thought Jarvis, how that, too, hadn't changed: on the day that Elsa had been asked to identify the clothing, he had gone to the Spar for food, which Robbie had devoured as if he were starving. Then, as now, he probably *had* been starving. That was one of the things that Jarvis had never understood: Elsa had seemed capable of subsisting for weeks without food. She was just one of those women who didn't eat a lot. She didn't seem to notice if she skipped a meal, or ate only once a day. As long as she had her cigarettes and her glass of wine in the evening, she was happy enough: food had never seemed to matter to her. It had mattered to a growing lad, and it mattered to the grown man now before him. 'You look as though you enjoyed that,' said Jarvis, taking his plate.

'Mike,' said McLaughlan, 'I'm in serious trouble.'

He had eaten Jarvis's food, had accepted his hospitality. And yet it was an effort to outline the events that had brought him there. He decided to start by explaining that he'd joined the police since Jarvis had last seen him. Jarvis greeted the news with disbelief, and McLaughlan showed him his badge: 'You'd know a fake if you saw one.'

'I can't believe it,' said Jarvis. 'What made you join?'

Good question, thought McLaughlan. He had often asked himself what had prompted him to join. A lot of people would have assumed it was simply so that he could get up his father's nose or prove himself to be nothing like him. But it wasn't that: he wasn't even sure that he could explain it to Jarvis, but it had something to do with the fact that, one night, a couple of months before he was found murdered, Jimmy had come down from Glasgow and he'd turned up at the house, looking for somewhere to stay for a couple of nights.

McLaughlan had opened the door to him, and when he saw it was Jimmy, he'd shouted out for his mother, then tried to close the door.

Jimmy had shouldered the door and had sent him flying. And then he had lunged down the hallway to pin him to the wall, his filthy, stinking breath in his face as he said, 'What's the matter, Robbie? Are ye no' glad tae see your uncle Jimmy?'

Jarvis had come out of nowhere to shove his badge in Jimmy's face: 'On your way now, Jimmy, or I'll be arranging a few days' accommodation, courtesy Tower Bridge.'

Jimmy had got the message. He'd backed off, and Jarvis had bolted the doors, the windows, against him.

That badge had seemed a magical thing to McLaughlan. Anything that could get rid of Jimmy had to have super-natural power. He had known even then that he would join the police, but he'd had to lie to get in. There wasn't a force in the country who would take the son of a villain. So he'd joined with Sussex, where the name McLaughlan meant nothing. None of their men had ever had the pleasure of breaking down the door, of putting their fist through the hull of the ship, of dragging his father out of the house at gunpoint, of leaving his mother crying in the hallway, offering to 'give her one' to brighten up her day. None of them knew what it felt like to stand in front of a judge for the Attestation Ceremony knowing that they could so easily have been standing in front of that same judge in very different circumstances. His entire life had been a long close call, and he owed so much to Jarvis.

'How did you get references?'

'One from school. One from the local Scoutmaster,' said McLaughlan.

And no national computer to spew his name into the lap of recruitment and inform them that he was the son of George McLaughlan.

'So what's the problem?' said Jarvis, and McLaughlan began to tell him, keeping it brief, keeping it to the point.

It's probable Swift murdered Ash.

It's probable that whoever divulged Ash's identity to Swift also divulged mine.

I knew I was being watched but they wouldn't believe me.

And then Doheny was shot.

After hearing him out, Jarvis sat back, and McLaughlan anticipated a barrage of questions that never came.

You come here, thought Jarvis, out of my past, and you tell me you've broken into your former home. You terrified the woman living there, and you terrified your wife and child. Your colleagues took you down as if you were a villain, and your friend and partner was shot in front of your eyes. You tell me all these things and you expect me to be able to do something to help you. But there's nothing I can do to help you, Robbie. This is the grown-up world, where people have to face up to the truth of their situation.

'What do you think I should do?' said McLaughlan, and Jarvis thought: I'll tell you one thing, Robbie, I'm not at all surprised it's come to this. No one with your background can hide their past for ever – sooner or later the truth was bound to come out. He reached into his pocket, brought out a wallet and took two-thirds of his pension out of it. 'Here – take this,' he said.

'Fifty quid? No.'

'Pay me back when you've got it. It'll buy you time, a meal, a bed for the night.'

'What do you think I should do?' repeated McLaughlan.

Jarvis thought, I think you should tell me what happened to Tam. I think I deserve to know. I was the father you never had. I put the clothes on your back, the food in your mouth, the roof over your head. I loved you, and fed you, and treated you as if you were my flesh and blood. And all you did was lie to me. You knew what was missing from the tin, but you never said a word. You knew what had happened to Tam. But you never told me. You knew that when I said I never wanted to see your face again, I was crying for you to help me, to read between the lines, to do for me just a fraction of what I'd done for you. But you walked away, and for twenty years you carried on walking, Robbie – until you needed help. And now you're back—

'I think you should contact Orme,' said Jarvis. 'Turn yourself in, admit your background, tell him how and where you got the gun, then give him the chance to help you.'

'I can't do that.'

'Up to you.' And as he pockets the fifty quid, you tell him something else, something he already knows but is currently denying to himself: 'You're finished, Robbie – it's over for you with the force.'

And now he walks out.

* * *

McLaughlan had wanted to shower before leaving, and Jarvis, with very good reason, wouldn't let him. He had reminded him of something he had forgotten: if he was innocent, as he claimed, then Forensic would find nothing on his clothes, in his hair, or on his skin to give him away as having shot Doheny, for firing a gun left its mark, not only on the victim but on the person who had fired the shot.

He was wearing the same clothes he'd gone out in the evening before. The minute he turned himself in, he would be stripped and his clothes would be sent for analysis. Forensic would find splashes of blood on his skin and on his clothes, some of them so minute they would be undetectable to the human eye, and the pattern in which those splashes of blood lay would divulge where he had been standing when Doheny was shot. Forensic would then consider the angle from which Doheny had been shot, and they would realise that there was a discrepancy, that McLaughlan *couldn't* have done it.

Turn yourself in, Jarvis had said, and McLaughlan had replied, 'I need to think.'

Well, now he had thought, and he knew that Jarvis was right. He should turn himself in. Just as Jarvis had said, he would be stripped and, ultimately, one of his colleagues would go to the house and get fresh clothes to replace those sent to the lab. But until that happened, he would be made to wear what looked like a hospital gown – and then would begin a relentless series of sessions during which he would be questioned by Orme.

It was always good to have the man being questioned at some kind of psychological disadvantage. Taking his clothes, making him feel inadequate and vulnerable, was one good way of doing it, but McLaughlan had no intention of being put at a disadvantage. He would go home, grab some clothes to take with him, then turn himself in.

He took a taxi home, and told the driver to stop at the top of the road after passing the house. It appeared to be in darkness, which meant that Claire hadn't come back, and he wasn't about to approach it from the front in case it was being watched.

He paid off the cab driver, then walked round the side of the house to an alley that divided it from the properties that backed on to it. It had once been an open thoroughfare, but residents had persuaded the Greater London Council to block it off with a metal, spike-topped gate. Somebody had a key to it. McLaughlan didn't know who.

He climbed the gate, getting a momentary view of the gardens flanking his own as he did so. All looked quiet. Especially his own garden, where he had to climb another gate in order to get in.

He found himself at the back of his own house, breaking in through an upstairs window, finding himself in a boxroom filled with clutter.

The door opened on to the landing. Was it really only yesterday that he'd been held face down on the boards? Was it really only yesterday that he had looked up at his wife and had seen such an expression of fear on her face it had shamed him? All he had wanted to do was protect the people who meant most to him in the world. What would they think if they could see him now, breaking in, walking down the stairs that the team he was so much a part of had forced him down with his hands behind his back?

His eyes were growing accustomed to the darkness.

There was something wrong – he couldn't put his finger on what. The family had always maintained that George could smell a stranger in the house. Essentially, it was primal – the instinct to smell the presence of an enemy. His house had been violated.

Perhaps he was sensing the search conducted by Orme, who would have checked for further weapons.

No, thought McLaughlan. Not Orme. It isn't Orme I can sense.

There was a shape at the door. Something on the mat. A large, bulky envelope. He bent and picked it up. No stamps. A hand delivery with his name on it – he didn't recognise the writing. What he *did* recognise was the fact that it was far too big for the letterbox. Whoever had delivered it had entered the house and left it for him to find.

The knowledge that whoever had left it might still be around heightened his senses. He took the envelope through to the sitting room, then heard the softest of thuds behind him. He turned and lashed out, the cat mewling its protest as his fist just brushed its tail. It ran beneath the sofa where it stayed, eyeing him with a mixture of surprise and mild contempt.

He checked and rechecked every room of the house. There was nobody there. And now he drew the blinds – not easy to do when staying clear of the window. But once they were drawn, he took a chance, and turned on the light. The first thing he saw was the envelope.

He examined it, but found that it was a standard A4 manila of a kind most commonly used by the legal profession. He sat on the sofa, put his thumb beneath the flap and ripped it open.

Something he recognised, something he didn't want to believe was there, sprang out a fraction. He pulled it out completely, and spread it on his lap. It was a child's tiny T-shirt and shorts.

McLaughlan just looked at them, not comprehending at first. And then the implications of what he was looking at kicked in, and he broke down. He held the clothes to his face, and he shouted into them. And when the phone began to ring, he left it.

It stopped, then started again. Then stopped, then started again. And eventually he slid off the couch and crawled across the floor, aware that if he walked across the room, his silhouette might be seen against the blinds by whoever was out there. And there *was* someone out there. He knew that now. Someone with a mobile phone, someone who had given him a minute to open the envelope before dialling his number. He lifted the phone off the hook.

'You took your time,' said Calvin.

'What do you want?' said McLaughlan.

There was a mocking note in Calvin's voice, the suggestion that perhaps McLaughlan wasn't thinking properly. '*Want*, Robbie? What do I *want*? What do you *think* I want?'

'You tell me,' said McLaughlan.

'I want *you*,' said Swift.

Chapter Thirty-three

The woman now sitting in front of Orme was possibly one of the best-looking women he had ever been in close proximity to. He had seen them, of course, from a distance: women who walked around Knightsbridge dangling small dogs from brightly coloured leads, their heels high, their legs as long as their mornings. Ladies who lunched, then filed complaints about men who broke into their houses in search of guns.

'Why did it take you three days to file a complaint?'

'He's a policeman. I wasn't sure anyone would believe me.'

Fair enough, thought Orme. After all, apart from a few disturbed bricks, there was little evidence that anything untoward had happened in the cellar. And there wasn't a mark on her – not outwardly, at any rate, but she shook as she spoke, and this wasn't the only reason Orme felt inclined to believe her: he now believed McLaughlan capable of anything.

There was no doubt that he had entered this woman's house under false pretences. There was also no doubt that he knew a gun was hidden in her cellar. Therefore, it was obvious he had some connection with the underworld, which revealed a side to McLaughlan that Orme had never before suspected was there. He had *links*. He had *connections*. He had *inside knowledge*.

If only this woman had come forward a day earlier, he thought. If she had, he would have kept McLaughlan at the station, which might have saved Doheny's life. Orme would also have paid Claire a visit earlier than he had, and she and Ocky would have been in a safe-house by this afternoon. As it was, Orme had spent the most traumatic twenty-four hours of his career consoling first Doheny's wife, then Claire, who was currently convinced she would never see Ocky again.

Orme hadn't been much use to her. He wasn't convinced himself.

Having persuaded her of the necessity of the safe-house, he had opened the door to the sitting room to find her mother standing in the hallway, looking guilty.

'Where's Ocky?'

'In the garden.'

They had gone into the garden together, Claire calling for Ocky, but Orme standing as if transfixed on the steps that led down from the kitchen. She had yet to see what he had seen, or perhaps she had yet to register its significance.

He had belted down the garden, had pushed his way through the trees, and had reached up. There, tied to one of the branches, was a silver, globe-shaped balloon, and all that Claire had been able to say when she saw it was 'Where did that come from?'

And then the implications had dawned on her, and she had run round the garden screaming for a child that

Orme had known even then was miles away. He had got on the radio, but had no description of the person who had abducted Ocky, the vehicle they were driving, or the direction they had gone in.

Orme had brought Claire back to the station with her mother. From there, they were taken to a safe-house, but the last thing Claire had said to him, was 'I don't know what's going on, but I do know Robbie, and I know you're wrong – he didn't shoot Doheny.'

'I never said he did.'

'You admitted you were considering the possibility.'

'That's my job,' said Orme. 'I'm paid to consider every possibility from every conceivable angle.'

He could only hope Claire's faith in McLaughlan would turn out to be justified. If so, he would come through whatever lay ahead, right down to losing his future with the force. And if she was wrong, then he didn't deserve her, and maybe he would find that he no longer had her to lean on. She was stronger than Orme had given her credit for, and Orme, who had sometimes wondered what it was about this plain, rather quiet woman that had attracted a man like McLaughlan, suddenly wondered if that was precisely where the attraction lay.

He had returned to the station ill-prepared for his second shock of the day: it had come in the form of this creature from a world that Orme had believed could only exist in magazines. She, like the pages depicting the kind of home she lived in, was glossy and polished, and she smelt very faintly of Cheltenham and varnish.

'What did he say when he grabbed you?'

'He said he'd fuck me if that was what I wanted, but only after I was dead.'

Charming, thought Orme. It sounded as though McLaughlan was losing his mind. But, then, the idea that this might be the case wasn't entirely new to him. It was now known that McLaughlan had stolen a gun, and the circumstances under which he had stolen it were violent. A woman had been assaulted. Doheny had been shot. Maybe he'd shot Doheny – Orme didn't know. The worrying thing was, he also didn't know whether, right at this moment, Ocky was safe. If Swift was behind his abduction, then he most definitely was not: a kidnap was a murder waiting to happen. If, however, McLaughlan had abducted his son, surely he was safe? Or safer. *Or was he?*

He spoke to Levinson, the psychologist whose services McLaughlan had rejected: 'Why would he abduct his son?'

'You say his wife told him she needed space?'

Orme confirmed it, but although he added that Claire was being supportive, Levinson said, 'He has no way of knowing, right now, that she's behind him. He may believe she's about to leave him, and men who suspect that their marriage may be history sometimes react violently to the prospect of being parted from their children. Maybe he's planning to start a new life, in a new place, a new country, but can't face leaving his son behind?'

'Is that likely, in his case?' said Orme.

'It's certainly possible,' said Levinson cautiously. And then, as if relishing giving bad news, he added, 'Did I mention that, in extreme cases, a person suffering from PTSD can sometimes become convinced they will shortly die?'

Orme, who had heard as much from other sources,

replied, 'He certainly seemed to think he was a marked man.'

'So typical of his condition – and in view of his condition, the news that he may have abducted his son is a worrying development.'

Orme, who was out of his mind with worry, didn't need to be told.

'You see, it rather indicates a sudden deterioration in his condition.'

'Meaning what?'

'Meaning it's imperative you find him before his condition deteriorates further.'

'Why?'

'There have been cases of subjects – predominantly male – committing suicide and taking their family with them.'

This was the last thing Orme had wanted to hear. *Please, God, let this guy be wrong.*

'We can't say with any degree of certainty why they do this, though analysis of their suicide notes suggests that they couldn't bear the thought of leaving their loved ones behind in a world so filled with pain.'

Orme was struggling with this one. Despite the way it currently looked for McLaughlan, the fact was, he couldn't bring himself to believe he would hurt Ocky. The child was his *life!* But maybe that was precisely what Levinson was driving at. Perhaps it was the very fact that Ocky was his life that put him in danger.

No, thought Orme. Not McLaughlan. He wouldn't hurt his child. And then the doubts crept in again. *He might if he's lost it, Leo.* But why would he leave a silver balloon tied to a tree in the garden? He asked the psychologist, who replied, 'He may have been trying to convince you that the balloon was a sign from Swift to say he'd got the boy.'

'What's the point?'

'It buys him time, and deflects you from him. If you're convinced you should be looking for Swift, you're far less likely to be looking for *him*.'

It made sense, thought Orme. And horrible sense at that. But McLaughlan wouldn't find it easy to hide – not for long. A man of six foot five is conspicuous. A man of six foot five who has a small child with him is even more conspicuous.

And then he reminded himself that it wasn't just McLaughlan who was missing: none of the Swifts were anywhere to be found. Even Sherryl seemed to have disappeared. The house in Berkshire was deserted. Someone had peered through the windows and had reported that Sherryl had gone without even bothering to clear up after the police had wrecked the place during the search. He explained this to Levinson, adding that the Swifts wouldn't have disappeared without good reason.

'I'd say the prospect of being repeatedly hounded by the police was a good enough reason,' said Levinson. 'They're probably just lying low.'

Levinson was convinced that McLaughlan was a loose cannon, a danger to himself and to those around him. Orme was not. He had to consider it, but he couldn't say he was convinced. He knew the Swifts too well, and knew that so much of what had happened bore the hallmark of a Swift campaign of terror.

Had they murdered Ash?

Probably, thought Orme.

Were they watching McLaughlan?

Possibly, thought Orme.

But he didn't know for *sure*, that was the trouble. And when you couldn't be sure, you couldn't take any chances.

Every force in the country was on the alert for McLaughlan, and everyone knew he might or might not have a child with him. Until such time as it was proved he wasn't dangerous, police and public alike were being advised not to approach him.

He might be totally innocent. But then again . . . thought Orme.

He turned his attention back to the chic, chic woman. 'You must have been very frightened.'

He thought he caught a glimmer of something flash through her eyes for a moment. 'I thought I was going to die,' she said.

And she smiled in a way that pushed Orme's testosterone level through the roof.

Chapter Thirty-four

The Gorbals of your childhood has gone for ever, yet you get off the train and you find your way to where the tower blocks stand. No need to ask directions. Something in your blood is pulling you back to your roots.

You knock on the door to the flat where Iris lived out her days. Nobody comes, though you know there's somebody in there – the walls are so fucking thin you can hear people think.

You kick the door from its hinges, and George is there in an instant, your mother right behind him. She thought you were police. Sad that even now she lives in fear of police ripping through the house like a bad infection. She tries to speak to you, but you haven't got time for niceties and you barge your way into the flat. He tells her to get in the back, and she does as she's told without question.

A younger George would be laying into you by now. But this is the older George. Big and brutal as ever, but nowhere near as strong. So he thinks twice about having a go, and all he says is, 'That was quite an entrance.'

The first thing you see is the model ship. The matches have darkened with age. Some of the rigging is broken. But it occupies pride of place. And the same old row of photographs *is running the length of one wall. Jimmy with his promoter. Jimmy with his trainer. Jimmy and George with Elsa and Iris, and other family members. You don't even know the names of half these people. But all of them were villains. None of them was straight. Even as a kid you knew they were bent. You remember these photos from childhood, the way you tried to grab them as a toddler, reaching up as any child might reach towards a photograph of any family member, pudgy fingers smearing the walls with jam, searching familiar contours for some sign that this was your tribe, that these were somehow your people.*

You never found it.

George sits on a couch that used to belong to Iris. There's a coffee table in front of it, and on it, an oblong tin that is as much a part of your childhood as the nightmare of Jimmy coming back from the dead. He opens it, pulls out a pinch of tobacco, performs a one-handed trick that Tam never managed to master. He puts the resulting work of art to his lips. Small. Tight. Neat.

'You've got a fucking nerve.'

A plume of smoke curls into the air like ectoplasm, a ribbon of blue so dense, you feel you could almost wrap it around yourself. And the smell of the tobacco takes you back to a time when telling him your troubles was automatic. Trouble at school. Trouble on the street. Trouble too big for a kid of ten to handle on his own.

You remember him saying that if anyone caused you a problem, it would be sorted. And suddenly you're afraid – but not of him. What you're afraid of is maybe hearing him say that he can't help you, that Swift is too big a villain, because if someone like him can't help you, nobody can.

'I said ye had a fuckin' nerve—'

You tell him you need a gun.

At least he hears you out – you'll give him that. He hears you out, then he asks why you can't run to Orme with your problems. You tell him why, and he's quiet now, then he starts to give you the kind of crap you've heard from other villains – how easily people who pride themselves on abiding by the law start breaking it when they perceive the law to be failing them. Why should he help you when all you've ever shown him is contempt?

You pull out the clothes and tell him you cut a deal with Swift – your life for Ocky's. The time and place were agreed. Swift will pick you up, and then he'll drop Ocky somewhere safe.

You had no choice but to agree, but you're not about to walk into that kind of scenario alone. When Swift or one or more of his henchmen turn up, you want to put up some kind of a fight, take a hostage, hold a gun to somebody's head, force one of them to tell you where to find Ocky.

'You never did a fucking thing for us. Well, now's your chance – your only chance to make some kind of amends.'

He twists the clothing around in his hands, lifts it to his face as if he would know for sure by the smell of it whether the child who wore these things is truly a McLaughlan. He might hate your guts, but Swift has grabbed his grandson, and this is something that stirs a primal instinct. Even so, he puts a condition on it. 'You'll tell me what happened tae Tam?'

You have a deal. Thirty minutes later, you also have a gun, a car, and a minder.

You're on your way to a rendezvous with Swift.

He knows every road from Glasgow to London. He's crossed the border at night, on foot or in cars, with or without headlights, *and always in the expectation that an unmarked saloon might come out of nowhere to overtake, then force him to a halt.*

He has no intention of climbing out of the car to lie face down in the road with those massive hands of his spread out on the tarmac. He has no intention of being stopped, and his guarantee is a nondescript vehicle driven with the utmost care. So you let him do the driving, but you ask him to put his foot down, and his only response is to ask you, 'What's the hurry?'

What's the hurry – when the only thing waiting for you is a long, slow death, with maybe a bullet to end it when you've reached the point of no longer being able to comprehend what these people are doing to you? Your lack of comprehension, of pain, will bore them. And only then will they kill you.

You tell him you're resigned to it. You've cut a deal with Swift. Your life for Ocky's. And Swift will keep his side of the bargain, provided you don't put one foot out of line. Anything less runs the risk of your son being killed. Very few villains are prepared to harm a child. But Swift is one who would have no compunction. He'll take the greatest pleasure in pulling back if he senses trouble. And after Ocky's body is found, there'll be nothing to prove that Swift ever had him. Your word alone won't constitute proof that Swift made the call you received at the house. There has to be firm evidence to get someone convicted. And Swift is a past master at ensuring he never leaves firm evidence of anything.

You need to sleep. Soon you will sleep for ever. You want to block out images of where Ocky might be and of what he might be going through. You also want to be wide awake for the single most important event of your life.

Your own death.

Chapter Thirty-five

The news that a senior member of Scotland Yard's clerical staff had been caught passing highly confidential information to the media's pet barrister rippled through the Met like typhoid. The implications didn't even bear thinking about, thought Orme.

He didn't yet know whether it had any bearing on police operations under his command, though he hoped it might ultimately explain how Calvin Swift had come by the information that Ash had informed on his son. Ultimately he would no doubt find out. Now, however, he had more immediate issues to deal with: Leach had sent word that he wanted to see him, and Orme went to the prison in the hope that he was about to divulge where the Swifts were.

He arrived to find Leach shaking gently, like someone with Parkinson's, but if Orme had hoped the man was about to divulge the whereabouts of the property, he was to be disappointed. 'I told you, I don't know.'

'Then why did you drag me out here? *Why are you wasting my time?*'

'There's something else – something I haven't told you.

If I tell you what it is, you won't make out that I wouldn't say where the Swifts were?'

'Let's have it, then we'll see,' said Orme, and because he had no choice but to agree to the terms, Leach caved in.

'The day we went to this property, Calvin picked us up outside Waterloo station.'

'Who do you mean by "we"?' said Orme.

'Me and Carl.'

Orme gave a nod.

'We were blindfolded and told to lie down in the back of a van. We were driven out to do a job. Then we were blindfolded again, and driven back to the pick-up point. That's where they dropped us off.'

'How long did the journey take?'

'About two hours.'

Two hours, thought Orme.

Common sense told Orme that Calvin wouldn't go to the bother of picking someone up and taking them on a two-hour journey just to fix a leaking pipe. There had to be some specific reason why he had chosen Leach. Whatever that reason was, it related to why Leach was so afraid, and he said, 'What was the job?'

Leach looked crushed by his own fear. 'I'm a bit of an expert in a particular field,' he divulged.

'And what particular field is that?'

'Lavatories,' said Leach.

'What?'

'Sewage, generally. That's what I used to do for a job before . . .'

Before he turned his hand to nicking cars, then robbing banks, thought Orme. 'Go on.'

316

'Calvin wanted a modern sewage system installed.'

'What was wrong with the old one?'

Leach shook his head at the memory of what he had dredged from the bowels of the cess-pit. 'It fed into a septic tank,' he said. 'Calvin wanted the tank cleaned out.'

'That's easy enough,' said Orme. 'You phone somebody. They come along with a lorry equipped to suck out the contents of the tank and take it away. You don't drive someone from London to do the job.'

As if he had anticipated that this was what Orme might say, Leach added, 'There was something in the tank – something he had to *remove* before he could get it professionally emptied.'

Orme was beginning to get the picture. He knew the Swifts of old. He could guess what had lain in that tank, and knew also that it had probably lain there for years.

'He made me climb in and start to feel for it,' said Leach, and Orme, who was beginning to know Leach quite well, recognised the tell-tale signs: any minute now, he was going to burst into tears.

Leach burst into tears. 'It was her,' he said. *'Barbara.'*

'Her body?'

Leach gulped. 'Not her body – her head. Her skull, I mean.'

'How do you know it was her?'

Leach was sobbing now. 'He took it from us, held it up for us to see, and he said, "Stuart's ma always said he looked more like her than me. She wouldn't say that if she could see herself now, eh?"'

If Calvin had hoped the comment might raise a laugh, he'd clearly been disappointed, thought Orme. Leach looked terrified by the mere recollection, but maybe he'd forced a smile, if only to ensure that he stayed alive.

He could just imagine Calvin holding up the skull of his late wife, just as he could imagine him holding up Ash's head and making facetious comments along the lines of: 'Notice in tomorrow's papers: "Top Boarding School Gets New Head" . . .' It was just his brand of brutal, simplistic humour.

He focused on finding out some basic facts. 'You say it took two hours to get to his place.'

'About that,' said Leach.

So, thought Orme, wherever the property was, it had to be somewhere in the home counties. He had given up hope of Leach telling him where it was. Maybe he genuinely didn't know. It was beginning to look that way.

'Vinny,' he said, 'it's possible Calvin may have abducted a child in order to lure someone to him.'

Leach stopped crying. He looked at Orme as if wondering what this had to do with him or his situation. Orme said, 'Now I don't know about you, Vinny, but I'd say your average villain, your average brutal villain, would stop short of hurting a child.'

Leach nodded agreement. There were very few villains who would hurt a child, and those who would knew only too well what would be waiting for them in prison.

'But I'd say,' said Orme, 'that Calvin isn't your average villain.'

Again, Leach nodded agreement.

'This kid is four years old,' said Orme. 'I've *got* to find him.'

Leach said nothing.

'So if you know where this property is, you have to tell me, Vinny. *Tell me!*'

Orme was an inch away from grabbing Leach and shaking him, but Leach's only response was to let a tear roll slowly down a chubby, pockmarked cheek. 'Mr Orme,' he said, 'I've got kids of my own. I might be a fuckin' robber, and I'm not up to much as a husband, but I love kids. I wouldn't do anything to protect someone who'd got his hands on one. If I knew where the Swift brothers were, I'd tell you. But I don't – I swear to you, I don't.'

Orme gave up. It looked as though Leach was telling the truth. He said, 'What did he do with the skull?'

Leach had no idea. We'll find it, thought Orme. First, however, they had to find the property Calvin had taken Leach to. Their chances of finding it quickly were remote. A two-hour drive out of London, and Leach had no idea which direction they'd gone in. Sussex, Essex, Oxfordshire, Berkshire, Hampshire, Wiltshire – *where*?

As he left the prison, his thoughts were on McLaughlan. Where are you? Is Ocky with you? Should I hope he is, or should I hope he isn't? What is the truth here?

Orme didn't know. And until he found out, he couldn't afford to take chances.

Chapter Thirty-six

It was four in the morning, and dark. McLaughlan had slept for most of the journey, but George had done all the driving and he was tired.

Little had been said as they drove through the night, and certain topics of conversation had been avoided altogether – such as the fight they'd had the last time they'd met. Jarvis's name hadn't been allowed to crop up in conversation, so McLaughlan hadn't said anything about having phoned him from the station before he boarded the overnight to Glasgow.

He had briefed Jarvis, and had told him what he intended to do. Jarvis had advised him against it. His advice was still to turn himself over to Orme, but McLaughlan had made up his mind to handle it his way. He had made Jarvis swear that he wouldn't contact Orme after they hung up. Jarvis had promised, but had said, 'If you don't want me to say anything, and you don't want me to do anything, why did you phone?'

McLaughlan had then come clean. 'There's something I wanted to say – something I should have said a long time ago. I just wanted you to know, you were good to me. Thanks, that's all.'

He had ended the call wondering why it was that people felt the need to say such things in times of personal danger. Maybe the threat of death was what it took to make people divulge their true feelings. Perhaps it sometimes enabled them to determine what their true feelings were. He didn't know: but if he had imagined that his thanks would be enough, he had been wrong. Jarvis had wanted something more than that. 'You can't do this without telling me what happened to Tam.'

McLaughlan had hung up. And now he regretted having phoned Jarvis at all. He imagined him thinking twice about the promise not to phone Orme, and he also imagined the countryside around them to be crawling with police.

If it was, he wouldn't know. But Swift would. Swift would have men watching the area from every conceivable direction. The minute they saw the unmarked 4 x 4s – such a fucking giveaway – crammed to capacity with men who could only be police, Swift would back off. And he had warned McLaughlan that there wouldn't be any second chances. 'You screw up, and make no mistake – he may be four years old, but I'll kill him.'

McLaughlan recalled again the girl in the wheelchair, smiling her greeting to everyone she passed on the Old Kent Road. She'd been extraordinarily pretty when Calvin first picked her up – seventeen, and too inexperienced to know what she was getting into. She had done a bit of rapid growing up at the point when she wanted to cut free and realised it wasn't quite as simple as that. *Women don't walk out on me, sweetheart.*

She had asked for, and got, police protection. Not that it made much difference. Few villains were as good at playing the waiting game as Calvin. Her vacant smile, her vacant gaze, only served to make her seem even younger, even more innocent than she was. And her mother would spend the rest of her life pushing her around in a wheelchair. Ocky, if he was lucky, would be killed outright. McLaughlan doubted Swift would show him similar mercy.

Anyone in his situation who claimed not to be afraid had to be lying. But fear was good. Fear could keep you alive. And it was one thing playing the hero in situations that gave you little time to think, but quite another to react to an immediate threat to yourself or to those around you. In moments of crisis, some people acted instinctively – they tackled armed robbers, dived into rivers, ran into burning buildings; in short, they sometimes gave up their life before realising they were at risk of losing it, and were described as extraordinarily brave. And maybe they were, in a way, but most people, given the time to weigh up their odds of survival would think twice. Nobody wanted to die – not even fathers who were prepared to do so in order to save their child. He wanted there to be options, but there were none. In holding Ocky, Swift held all the cards.

Calvin had given instructions: McLaughlan had been told to drive to a particularly rural part of Berkshire where he followed detailed directions and found himself on a country road that came to a dead end. 'There's a gate on your right,' Calvin had said. 'It leads to a field. Stand in the centre of the field. I'll come to you.'

The headlights of the car had picked out a five-barred

gate. George turned off the lights and the engine. He and McLaughlan got out of the car, climbed the gate, and walked into the field, the grass short, the ground hard with recent, heavy frost.

George, who was armed with a semi-automatic, had chosen to stand with his back to one of the hedges. He watched as McLaughlan obeyed Swift's instructions by walking into what he thought was probably the centre of the field. He could make out the shape of the boundaries, but little else. Scattered cloud cut much of the light from the sky, and from where he was standing, he couldn't make anything out against the skyline.

Swift had been clever, he thought. When someone was standing in a field, and they didn't even know for sure what surrounded them, they found it all the more difficult to defend themselves. There was something very isolating about standing in a position that exposed you from every side, and it went against his every instinct to stay there.

He listened for a car. What he heard was a helicopter. He looked up, and saw its lights. They defined its shape and size, and he knew straight away it was huge – ex-military, perhaps.

It came in to land only yards from where he was standing, and McLaughlan was almost blown away by the velocity of the air coming off the blades. They slowed, but they didn't stop. It could rise up into the sky again at the slightest sign of a problem. Swift was taking no chances, thought McLaughlan.

Whatever the helicopter's origins may have been were hard to tell: like the trials bike used in the murder of Doheny, it had been sprayed completely black. No code or registration to identify who owned it or where it came from. No logo. Nothing whatsoever to link it to the Swifts.

It took him every ounce of courage he possessed to climb inside, and the minute he climbed through the doorway, he was grabbed.

He didn't resist as his hands were bound, but he stiffened as a hood was pulled over his head. He hadn't expected the hood, and it came down over his eyes like a cold, grey shock. But that was nothing to what he felt when a rope was placed over the hood, the knot positioned deliberately under his left ear, then tightened – a classic hangman's noose.

It was then that McLaughlan knew what they planned to do to him, and he also knew how Ash's head had come to rest in the grounds of a public school. Perhaps, in the next few minutes, his own head would land in a place where the Swifts would deem it unwise to land to make a search, and his body would swing from a motorway bridge on the approach to Heathrow Airport.

The rhythm of the blades increased, and the helicopter lifted from the ground. He sensed the moment at which it cleared the trees, and a thought crept into his mind: *Robbie McLaughlan – tonight is the night you die.*

To stand in the field and watch the helicopter sweep away from view made him feel helpless. And he wasn't a man who was used to feeling helpless.

He realised now that, by making certain assumptions, he and Robbie had left themselves wide open: they had assumed that Swift or whoever he sent would arrive by car. They had been wrong. They had assumed that, at some point in the proceedings, the vehicle or the people in it would be vulnerable to attack. Again they had been wrong.

The only consolation lay in the fact that not even a police back-up would have made much difference. Armed police could have fired on that helicopter without so much as denting the armoured exterior. And at the first sign of trouble, the Swifts would have lifted off – and there would have been no actual proof to connect them with it.

The lights on the helicopter were fading into the distance. Soon he would lose sight of it altogether, but he kept it in view as long as he could because he knew he had no choice now but to involve the police, and they would want to know what direction it was flown in after the pick-up.

Cloud finally hid it altogether, and this was the point at which he might have turned and made for the car.

But something stopped him from turning. Something that was being pressed hard against his temple.

In all his career, he'd never had a gun pressed against him, but he felt one now, and he knew it for what it was. 'George,' he said, and he felt the gun withdrawn.

George McLaughlan couldn't have been more stunned. 'Jarvis?' He'd seen his shape against the gate, and had thought he was someone working for the Swifts. 'What are you doin' here?'

'Same as you,' said Jarvis. 'Trying to stop the Swifts from killing your son.'

It wasn't easy to study him in the darkness, but Jarvis's first impression was that George was still a power-house of a man. He'd still take some of Whalley's men if the situation arose, thought Jarvis, grimly.

He withdrew the gun, which was small consolation to Jarvis, who wouldn't have trusted him not to change his mind and pull the trigger. George had never come after him, and Jarvis didn't know why. He wasn't about to ask. Instead, he told him quickly that Robbie had phoned him from the station, telling him where and when he'd arranged to meet Swift, and adding: 'I need you to watch and tell Orme if Swift pulls a fast one and we both get killed.'

After Robbie's call, Jarvis had been deeply tempted to contact Leonard Orme. He didn't know him, but from the little Robbie had told him, Jarvis got the feeling he was a fair and reasonable man.

He hadn't contacted Orme. Not because he'd promised he wouldn't, but because he had known that Robbie would never forgive him if Orme turned up with back-up and Ocky got hurt as a result. He would never forgive *himself*.

He outlined this as they left the field and got into George's car, backed it down the lane that was too narrow for a three-point turn, and pointed it in the direction Jarvis had said they should go.

'You can't rescue someone when you haven't a clue where they are,' said George.

He had a point, thought Jarvis but, then, he had information that neither George nor Robbie nor the police in all probability was privy to. 'Remember Hunter?' he said.

George, who was doing the driving, gave a nod.

'After he came out of prison, he wrote a book.'

'Each tae their own,' said George. 'Personally, I preferred to carry on where I left off wi' ma trade.'

'Quite,' said Jarvis. 'Well, not everyone is fortunate enough to be in the position to pick up the threads of their chosen profession after coming out of prison, so Hunter wrote a book on some of the more notorious villains he came across as a copper.'

'Do I get a chapter tae maself?' said George.

'No, but you do get a mention,' said Jarvis. 'More to the point, the Swifts get a mention, though not much of one.'

'You surprise me,' said George. 'I'd a thought they'd a warranted a book tae themselves by now.'

'No doubt someone will write one soon enough,' said Jarvis. 'But Hunter put this book together almost thirty years ago. The Swifts were in their twenties then. They hadn't yet made their mark. They'd made a bit of money, though, working as runners for a well-known East End firm.'

'Your friends and mine?' said George.

'Yours, maybe,' said Jarvis.

'Get tae the point,' said George.

'Hunter mentioned them, but said very little. As I say, there was little to be said at the time, they were just a couple of runners. His only reason for mentioning them at all was to illustrate how much money a couple of kids like them could make doing the kind of work they were doing for the kind of people they were working for.'

'Surprise me,' said George.

'Enough to buy themselves an old farmhouse in Berkshire.'

'Where?'

'The book didn't say,' said Jarvis.

'So what fuckin' use is that?'

'I phoned Hunter,' said Jarvis, but he didn't add what Hunter had said when he heard his voice on the line. 'Don't tell me you're still mixed up with the McLaughlans – I'd have thought you'd have learned your lesson.'

Jarvis said, 'I asked him what he knew about the Swifts. Turned out he knew quite a bit.'

'Hunter would,' said George.

'I outlined the problem and asked him whether he knew of any properties they might own without it being general knowledge. He said he'd made a note of a few interesting facts that had come to his attention over the years. He didn't have them to hand. He'd have to phone me back.'

Jarvis had pictured Hunter rummaging through box files stored in the attic of a house that was somewhat modest by comparison with that which he had owned prior to being busted. He said, 'He phoned me back within the hour. According to his notes, they still owned the farmhouse where Calvin and Barbara lived through-out their marriage. It was close enough to Newbury for Ray to be able to picture himself as part of the local racehorse scene. I think he even had plans to build stables and a gallops. Then Barbara disappeared, and Calvin got nicked for armed robbery. The farmhouse stood empty for a while. And then it was sold – only Hunter doesn't think it was ever sold.'

'Why make it look as though it was?'

'Come on, George, you know as well as I do that it's useful for people – dare I say it, people such as yourself? –

to have places to run to, places to hide, places that simply aren't associated with them.'

'He was a good copper, Hunter – always knew what everyone was up tae, and where they were livin'. You had tae admire the man.'

Jarvis doubted the Met held quite so high an opinion of Hunter as George did, but didn't say so.

'Did he give an address?' said George.

Jarvis pulled a piece of paper from his pocket. He gave it to George, who reached for a map and shoved it on to his lap. 'Find it,' said George.

'No need,' said Jarvis. 'I know *exactly* where it is. Take a left.'

McLaughlan stood with his back to the cold night air. The rope around his neck had been tied to a metal loop above his head. If he fell through the open doorway, the fall would break his neck.

So this is it, thought McLaughlan. This is how it's done. He pictured himself as he imagined he would be in the moments to come, swinging by the neck from a helicopter in flight.

They were beating him now, a rhythmical punching and kicking to every part of his body. Then he felt himself grabbed by the shoulders and shoved towards the door.

Although his hands were bound, McLaughlan started to fight, using his head, shoulders, anything to stop them from getting a hold on him.

He knew himself to be immensely powerful, but he also knew that this was a battle he could never win. They pushed him towards the doorway, and powerful though he was, he didn't stand a chance against them all. They crashed against him in unison, and just for a moment, he hovered on the very edge—

—then he fell. Not quickly, but slowly, or so it seemed to McLaughlan, and he waited for the rope to do the business.

Chapter Thirty-seven

Swift, thought Jarvis, wouldn't have wanted to be airborne longer than he needed to be. He had flown low, and no doubt without permission. He had also stayed remarkably close to home, for it had taken less than an hour to drive from the field to the farm. Therefore, thought Jarvis, the helicopter had probably been airborne for fifteen minutes, if that.

They hid the car in trees at the top of a lane, and after leaving it, George and Jarvis had walked across the fields towards the farm.

The exertion of climbing gates and crossing fields had brought Jarvis out in a sweat. If nothing else, the ease with which George covered the ground made him feel even older than he was. Nothing changes, thought Jarvis. Here we are, two old men, and he still makes me feel physically inadequate.

Periodically, George eased his pace to enable Jarvis to catch his breath, and during a moment's rest, Jarvis said, 'How come you never came after me? All these years you never bothered – why?'

So far, neither had mentioned Elsa, and even as he

asked the question, Jarvis wondered if he was making a serious mistake referring to her at all.

George replied by asking a question of his own, one that Jarvis didn't feel inclined to answer. 'She said you walked away without a word?'

Jarvis said nothing.

'Come on, Mike. I let you alone. The least y' can do is tell me why you left her.'

Jarvis thought back to the tin. He'd been rooting around inside it for a roll of Sellotape. In order to find it, he had pulled out Tam and Robbie's birth certificates. He had to have seen them a dozen times before. Only this time he glanced at them, and something caught his eye: much as he expected, George was named as their father, and their surnames were McLaughlan. Elsa's name, however, was given as Richards, and he suddenly realised that Tam and Robbie had been born before she and George were married. If so, she'd never said anything, but that was hardly surprising: back then, there was still some shame attached to having given birth to an illegitimate child, so it wouldn't have been something she wanted to broadcast.

He had started to search the tin for something else – something he had never looked for before. And how well he remembered the moment that he sensed she had entered the kitchen. He hadn't had to look to know she was watching him from the doorway. 'What are you looking for?'

He could have said 'a button, a pin, the Sellotape'. Instead, he told her the truth. He handed her the birth certificates, saying, 'You never told me the boys were born out of wedlock.'

Such an old-fashioned term, thought Jarvis. *Born out of wedlock!* Just saying it made him feel like a maiden aunt. But Elsa's response had been equally old-fashioned: she'd blushed, and she'd stammered, 'I wasn't sure how you'd feel about it.'

'It wouldn't have bothered me,' said Jarvis. 'In many ways, it would have made things easier.'

'What makes you say that?'

'We could have got married. We wouldn't have had to wait for George to come out so that you could feel less guilty about filing for divorce.'

The blush grew more vivid.

'As it is,' said Jarvis, 'we *do* have to wait, don't we?'

She'd handed the certificates back. 'I thought we'd agreed. Why go on about it?'

But Jarvis wasn't finished. 'Where's your certificate, Elsa?'

'What would you want with my birth certificate?'

'Not your birth certificate. Your *marriage* certificate. Where is it?'

'It's in there.'

'No,' said Jarvis. 'It isn't.'

'It must be.' She'd taken the tin, and he'd watched her make a drama of searching for something that didn't exist. He had placed his hand over hers to stop her from the pointless, useless scrabbling through bits of string and packets of thread, and he'd said, *'Don't.'*

The way he'd said it. 'Mike—' she began, but Jarvis was already leaving the kitchen. She followed him into the hallway and watched him put on his coat. And she shouted after him as he left the flat. *'Mike.'*

There had been a note of panic in her voice, but the

panic wasn't that of a woman who felt she was losing the man she loved: the panic was born of a vision of mounting bills, of having to move to a smaller place in a poorer area. *'Mike!'*

'I asked her to marry me,' said Jarvis. 'Not once, but dozens of times. Her answer was always the same.'

Jarvis stopped talking. He was watching George. In one massive hand, he was holding the gun. In the other, he held a pinch of tobacco and a cigarette paper. He rolled a cigarette with a flick of his fingers. It fascinated Jarvis, who felt it was the kind of trick a man only learned in prison. George must have learned it young. He'd spent a lifetime perfecting it. He put the cigarette to his mouth and smoked it while he was still confident that they were far enough away from the farmhouse for it not to attract attention. 'You were saying,' said George.

'She told me she couldn't file for divorce while you were still inside. I believed her. I was willing to wait. I had no choice. And then, one day, I just happened to look in the tin.'

George gave a nod. He knew the tin that Jarvis was referring to.

'I realised you weren't married when the boys were born. It made me curious. I started to look for a marriage certificate.'

'You wouldn't have found one,' said George.

'No,' said Jarvis. 'I realise. And then I realised something else – something I should have realised years ago.'

'And what was that?' said George.

'I realised it was never going to matter what you did *to* her or what I did *for* her, she would always belong to you.'

George said, 'A minute ago, ye asked me why I never came after you.'

Jarvis nodded.

'I always knew you were never a threat tae me.'

Of all the things he could have said to put me down, thought Jarvis, that was perhaps the worst.

He crouched in a small space in total darkness. But darkness was something McLaughlan was better equipped to deal with than most. As a child, he had sometimes lived for days in the cellar, and at night it had been completely dark – no streetlight, no moon, no headlights from passing vehicles.

The walls of the cellar had been brick, and the walls of the space he occupied now were also brick. Familiar things, thought McLaughlan, though the cellar had been big enough to walk around whereas this was maybe ten by ten at most.

He couldn't stand up, so he squatted on his heels, his hands still tied behind his back. He touched the ceiling with his face. It was metal. He pushed it. It didn't move. It felt like corrugated iron, but if that was what it was, it had to be weighted down with something. He couldn't work out where he was or how he came to be there. All he could remember was falling to what he had thought would be his death.

He had regained consciousness to find himself lying on his back. The hood had been taken off his head, but the rope still hung round his neck like an umbilical cord. Calvin had used it to yank him to his feet, and then McLaughlan saw that he was standing in a field by the side of a house. The helicopter was close by, and Ray and two other men stood near it, talk-ing.

He had found it hard to focus. Calvin had been a blur, but his words had been clear enough: 'You think we'd hang you, eh?'

McLaughlan was too disoriented to work out what they'd done to him.

'Not yet, McLaughlan. We have plans for you.'

All this, he could cope with, rationalise and plan against. What he couldn't deal with was that, quite close by, a child was sobbing. His crying was interminable, a gut-wrenching, desolate sound.

He knew that cry. He knew it was Ocky. He shouted out and banged at the metal ceiling with his head.

If anything, the sound of the crying grew louder.

George heard the sound of a small child crying long before Jarvis did. Better ears? Better genes? Jarvis didn't know. George had always had more of the animal about him than most men. Despite his age and size, he had crossed the fields like a deer, his footfalls light, his movements amazingly assured.

Jarvis had stumbled after him, and probably would have stumbled into the farmhouse itself if George hadn't stopped him. He lifted a hand, and Jarvis stood stock still.

George had heard the sound of crying. Now Jarvis heard it too. It drew them to a field at the side of the house.

Here, the ground was rutted, as if it had gone uncul-tivated for years. A mound in the land gave Jarvis the impression that perhaps this had once been a Bronze Age settlement, that the mound would prove to be a burial site. But if it was a burial site, someone had a funny way of paying their respects.

A cassette recorder lay by the side of the mound. A tape was playing, and the recording was that of a child who was crying inconsolably.

'Bastards,' said Jarvis.

They walked towards the tape, and Jarvis reached down as if to switch it off, but George stopped him. 'Mebbe they can hear it from the house. If we turn it off, it'll act as a warning.'

How strong the instinct is to stop a child from crying, thought Jarvis. But George had a point, and he left it.

George then touched the grass that covered the ground. Jarvis did likewise and found that, unlike the grass that grew beneath their feet, it was soft. George took hold of a handful and pulled. A square of turf came neatly away from the rest.

Jarvis joined him now in lifting the turf from the mound. Beneath it were sheets of corrugated iron. They pulled one away.

They peered into the septic tank. 'Robbie,' said George, and as he spoke, Jarvis saw someone come out of the darkness and lash out at the gun in George's hand.

George dropped the gun and spun round to find Ray Swift standing behind them with a baseball bat. He was trying to keep his eye on them, yet scanning the ground to see where the gun had fallen.

George tore the bat away from him and threw it out of reach. Ray weighed him up, then smirked, because what he saw before him was a man who was a good fifteen years older than he was. 'Come on, then,' said Ray. 'Have a go.'

George needed no further prompting. He squared up to Ray, who jabbed at his face. George ducked out of the way, and Ray tried again.

This time, a punch slid off George's chin as if his skin were greased, and Ray yelled out, 'You fucker,' more surprised than afraid. George looked too old to move that fast, and Ray, lulled into a false sense of security, launched himself at him, the attack frenzied, the blows badly timed.

George held them off by raising his arms, brushing them away as if a child were having a mock-fight with him. Jarvis got the impression that, at any moment, George could have grabbed Ray's wrists, and batted him round the head with the flat of his own hands. A child's game. Something that would delight a kid who would revel in his father's strength and dominance.

And then, it seemed to Jarvis that George grew bored, or angry, or both. Or maybe he'd just been holding back the rage he'd felt from the minute Robbie told him the Swifts had Ocky. Whatever the case, he suddenly threw a massive punch at Ray, and although Jarvis knew it wasn't possible, he half convinced himself that he felt the air around him shift accordingly. George had thrown a punch, and Mother Nature herself had got out of the way.

In witnessing the power behind that blow, in hearing it connect with a jaw bone that shattered as if it were china, Jarvis couldn't help but think of Jimmy. He'd seen him fight in London as an amateur, and even then, young though he was, it had been obvious that Jimmy was destined for greatness.

Ray rocked on his heels, and his knees began to shake. Jarvis had seen footage of men reacting in precisely that same way mere seconds after being shot in the head. Any minute now, thought Jarvis, and Ray would crumple to the ground. But Ray had no such intention. He stood there, reeling, as Jarvis jumped into the septic tank and started to untie Robbie.

The minute he was free, McLaughlan felt round the floor of the tank for the gun. He picked it up, then he and Jarvis climbed out.

Ray was still on his feet. For his own sake, Jarvis hoped he would swallow his pride and succumb to what must be an almost overpowering urge to fall to the ground and curl up into a foetal position. If he did that, he'd be all right, thought Jarvis. George might paw him around a bit like a grizzly, but he'd leave him alone. If, however, Ray put up a fight, George would maul him to death.

Ray, unaware of the etiquette that might serve to save his life, pulled himself together. He blinked at George a couple of times, then raised his fists again. And instantly George took him by the scruff of the neck and began to deliver a beating. There was something utterly primal and brutal about it, thought Jarvis. This was the kind of beating a boxer could give an opponent when what mattered wasn't so much the winning as the exacting of revenge. The Swifts had abducted his grandson. They'd tried to murder his son. To add insult to injury, this particular Swift had had the audacity to whack him with a bat. George wasn't so much incensed as deeply pissed off. The only consolation, thought Jarvis, was that Ray was beyond all knowledge of what was being done to him. He was upright, because George was holding him up by the throat. But he was unconscious when George delivered a final, fatal blow.

Whether he meant to kill him, Jarvis couldn't say. He only knew that the force behind that blow broke Ray Swift's neck. George let him go, and he fell to the ground with what sounded like the cracking of a branch, but the crack had come from a shotgun fired by Calvin.

Jarvis and McLaughlan threw themselves to the ground. George had no time, no warning, and he went down from a gunshot wound to the stomach.

The instant Calvin turned the gun on them, McLaughlan shot him dead. So quick, thought Jarvis. No drama. No time to think. Thirty seconds ago, Ray had invited George to 'have a go'. In just under half a minute, two men lay dead, and one was probably dying.

Sherryl ran out of the house as McLaughlan leaped to his feet and grabbed the gun from Calvin. He ran to George who was writhing in agony. 'Go get Ocky,' gasped George.

McLaughlan ran up to Sherryl and turned the shotgun on her. 'Don't fuck me around, where is he?'

Sherryl was looking past him to where the bodies of Ray and Calvin lay. She opened her mouth to speak, but couldn't, and McLaughlan tossed the shotgun over to Jarvis. 'Don't trust her,' he said, and Jarvis replied with a warning of his own, 'Don't forget there may be people around.'

Sherryl ran to the bodies of her father and uncle, and then she started to shout, as if she could somehow yell them back to life.

Jarvis felt for her, and would have tried to comfort her if he could. But he reasoned that Robbie wouldn't have

342

warned him against her without good cause, so he kept
his distance. He ran over to George and saw that he was
bleeding from the stomach. This is it for him, thought
Jarvis, who looked at the house as Robbie reached the
door. Sherryl had left it open. There were lights on in
every room. He saw him enter the kitchen as if expecting
armed men behind the door.

He heard a young child crying, and Jarvis realised they
hadn't stopped the recorder. The tape had rewound itself
automatically. The replay of crying began all over again.

It took McLaughlan only moments to work out that the
house was empty. The men who had helped to beat him
up in the helicopter had left after doing the job for
which Calvin had paid them handsomely, no doubt, and
in cash.

Having edged up the stairs, he came to a door that was
locked. He kicked it open and turned on the light. A small
form lay in the bed the blankets obscuring his face.

McLaughlan pulled the blankets back, and Ocky stared
up at him, his eyes filled more with bewilderment than
fear. 'Daddy.'

He picked him up, held him close. And carried him
out to Jarvis.

George lay on his back on the grass. The tape had been
switched off, but the sound of sobbing still predominated.
This time, it came from Sherryl, and her crying was no
recording.

McLaughlan looked at the wounds to his father's stomach. He was no expert, but he knew that any stomach
wound was serious. People could die quickly. Or they

could die quite slowly. Some died of blood loss or shock, and those who didn't usually died of gangrene. 'We have to get you to a hospital.'

'No,' said George. 'No hospital.'

Jarvis tried to reason with him, but George wouldn't have it. 'I killed the man – that's a life sentence. I can't face another stretch. Take me home,' said George. 'Take me back tae Glasgow.'

McLaughlan stood up with Ocky still in his arms.

'You'll keep your word?' said George. 'You'll tell me what happened tae Tam?'

Ocky was whimpering quietly. McLaughlan passed him to Jarvis, then helped his father to the car. He laid him down in the back as best he could, but George, huge as he was, could only lie there doubled up with pain.

Jarvis got in the front beside McLaughlan, Ocky on his knee. 'Maybe we ought to get him to a hospital whatever—'

'No,' said George. 'No hospitals. No police. No Barlinnie. *I've had enough.*'

McLaughlan backed the car away from the farmhouse. Just for a moment, Sherryl was caught in the headlights of the car. She was bending over the body of her father, and suddenly it was as though Jarvis came to his senses.

'We can't just leave—'

'We can.'

'We have to call the police. They'll want statements.' George lay in the back of the car. He groaned as the car started moving. 'We've got to get him to a hospital.'

'You heard the man,' said McLaughlan. 'No hospitals.

344

No police. No charges, trials, or sentences for murder. He's had enough.'

'But we can't just leave, it's illegal.'

McLaughlan stopped the car. 'Now's your chance,' he said. 'If you want to get out, go back, then go ahead.'

'What about you?'

'I'm going to Glasgow,' said McLaughlan. 'I'm taking him home. I'm taking him to the spot where Tam—'

He didn't finish, but he didn't have to, and Jarvis needed no further persuading: for thirty years the mystery surrounding Tam's disappearance had been gnawing away at him. This might be the only chance he ever got to find out what happened. Sherryl could carry on crying, and the police would have to wait. Ray and Calvin weren't going to grow any deader between now and the time that the police arrived at the scene. 'All right,' he said. *'All right.'*

George was lapsing into and out of consciousness. For the most part, Jarvis said little. McLaughlan said even less. Ocky clung to Jarvis and fell asleep.

At one point, George came round, and Jarvis heard him call, *'Jimmy!'* He tried to turn to look at him without disturbing Ocky.

George was barely conscious. For some miles, he'd been rambling, and little of what he'd said had made much sense. But suddenly he said something that made absolute sense, and Jarvis spun round, waking Ocky in the process. 'What was that, George? What was that you said?'

Whether he was aware of who or where he was, Jarvis didn't know. Perhaps he didn't even realise what he had said. Either way, it constituted a confession of sorts, and Jarvis was reminded that, thirty years ago, Whalley had been driven to distraction by the fact that several months after Jimmy's murder, all he could say for certain was that Jimmy had either walked into the gym with his killer, or had opened the door to him later.

According to the pathologist, there had been no bruises on Jimmy's body to suggest a struggle. There was also nothing to suggest that he had been tied to what Jarvis referred to as the Christine Keeler chair. In short, these factors indicated that Jimmy had either sat on the chair at gunpoint or of his own free will.

Whatever the case, he had sat facing the cabinet that held the trophies, photos and newspaper clippings. He had then been shot through the back of the head and had fallen from the chair. Nothing was stolen, and nothing had come to light to give Whalley a lead with regard to who might have killed him or why. 'Like I said before,' said Whalley. 'It looks tae me like a revenge killing – like the kind o' thing someone might do tae an informant. What do you think?'

Jarvis hadn't known what to think.

Until now.

'What was that you said, George?'

And George repeated what Jarvis had thought he heard him say: 'He wanted those newspaper cuttings tae be the last thing he saw.'

That was almost exactly what Whalley had said. 'George,' said Jarvis, 'what are you talking about?'

'He couldnae stand tae live like that any longer,' said George. 'He wanted tae die like a man, not like some nancy-boy with a bottle o' pills. He begged me tae shoot him, but not at home. He couldnae do it tae Iris.'

He lapsed back into unconsciousness.

Jarvis looked at Robbie.

McLaughlan kept his eyes on the road, and said nothing.

Chapter Thirty-eight

Orme had often had cause to regret giving an order along the lines of 'If anything happens on this one, I want to know immediately – even if it means waking me up in the middle of the night.' It had all too often resulted in his wife pulling a pillow over her head and leaving him to deal with a call that hauled him from his sleep, and then from his bed.

The news that Thames Valley had contacted the Met to report that Calvin and Ray Swift had been murdered jolted him wide awake. 'Come again?' said Orme.

His wife, her voice heavy with sleep, said, 'Leonard?'

Orme put a finger to his lips and she asked nothing further, but he listened as the person giving the information explained that an hysterical Sherryl Swift had called the police to say that her father had been beaten to death and that Calvin had been shot.

Thames Valley checked it out, and because the victims were notorious London villains they immediately informed the Met's Serious Crimes Squad.

'What does Sherryl say happened?' said Orme, and if the person he was talking to picked up on the fact that he wasn't necessarily prepared to believe a word, he didn't say so.

'She says Ray heard a noise and went outside to investigate, followed by Calvin. Seconds later, Sherryl heard a shot. She looked out the window, and saw a car being driven away. She went downstairs and found Ray and Calvin out the back, dead.'

'I don't suppose she has any idea who killed them?'

'If she knows, she isn't saying.'

She'll have her reasons, thought Orme. 'You said something about her looking out the window, and seeing a car being driven from the scene.'

'We've put out an alert.'

'She gave a description?' said Orme.

'Better than that – she got the registration.'

That was seriously quick thinking, thought Orme.

'Ten-to-one it's been stolen, but the bloke the killer stole it from just happens to be a villain – George McLaughlan. He's one of your boys from Glasgow, old school, but a real heavy in his day. Grievous bodily harm, armed robbery . . .'

McLaughlan! thought Orme. He couldn't believe what he'd heard. They're related. They have to be. And if this George McLaughlan had previous for armed robbery, it seemed likely that he may have had dealings with the Swifts. Maybe George and Robbie McLaughlan had long been involved with the Swifts.

It was such a revelation to him that he couldn't get a grip on it. What if I'm wrong? he thought suddenly. But it all fitted together too well for him to be wrong.

He suddenly saw it all: the Swifts and the McLaughlans had been doing business for some time. Then business relations had soured for some reason. Ash had tipped off Robbie McLaughlan with regard to the impending bank job. McLaughlan had shot Stuart. Calvin had come after him. He'd panicked, got his hands on a gun, and tried to protect himself.

Maybe McLaughlan had abducted his son with a view to disappearing and starting a new life, or maybe the Swifts had abducted him and McLaughlan had gone after them. He clearly knew where to find them, which was more than Orme did. There'd been a fight. He'd murdered them. And now he was on the run.

Orme was told that the vehicle was heading north. It was being followed from a distance by an unmarked car, but the driver had been told not to approach it, much less try to pull it over, because it looked as though McLaughlan had two male passengers and a child in the vehicle with him.

Ocky, thought Orme. Question was, had McLaughlan rescued him from the Swifts, or had Ocky been with him all along? As for the two male passengers, Orme couldn't even hazard a guess as to who they might be.

Thames Valley were waiting for him to give some decision with regard to how he wanted this handled, and Orme was profoundly grateful to have solid procedure to fall back on at times like this. He gave the only order possible.

'Continue to follow the vehicle, but remember, McLaughlan is a police officer – he'll be watching for a tail. If you think he's spotted you, back off. Better to lose him than to risk the child getting hurt. We follow him to his destination. At that point, we bring someone in to negotiate with him, see if we can get him to let Ocky go.'

The words *heading north* had stayed with Orme, and he recalled that the address on the vehicle registration had been given as Glasgow. He added, 'If it starts to look as though he's heading for Glasgow, organise a helicopter to get me down there, and ask Strathclyde to make armed back-up available.'

Chapter Thirty-nine

Nothing much had happened to change the place, thought Jarvis. Same river. Same stink. Same junk in the canal. Same notice on the locks telling kids to keep off. Thirty years on, and no one had got it together to build on the land. No money to do it, probably.

They walked along the banks of the river with Ocky at their heels, Jarvis and McLaughlan taking the bulk of George's weight. The bleeding was worse now that he was moving, and Jarvis said, 'You sure about the hospital?

'Cannae face another stretch, Mike. Let me alone, eh?'

He was anticipating surviving, only to have to face a life sentence, thought Jarvis. And that was what he would get. Any Crown Prosecutor worth his salt would call the pathologist as an expert witness, and the pathologist would say that Ray Swift's injuries were so extensive that there had to have come a point when he could no longer defend himself. 'It is therefore not unreasonable to assume that the defendant, George McLaughlan, intended to kill him, my Lord.'

They stumbled along the riverbank for almost half

a mile, McLaughlan now straining to take his father's weight.

He set him down on the banks of the Clyde at a point where the river began its graceful curve. From here, thought Jarvis, it would flow fifteen miles to the city. It would widen, and deepen, and strengthen, a vast, impressive waterway. 'It's quite some river,' he said.

McLaughlan took off his coat and used it to cover his father. It was bleak here. No shelter to speak of. And the wind that whipped the surface of the water into waves came straight from the sea.

Ocky was cold. He clung to Jarvis for warmth as much as security, and Jarvis held him under his coat. He didn't like to think of a child going through what he'd gone through in the past few days. But he was very young, thought Jarvis. He wouldn't understand a lot of what had happened, and with luck he would forget most of it in time.

George, barely conscious, said something McLaughlan didn't catch. He bent down to hear him, and heard him whisper, 'Crackerjack.'

Jarvis had heard it said that those who were dying sometimes saw the spirits of the people they had been closest to in life, and he wondered whether this was what was happening with George. But then he realised that George was just confused: he wanted to know whether this was the place where he'd dumped Crackerjack's body, and if so, what they were doing there.

McLaughlan reminded George that they had a deal: he'd promised to take him to the place where he had last seen Tam. This was the place.

Jarvis asked why he and Tam had gone there, and

McLaughlan replied that they'd gone to find Cracker-jack's body.

'How did you know where it was?' said Jarvis, and McLaughlan thought back to the moment when he and Tam had stood at the top of the stairs that led down into the cellar. Elsa had been almost frantic, scared the police would show up on the doorstep any moment. George had tried to calm her down by promising to get rid of the body the minute it grew dark. He said: 'We overheard when he told our mother where he planned to dump the body.'

'What made you come looking for it later?'

'Curiosity,' said McLaughlan.

'We wanted to see what it looked like.'

They hadn't known exactly where the body was, but they knew the area well enough, and it hadn't been all that difficult to find it. They had been appalled by how decomposed it was. It had lain out there for a couple of months, and if they hadn't known it was Crackerjack, they wouldn't have recognised it. The sight of it had given McLaughlan nightmares worse than any brought on by Jimmy. 'It stank,' he said. 'You'd have thought the smell alone would have led someone to it, but this has never been the kind of place where people walk their dogs.'

Jarvis could well understand why the average person wouldn't want to wander across an expanse of land like this. It didn't lead to anywhere of interest. It merely flanked a section of the Clyde that was neither beautiful nor valuable as such. There were many such places that decent people ignored as if by instinct, leaving them to the dealers, the villains, and *leavers of the dead* – elements of society who had a use for such places as these.

McLaughlan added, 'We'd found it, but we weren't all that sure what to do next. Tam wanted to stay a while longer. But I wanted to go – I was scared we'd miss the train – so we started back along the tow-path, but the bank wasn't very stable. Tam got close to the edge. He fell in.'

McLaughlan stopped right there. And then, as if he were making some comment about the weather, he added, 'He drowned.'

He stared out over the river, and in following his line of vision, Jarvis realised that anyone falling in would have one hell of a job getting out. Swift and deep, and laced with lethal currents, it was a killer. The river had swallowed Tam, had swept him to his death.

But how come it hadn't spat him out on the doorstep of the city?

There *has* to be more, thought Jarvis. But perhaps now wasn't the time. All he said was, 'Why in God's name didn't you *tell* anyone?'

'How could I?' said McLaughlan. 'How could I explain how we knew where Crackerjack's body was without admitting that we'd overheard our father saying where he intended to dump it? I didn't want to be the one to implicate him in the robbery. I didn't want to be the one to lead the police straight to him.'

'But why were you so keen to protect him?' said Jarvis, and McLaughlan reminded him of nothing so much as one of Robert Maxwell's sons when he replied, 'He was my father. I loved him.'

He was your father, thought Jarvis. Of course you loved him. And he thought back to the moment when Robbie had stood at the top of the stairs with Iris, watching as armed police marched George to the van at gunpoint. *'They've got my dad.'*

'After he was jailed, I wanted to tell the truth, but Elsa was hanging on to the idea that Tam was alive. I didn't know how to tell her I'd known all along he was dead. I was ten years old. I didn't know how to deal with it. And then the years went by, and things got worse, not better. She kept insisting Tam had gone to Australia, that one day he'd come back. I couldn't stand to think what it would do to her.'

My God, thought Jarvis. Why didn't I see all this? I thought I knew him so well. How little we know the people we think we're closest to.

He caught the slightest movement on the periphery of his vision and turned. What he saw surprised him. At first glance, he would have said that the topography of the area was such that it was impossible for anyone to stalk and hide, and stay well out of view, but this was not so. The ditch to either side of the railway embankment provided cover, and armed police had used it to get to within yards of them.

One of them shouted, 'Armed police. Move away from the gun.'

McLaughlan didn't move.

'Robbie,' said Jarvis, but McLaughlan's only response was to sink to his heels. He did it very slowly, and it wasn't a threatening movement, but the very fact that the gun was at his feet increased the tension. Jarvis almost felt a dozen fingers on the triggers of a dozen automatics. It wasn't a pleasant feeling to be in the line of so much fire.

Right now, thought Jarvis, the police don't know the

truth. When I tell them that Swift had Ocky, and that they lured Robbie to the house with a view to murdering him, the pieces will fall into place. They'll realise Swift hired a hitman, that the hitman shot Doheny in error, that in arming himself, Robbie was merely trying to defend himself and his family.

But that won't save his job, thought Jarvis. He may not have lied about his background when he joined the force, but he certainly concealed it, which was just as bad in a way. And there was no escaping the fact that he had tricked his way into his former home, or that he assaulted the woman now living there. He left the scene of Doheny's murder, and went on the run from police.

From the little Robbie had told him about Orme, Jarvis had reason to believe that he would help him as much as he could, but that he wouldn't bend the facts. The best that Robbie could hope for was that charges wouldn't be brought, but maybe that wouldn't bother him in the end. Maybe, thought Jarvis, in ridding himself of the secrets he'd kept hidden, he would enable himself to move on.

He hoped so. He also hoped that, whatever happened, Robbie would give him the chance to get to know Ocky – he was the closest he would ever come to a grandson of his own.

McLaughlan was still crouching a few feet from the water. He pulled at the coarse, almost olive-green grass that formed in clumps on the bank, and he spoke his thoughts aloud:

I don't know anyone else who took their kid brother around the way you used to take me, but I was too young at the time to realise how good you were with me. I took it for granted.

Iris once asked if you minded me constantly tagging along, but all you said was you liked to have me around. Even now, all these years later, I don't think I've come across anyone who really likes having me around, not the way you did. But I don't expect it from anyone else. That kind of easiness only comes once in a lifetime. You only have it with one person. And I had it with you.

Finding Crackerjack's body was your idea, and it was the one occasion when you felt I should stay at home. But I kept on until you said you'd bring me along, and in the end, you gave in.

You warned me not to breathe a word, and we said we were going to Glasgow to find our dad. We never even looked for him, remember? Even if we had, we wouldn't have found him. But we found Crackerjack, no problem. We knew this place like the backs of our hands, and finding him was easy enough for us.

It was the first time I'd ever seen anyone dead, and it scared me. His body had been there for weeks, and he didn't look anything like the man we'd known. I poked his face with a stick and his cheek split apart like the skin on an overripe fruit. I ran away, but you coaxed me back in the end.

You used the stick to lift his shirt. The bullet-holes ran in a diagonal line from his stomach to his shoulder. And you said he had to have been strong to have survived as long as he did. Anyone else would have died in minutes, you said. But not him. And you were proud of him for that.

You'd liked him. He used to slip you five bob now and then. He told you jokes, and he gave you bottles of beer. He made you feel like a man but, most of all, he made you feel like a 'someone'. And when you're the son of a robber, you welcome anyone showing you respect of any kind – because that's what's so lacking in coppers who shove their fist through a model that *it's taken you months to make. You were only the son of a robber. What did it matter if they wrecked your ship? Who was going to stop them?*

You said we ought to bury him, that his wife and kids would like it, so we dug around for a while, but all we had was a piece of tin to dig with. It didn't really work, and we threw it away. But you dangled the crucifix over him and we said a prayer for his soul. You said you'd been to a funeral once, so you knew what had to be said: 'Our father in heaven . . . He wasn't all bad. He was good to his wife and kids. He didn't always get things right. He did his best. Amen.'

Then we headed back down the tow-path, and the tide had gone out completely. It was almost as if the storm had sucked the river from its bed.

The mud was black and glutinous, the consistency of tar. I stopped to throw some stones in it, and you twisted round to tell me we'd miss the train. The next thing I knew, you'd slipped – but you didn't fall, and you looked like somebody learning to skate, slithering sideways, your arms outstretched as if to balance yourself.

You started to sink the minute you hit the mud, but you didn't sink deep. Not at first. At first, you sank to your knees. And then you sank to your thighs – not smoothly, but in a series of jerks, as if something beneath the mud was pulling you under.

You laughed. I'll never forget that laugh. It was a high, nervous laugh. I'd never heard you laugh like that before, and you just said, 'Fuck!'

I don't think I said anything. I was too surprised. That's all it was at first – surprise, not shock or fear. Something out of the ordinary had happened, and we were surprised. We'd sort it out. We'd laugh it off. We'd get cleaned up, get home, and maybe, only later, would we realise—

You called to me and said, 'I can get out – all I need is a minute,' but a minute was all it took for you to sink as deep as your chest.

The look on your face – I was so scared I couldn't even stand up. I sat on the bank and I started to bawl, and you told me to run for help. But we were miles from the road. I knew that if I left, you'd be dead before I got back. And I wanted to stay. Those were going to be the last few minutes that I would have a brother. I wanted them to last for ever. And all the time I was yelling at you to do something, anything, to get yourself out.

Then just for a moment, the sinking stopped, as if you'd reached bedrock, something that would keep you stable until I could bring help. You stayed like that for twenty seconds or so. And then you sank quite suddenly and the mud was up to your neck. You knew then. And I knew it too – nothing was going to get you out of there. The mud stank like shit, but your fear rode over the top of it and reached me in waves of terror.

I crawled down the bank, as close as I could get. You yelled at me not to, but I thought that if only I could just get that little bit closer – just hold my hand out – that somehow you'd manage to reach it. You almost did at one point. That was maybe one of the worst things about it. Just an inch more. And then you had an idea – you yanked the cross from your neck, and you tossed it to me. I grabbed the crucifix. The chain formed a bridge from your hand to mine. I thought it was going to save you.

Looking back, I can't believe I thought it would hold your weight, or that I could hang on until somebody came and keep you from sinking deeper. But when you're desperate, you don't have time for logic, and I pulled on that chain as if I could pull you out. It snapped like a thin piece of cotton.

You told me not to worry, that it wasn't my fault, and then the mud was up to your mouth, and you didn't dare move. You lifted your face to the sky, and that was all I could see of you, as if someone had put a mask on the surface of the mud. It sank, and an impression was left, as if your face had marked the mud in a way that would stay there for ever. I watched the impression disappear. And then I ran away.

McLaughlan was still crouching on the bank, the gun at his feet. The fact that he wasn't holding it was no consolation to Orme. He knew how quickly someone could grab a gun, and knew, also, the devastation they could cause before they were shot or disarmed. He might have to shoot him. He might have no choice. But first, he would try to talk him into giving himself up.

He used the tone of voice that he had used when trying to coax Stuart Swift into giving up the child. 'Robbie, we need to talk.'

McLaughlan eased himself slowly to his feet, away from the gun, then away from the river. He reached out for Ocky, and Jarvis passed him over.

Orme and his men lowered their weapons as Jarvis and McLaughlan walked towards them, then followed them down the path to a fleet of cars.